Praise for *Gold Boy, Emerald Girl*

Winner of the Northern California Independent Booksellers
2011 Book of the Year Award for Fiction

Finalist for the Story Prize

"[Yiyun Li] succeeds in making the details of a very particular (and very sharply drawn) time and place express something broader and more universal. . . . As in reading Chekhov, one is struck by how profoundly important the lives of ordinary people are made to seem, and by what a sizable chunk of existence—an entire life or several lives—has been compressed into a few pages. . . . How art affects us—the way it stuns the clamorous world into silence on our behalf—echoes throughout Yiyun Li's stories, which themselves have the power to create hushed intervals that resonate with emotion. . . . *Gold Boy, Emerald Girl* is an example of the treasure an artist can fashion from the raw materials of ordinary existence."

—Francine Prose, *The New York Times Book Review* (Editor's Choice)

"Fascinating . . . [The] characters' vivid interior worlds—full of loss and hard-won wisdom—lift smart subject matter into masterful storytelling." —*O: The Oprah Magazine*

"Appealing and lucid . . . [*Gold Boy, Emerald Girl*] radiates love, passion and kindness. . . . [It] well deserves a celebration with its sophistication and honesty, which often derive from a deep understanding of the history, culture and politics of China, and of their impact on ordinary people." —*San Francisco Chronicle*

"Breathtaking . . . starkly wondrous . . . gorgeous fiction . . . [Li] is an impresario of our essential loneliness. Still, these nine stories are not sad, but astringently beautiful." —Cleveland *Plain Dealer*

"Delectable . . . subtle and assured . . . [Li] finds the pulse points in the lives of her Chinese and Chinese-American characters and renders her findings with empathy and exactitude." —*Elle*

"Masterly . . . nuanced . . . [Li's] eloquent understanding of people struggling to help one another 'make a world that would accommodate their loneliness' feels universal." —*Vogue*

"Li vividly illuminates the struggles of the modern Chinese. . . . Despite cultural differences, they share much with us all." —*People*

"[Li will] remind you of what it's like to be human in today's increasingly fragmented world." —*Marie Claire*

"Li displays a staggering poise and grace in her latest collection of short stories. . . . The yarns spun in *Gold Boy, Emerald Girl* prove to be as varied as humanity itself." —*Time Out New York*

"Yiyun Li is a phenomenal writer. . . . [*Gold Boy, Emerald Girl*] beautifully captures her native country in transition."
—The Daily Beast

"A stellar assortment of stories . . . further proof that Li deserves to be considered among the best living fiction writers."
—*Kirkus Reviews* (starred review)

"Brilliant . . . a frighteningly lucid vision of human fate."
—*Publishers Weekly* (starred review)

"[Li's] writing is precise, thoughtful, and powerful in its ability to make universal sentiments . . . palpable in any context."
—*San Francisco* magazine

"[Li's] writing is minimal, yet packed with detail. At times, it feels like she is reporting in the manner of a journalist; at others she

teeters on the verge of lyricism, often walking this line within a single paragraph."
—*The New York Observer*

"Moving . . . Li's stories achieve a poignant blend of the tragic and the commonplace that is all her own."
—*Sacramento News & Review*

"It is nothing short of amazing how Yiyun Li creates her worlds. . . . Li's stories have the satisfying reach of a novel too and are surprisingly contained in their short form. . . . Gentle philosophical landings, carefully articulate in their portrayal of human struggle."
—*The Oregonian*

"Wonderfully amazing short stories."
—*Daily American* (Somerset, Pennsylvania)

"[Li's] lucidity and eloquence make this collection a literary pleasure."
—*BookPage*

"Dark yet covertly witty and caring . . . In several tales, including the funny, bittersweet title story, adjustments are made, solutions are found, and friendship and love survive like plants pushing through asphalt."
—*Booklist*

"This is work that lasts. These sly women, punished men, these worried, worrying, surprising characters, are held aloft and illuminated in Yiyun Li's strong and magical prose."
—Amy Bloom

"In the most dismal circumstances and with the most unlikely subjects—the old, the forgotten, the bookish, the unattractive—Yiyun Li has the rare ability to conjure hope. She writes with precision and delicacy about the Chinese diaspora and about the new China, and in doing so she writes about us all."—Mona Simpson

ALSO BY YIYUN LI

The Vagrants

A Thousand Years of Good Prayers

Gold Boy,
Emerald Girl

Gold Boy, Emerald Girl

• • • • •

Yiyun Li

RANDOM HOUSE TRADE PAPERBACKS | NEW YORK

Gold Boy, Emerald Girl is a work of fiction. Names, characters, places, and incidents are the products of the author's imagination or are used fictitiously. Any resemblance to actual events, locales, or persons, living or dead, is entirely coincidental.

Published in the United States by Random House Trade Paperbacks, an imprint of The Random House Publishing Group, a division of Random House, Inc., New York.

RANDOM HOUSE TRADE PAPERBACKS and colophon are trademarks of Random House, Inc.
RANDOM HOUSE READER'S CIRCLE & Design is a registered trademark of Random House, Inc.

Originally published in hardcover and in slightly different form in the United States by Random House, an imprint of The Random House Publishing Group, a division of Random House, Inc., in 2010.

The following stories that appear in this work have been previously published:
"Kindness" was originally published in *A Public Space*
"A Man Like Him" and "Gold Boy, Emerald Girl" were originally published in *The New Yorker*
"Prison" was originally published in *Tin House*
"The Proprietress" was originally published in *Zoetrope: All-Story*
"House Fire" was originally published in *Granta*
"Number Three, Garden Road" was originally published in *Waving at the Gardener: The Asham Award Short-Story Collection*
"Sweeping Past" was originally published in *The Guardian*
"Souvenir" was originally published in the *San Francisco Chronicle*

Library of Congress Cataloging-in-Publication Data
Li, Yiyun.
Gold boy, emerald girl : stories / Yiyun Li.
p. cm.
ISBN 978-0-8129-8015-8
eBook ISBN 978-0-679-60406-8
I. Title
PL2946 Y59G65 2010
813'.6—dc22 2009047298

Printed in the United States of America

www.randomhousereaderscircle.com

2 4 6 8 9 7 5 3 1

Book design by Victoria Wong

For Brigid Hughes

Contents

Kindness.. 3

A Man Like Him.. 81

Prison.. 101

The Proprietress.. 131

House Fire.. 151

Number Three, Garden Road.. 169

Sweeping Past.. 187

Souvenir.. 198

Gold Boy, Emerald Girl.. 204

Acknowledgments.. 223

A Reader's Guide.. 225

Gold Boy, Emerald Girl

Kindness

ONE

I AM A forty-one-year-old woman living by myself, in the same one-bedroom flat where I have always lived, in a derelict building on the outskirts of Beijing that is threatened to be demolished by government-backed real estate developers. Apart from a trip to a cheap seaside resort, taken with my parents the summer I turned five, I have not traveled much; I spent a year in an army camp in central China, but other than that I have never lived away from home. In college, after a few failed attempts to convince me of the importance of being a community member, my adviser stopped acknowledging my presence, and the bed assigned to me was taken over by the five other girls in the dorm and their trunks.

I have not married, and naturally have no children. I have few friends, though as I have never left the neighborhood, I have enough acquaintances, most of them a generation or two older. Being around them is comforting; never is there a day when I feel that I am alone in aging.

I teach mathematics in a third-tier middle school. I do not love my job or my students, but I have noticed that even the most meager attention I give to the students is returned by a few of them with respect and gratitude and sometimes inexplicable infatuation. I pity those children more than I appreciate them, as I can see where they are heading in their lives. It is a terrible thing, even for an indifferent person like me, to see the bleakness lurking in someone else's life.

I have no hobby that takes me outside my flat during my spare time. I do not own a television set, but I have a roomful of books at least half a century older than I am. I have never in my life hurt a soul, or, if I have done any harm unintentionally the pain I inflicted was the most trivial kind, forgotten the moment it was felt—if indeed it could be felt in any way. But that cannot be a happy life, or much of a life at all, you might say. That may very well be true. "Why are you unhappy?" To this day, if I close my eyes I can feel Lieutenant Wei's finger under my chin, lifting my face to a spring night. "Tell me, how can we make you happy?"

The questions, put to me twenty-three years ago, have remained unanswerable, though it no longer matters, as, you see, Lieutenant Wei died three weeks ago, at forty-six, mother of a teenage daughter, wife of a stationery merchant, veteran of Unit 20256, People's Liberation Army, from which she retired at forty-three, already afflicted with a malignant tumor. She was Major Wei in the funeral announcement. I do not know why the news of her death was mailed to me except perhaps that the funeral committee—it was from such a committee that the letter had come, befitting her status—thought I was one of her long-lost friends, my name scribbled in an old address book. I wonder if the announcement was sent to the other girls, though not many of them would still be at the same address. I remember the day Lieutenant Wei's wedding invitation arrived, in a distant past, and thinking then that it would be the last time I would hear from her.

I did not go to the funeral, as I had not gone to her wedding, both of which took place two hours by train from Beijing. It is a hassle to travel for a wedding, but more so for a funeral. One has to face strangers' tears and, worse, one has to repeat words of condolence to irrelevant people.

When I was five, a peddler came to our neighborhood one Sunday with a bamboo basket full of spring chicks. I was trailing behind my father for our weekly shopping of rationed food, and when the peddler put a chick in my palm, its small body soft and warm and shivering constantly, I cried before I could ask my father to buy it for me. We were not a rich family: My father worked as a janitor, and my mother, ill for as long as I could remember, did not work, and I learned early to count coins and small bills with my father before we set out to shop. It must have been a painful thing for those who knew our story to watch my father's distress, as two women offered to buy two chicks for me. My father, on the way home, warned me gently that the chicks were too young to last more than a day or two. I built a nest for the chicks out of a shoe box and ripped newspaper, and fed them water-softened millet grains and a day later, when they looked ill, aspirin dissolved in water. Two days later they died, the one I named Dot and marked with ink on his forehead the first one to go, followed by Mushroom. I stole two eggs from the kitchen when my father went to help a neighbor fix a leaking sink—my mother was not often around in those days—and cracked them carefully and washed away the yolks and whites; but no matter how hard I tried I could not fit the chicks back into the shells, and I can see, to this day, the half shell on Dot's head, covering the ink spot like a funny little hat.

I have learned, since then, that life is like that, each day ending up like a chick refusing to be returned to the eggshell.

I was eighteen when I entered the army. Lieutenant Wei was twenty-four, an age that I now consider young, though at the time she seemed much older, a lifetime away from me. The day I arrived at the camp, in a midsize city plagued by hepatitis and pickpockets, I came with a single half-filled suitcase. The army had sent an extensive list of supplies that would be issued to us: toothbrushes and towels and washbasins, mess kits, thermoses to be shared among a squad, uniforms for all seasons—we used to joke that, had the army known the sizes of our bras, they would have ordered them too, dyed the same green as our socks and underpants.

A few men and women in uniform loitered under a tree. I had taken a night train, making a point of leaving home and arriving at the camp at the earliest time allowed. My father had seen me off at the train station, shaking my hand solemnly through the open window when the train whistled its signal of departure; my mother had not come, citing illness, as I had known she would.

After I registered, a woman officer, about a head taller than I was, her hair cropped short, introduced herself as Lieutenant Wei, my platoon leader. She had on a straw-colored uniform shirt buttoned to the top, dark green woolen pants, and a crimson tie. I did not cringe under her severe stare; I had lived, until then, beneath the unrelenting eyes of my mother. Decent if not strikingly beautiful—sometimes during a meal she would study my face and comment on it; in the evenings when my father was working the night shift, she would remark on my adequately developed curves. I had learned that if one remained unresponsive in those situations one could become transparent; when my mother's eyes peeled off my clothes piece by piece they would meet nothing underneath but air.

After I changed into my uniform, Lieutenant Wei ordered me to mop the barracks. Yes, I replied; yes, Lieutenant, she corrected me. Yes, Lieutenant, I replied readily, and she looked at me for a long moment, then turned around as if disgusted by my lack of defiance.

I was the first one of our platoon to have arrived, and I walked through the aisles between the bunk beds, studying the names taped to the metal frames. The company was housed in a three-story building, with each platoon occupying a long floor and bunk beds lining both walls, separated into four squads by washstands and desks. I would be sharing a bunk bed with a girl named Nan: We each had a white sheet, underneath which was a thin straw mattress; a quilt and a blanket, both dark green, folded as though they were sharply cut tofu. There was no pillow, and soon we would all learn to wrap up our outside clothes—dresses and shirts that were forbidden in the barracks—into pillows at night. Next to my bed was a window opening to the courtyard, where trees whose names I had yet to learn stood in a straight line, their branches pointing upward in a uniform manner.

Lieutenant Wei came back later and ran a palm over the floor. Do not think this is your home, she said, adding that I'd better prepare to shed a few layers of skin. When she ordered me to mop the floor again, I replied, "Yes, Lieutenant."

"Louder," she said. "I can't hear you."

"Yes, Lieutenant."

"I still can't hear you," she said.

"Yes, Lieutenant," I said.

"You don't have to yell in my face. A respectful and clear reply is all we need here."

"Yes, Lieutenant," I said. She stared at me for a long moment and said that a soldier shed sweat and blood but never tears. I waited until she left before I dried my face with my sleeve. It was my father's handshake through the open window that I had cried for, I told myself, and swore that I would never again cry in the army.

TWO

A DREAM HAS occurred repeatedly over the past twenty years, in which I have to give up my present life and return to the army. Always Lieutenant Wei is in the dream. In the early years she would smile cruelly at me. Didn't I tell you that you would be back? The question was put to me in various ways, but the coldness remained the same. The dreams have become less wicked as the years have gone by. I'm back, I tell Lieutenant Wei; I always knew you would come back, she replies. We are older, having aged in my dreams as we have in real life, the only remnants of a previous life among a group of chirrupy teenage girls.

These dreams upset me. Lieutenant Wei's marriage, two years after I had left the army, and her transfer to another city, which would know her only as a married woman and later a mother, and then would see her die, must have wiped her history clean so she could start collecting new memories not about young, miserable girls in the camp but about happy people who deserved to be remembered. I never showed up in her dreams, I am certain, as people we keep in our memories rarely have a place for us in theirs. You may say that we too evict people from our hearts while we continue living in theirs, and that may very well be true for some people, but I wonder if I am an anomaly in that respect. I have never forgotten a person who has come into my life, and perhaps it is for that reason I cannot have much of a life myself. The people I carry with me have lived out not only their own rations but mine too, though they are innocent usurpers of my life, and I have only myself to blame.

For instance, there is Professor Shan. She was in her early sixties when I met her—but this may be the wrong way to put it, as she had lived in the neighborhood for as long as my father had. She must have watched my generation grow up, and studied every one of us before singling me out—I like to imagine it that way; you see, for a lonely woman, it is hard not to make up some scenario that allows her to believe herself special in some minor way.

Professor Shan was in her early sixties and I was twelve when she approached me one September evening. I was on my way to the milk station. "Do you have a minute?" she asked.

I looked down at the two empty bottles, snuggled in the little carrier my father had woven for me. He had painted the dried reed different colors, and the basket had an intricate pattern, though by then the colors had all paled. My father had a pair of hands that were good at making things. The wooden pegs he put on the foyer wall for my school satchel and coat had red beaks and black eyes; the cardboard wardrobe had two windows that you could push open from the inside, a perfect place for me to hide. He had built my bed too, a small wooden one, painted orange, just big enough to fit in the foyer alongside the wardrobe. We lived in a small one-room unit, the room itself serving as my parents' bedroom, the foyer my bedroom; there was a small cube of kitchen and a smaller cube of bathroom next to the foyer. Later it occurred to me that we could not afford much furniture, but when I was young I thought it was a hobby of my father's to make things with his own hands. Once upon a time he must have made things for my mother too, but from the time my memory begins, their bedroom had two single beds, my father's bare and neatly made and my mother's piled with old novels, perilously high.

"Do you have a minute? I am asking you," the old woman

said again. I had developed a look of distractedness by then, and she was not the most patient woman.

I was on the way to the milk station, I stammered. "I'll wait for you here," she said, tapping on the face of her wristwatch with a long finger.

When I was out of her sight I took my time examining the trees by the roadside, and the last blossoming wildflowers. The line at the milk station was long, and that was what I told her when I reported back to her late. I addressed her as Teacher Shan, and she corrected me, telling me to call her Professor Shan. She led me up flights of stairs to her flat on the fifth floor. It did not occur to me that there was anything odd about this. The only thing my mother had warned me about, when I had had my first period a month earlier, was not to spend time alone with a man.

Professor Shan's place, a one-room unit also, seemed more crowded than ours even though she lived there by herself. Apart from a table, a chair, and a single bed, the room was filled with trunks: dark leather ones with intricate patterns on the tops and sides, wooden ones with rusty metal clips, and two matching trunks—once bleached but by then more yellow than white—made of bamboo or perhaps straw, I couldn't tell which. On each trunk there were books. She moved a pile of books to make a spot for me to sit on her single bed, and then took a seat in the only chair in the room. Up to that point I had not studied her, but I realized now that she was a beautiful woman, even at her age. Her hair, grayish white, was combed into a tight bun, not a single strand running loose. Her face—the high cheekbones, the very prominent forehead, and the deep-set eyes—reminded me of a photograph of a female Soviet pilot in my textbook. I wondered if Professor Shan had some mixed blood. It was a secret joy of mine to study people's faces. I must take after my mother, who, apart from studying my face at meals—the table placed between the two beds in my parents' bedroom—rarely took a bite. Sometimes, waiting for us to finish eating, she would comment on the people passing by outside our window: *Oily and puffy as fresh fried dough*, she described a woman living a floor above us; the man next door had a long and bitter-looking face, like a cucumber.

My mother was the prettiest woman I had known until then, with almond-shaped eyes in a small, heart-shaped face, a straight and delicate nose, and, as I later learned from her collection of romantic novels from the early 1900s, a cherry-petal mouth. When she grew tired of watching the world, she would study her own face in an oval mirror that she kept close to her all day long. "A princess trapped in the fate of a handmaiden," she would say to no one in particular. My father, eating silently, would look up at her with an apologetic smile, as if he were a parent responsible for his child's deformed body.

My father had married late in his life, my mother early, he at fifty and she at twenty. Two years later they had me, their only child. When I was in elementary school, other children often mistook him for my grandfather, but perhaps that was because he had to be a parent to my mother, too. Together my mother and I made my father grow old fast. You could see that in his stooped back and sad smile.

"Do you always let your mind wander in front of your teachers?" Professor Shan asked, though I could see the question was more an amusement than a criticism. In her youth, she must have been more beautiful than my mother. I wondered what my mother would think, if she knew my opinion. One thing I was certain of was that my mother would not get along well with Professor Shan, eccentricity being both women's prized possession.

I was aware of Professor Shan's existence as much as I was aware of the other people in the neighborhood: If you live in one place long enough, you do not need to seek gossip and rumors; stories, all sorts of tales, will come to find you. Even for a family like ours, with a mother who rarely talked to people and a father who was, in my mother's words, *quiet as a dead log,* stories would come in eavesdropped form while I waited in lines—and it seems that I spent my childhood perpetually in lines, waiting for eggs, cooking oil, meat, soap, milk, and other rationed goods, waiting to pay the rent and utilities, waiting to get my mother's prescription filled at the pharmacy. That was where I had first heard bits and pieces of Professor Shan's story, even before I met her: She had taught high school English in another district before her retirement. She had a son and a daughter, who, after graduating from college, had both vanished, reappearing every once in a while as visitors from America. People could not agree on how they had managed to leave the country, though the most reasonable explanation was that Professor Shan had relatives on her mother's side who had fled to the States. Once upon a time there had been a husband, a much friendlier person than Professor Shan, but he had disappeared, too, and it was said that he had been sent to the American relatives just as their children had been; it was also said that he had taken up with a younger woman and started a Chinese restaurant with her in New York City, which might be true, as he was never seen in the neighborhood again.

In any case, sitting in Professor Shan's room on that first day, I could not imagine that the place had once been occupied by a family. There were no framed photographs or letters bearing foreign addresses, and the room, packed with the trunks, seemed too small even for Professor Shan by herself. She studied me while I looked around the room, then picked up an old book and turned to a random page. "Read the line to me," she said. The book was the first one in a series called *Essential English*, which Professor Shan had used to learn English fifty years ago. The page had a small cartoon of a child on a seat, the kind one would find in a luxury theater. In the cartoon, the child, who was not heavy enough to keep the seat from folding back, smiled uncertainly on his high perch, and I felt the same. I had entered middle school earlier that month, and had barely learned my alphabet.

When I could not read the caption, Professor Shan put the book back with the other volumes, their spines different colors that were equally faded. "You do know that you are not your parents' birth daughter, don't you?" She turned and faced me. "And you do know that no matter how nicely they treat you, they can't do much for your education, don't you?"

I had not doubted my blood until then—I knew that my parents were different from most parents, but I had thought that it was their age difference, and my mother's illness. Moyan: My mother sometimes said my name in a soft voice when my father was not around, and I would know that she had some secrets to tell me. A man can have children until he is seventy, she would say; a woman's youth ends the moment she marries. Moyan, do not let a man touch you, especially here and here, she would say, gesturing vaguely toward her own body. Moyan, your father would get you a stepmother the moment I died, she would say, narrowing her eyes in an amused way; do you know I cannot die now because I don't want you to live under a stepmother? In one of these revelatory moments she could have said, Moyan, you were not born to us; we only picked you up from a garbage dump—but no, my mother had never, even in her most uncharitable moment, said that to me, and in fact she kept the secret until her death, and for that alone I loved her, and love her still.

"If your parents haven't told you this, someone else must," Professor Shan said when I did not reply. "One needs to know where she came from, do you understand?"

In my confusion I nodded. I am fortunate to be slow in responding to news—I have avoided much drama in my life, as the impact, if there is any, comes much later, in solitary meditation.

"I was an orphan myself." Slowly, over the next three years, her story would come in full. Her mother, a woman who had stayed unmarried to take care of her own aging parents, had inherited their small china shop when they died; by then she was too old to get married. She went to a Shanghai orphanage in the deadly winter of 1928 and adopted the only girl who was not suffering pneumonia. She named the young girl Shan Shan; she had no family name, as there was not one she could claim. McTayeier School for Girls, the best school in Shanghai, was where Professor Shan had been educated, the school's name spelled out for me to remember, "The McTayeierans," the song she and her classmates had sung at school gatherings, sung to me. In her early twenties, Professor Shan had been hired by a teachers college but was fired when her dubious history was discovered. People who think they know their own stories do not appreciate other people's mysteries, Professor Shan explained; that is why people like you and me will always find each other. Those words, first said to me in the early days of my visits, are what made me go back to her every day at five o'clock.

She read to me. She scoffed at my English textbook, and told me to start on the first volume of *Essential English*. She never checked my progress, and after a while I realized it did not make any difference to her that I only looked at the illustrations. Instead she read her collection of novels to me. We began with *David Copperfield,* she sitting in the only chair in the room, I on the bed. Intimidation kept me focused at first, as sometimes she would look up sharply in mid-sentence to see if my eyes were wandering to the trunks, or the trees outside. I worried that she would find me a fraud and dismiss me. I did not like her or dislike her yet, but I was in shock, unable to process the fact that I was not related by blood to my parents, and Professor Shan's reading voice, with a melody that was not present when we talked, was soothing in a way that my mother's voice never was. Professor Shan would read long passages, stopping only when she seemed pleased, and then translate for me. Her translation seemed shorter than the original English, but even those brief Chinese words gave me a joy that I did not get elsewhere—she used phrases that belonged to a different era, a language more for the ancients than the living, and before long I began to mimic her. I had never been a talkative person, but now I had even fewer words, for the ancients had the most efficient ways of saying things. My schoolmates found it laughable but I persisted, ignoring teenage slang for a mixture of language used in ancient poetry and eighteenth-century romance novels. My father, who was not an educated person, did not seem to find it odd, perhaps having little idea how education could change one's speech, but my mother, more than once, studied me after my father and I exchanged some words. I knew I had invaded her territory—after all, she was the one who read ancient poetry and centuries-old novels to pass the time. She could not make up her mind about how to accept my change, I could see, just as I could not make up my mind about the news of her not being my birth mother.

THREE

BY OUR THIRD week in the army everyone in my squad had received a letter from home; a few had received additional letters from their friends. Without fail all of them cried when they read them. Ping, the youngest among us, fifteen and a half, doubtless a genius to have graduated high school that young, read aloud her father's letter between sobs: "After you registered and went into the barracks, Baba cried on the way to the train station. The night train from Wuhan to Beijing was fully packed, and Baba stood for eighteen hours, but that, compared to Baba's little darling's suffering in the army, was nothing. I have the calendar on my wall, and every morning I mark a day off, knowing it is one day closer to our reunion."

I was the only one, by the fourth week, not to have received a letter. "Are you sure you don't want to write to your parents again?" asked Nan, who stood next to me in line for the formation drill and slept in the bunk bed above me. "Your last letter might have got lost, and they might not have the address to write to you."

I shook my head. I had sent a postcard to my parents the first week, saying nothing but that I had arrived safely. My father was not the type to write a letter, and secretly I was relieved that my father was not like Ping's, who would continue sending letters filled with unabashed words of love, which Ping never hesitated to share. My mother might write me, on a whim, a letter filled with quotations from ancient poems, but then again, she might have decided to cut me out of all communications.

At the end of the week I was summoned to Lieutenant Wei's room. It was a Sunday, and we had the morning off from drills. She motioned for me to take the only chair, and I moved it away from her before sitting down in the middle of the room. There was a single bed on my left, with an army-issue quilt, blanket, and sheet. There was no pillow on her bed, and I wondered if she wrapped up some old clothes as we did at night, or if she had a pillow hiding in her closet. On the wall next to the bed were a few framed photographs. A black-and-white one stood out. A young girl, thirteen or fourteen, looked away with a smile, as if she had been teasing the photographer. "That was taken the summer before I enlisted," Lieutenant Wei said as she studied me. "Have you been out to town yet?"

"No, Lieutenant," I said. She only had to check her chart to know that I had never requested one of the two-hour permits to visit town on Sundays.

"Why? The town is too small for someone from Beijing to visit?"

I thought about the question, which, like all questions put to us by an officer, could have many traps. There was no particular reason, I said. I could have said that I wanted to give the opportunity to the other girls, who were more eager to have the two hours of freedom, but that would have led to more questioning. I had learned, in the past few weeks, that an officer's friendliness was not to be trusted. Lan, a girl whose hometown was in the same province as Lieutenant Wei's hometown, once had an amicable chat with Lieutenant Wei at a drill break, but five minutes later, when Lan made the mistake of turning right when the rest of us turned left, Lieutenant Wei ordered her to leave the formation and do a hundred turn-lefts. Even worse, Lan was to give herself the drill command, and by the time she reached thirty, her voice was choked by her tears. Lieutenant Wei, while the rest of us watched with anxiety, told Lan that if she did not make the command clear and loud to all who were witnessing her punishment, it would not count. Similar incidents had happened to others: A girl was ordered to stand in the middle of the mess hall during a meal after she had laughed at a joke told quietly to her by a squad mate; another girl was asked to read a self-criticism in front of the company because she had claimed the food from the mess hall was better suited for feeding pigs than human beings. These punishments were measured out not only by Lieutenant Wei and the other junior officers, but also by Major Tang, the commander of our company, who, as the only male officer, liked to storm through the barracks for unannounced inspections.

When I did not reply, Lieutenant Wei changed the topic and said that she had heard that I hadn't yet received a letter from home. I wondered who had reported this to her, but perhaps this was how the army worked, details about our lives recorded by informants among us. My parents are not the type to write letters, I said.

"Is that a problem for you?"

"A problem, Lieutenant?"

"Would you like to phone them?" Lieutenant Wei said. "I could arrange for you to make a phone call to your parents if you wish."

My parents did not own a telephone. The nearest public telephone was a few blocks from our building, guarded by a brusque middle-aged woman. A message would be taken but would not be delivered until the end of the day; she was paid as a government worker, her salary at a set level, so she rarely inconvenienced herself to deliver even the most urgent messages. Once in a while when the residents filed complaints, she would for a week or two put the callers on hold and send her teenage son around the neighborhood. "A phone call for number 205," he would call out in front of a building, his voice no longer a child's but not yet a grown man's. He was said to be slow, so no school would admit him, and he spent his days, if not as a companion to his mother, then running around the neighborhood and intimidating young children with incoherent ghost stories. My mother would never respond to such a boy calling our flat number in that manner, nor would she be willing to make a trip to the phone booth to call me back.

I told Lieutenant Wei that there was no need to make a call, as my parents did not have a telephone at their place.

"And a neighbor? A friend living nearby?" Lieutenant Wei said. "Anyone who could receive a phone call on their behalf so they know you are well?"

The only telephone number I knew—though I had never used it—was Professor Shan's. It was written on a slip of paper, in her neat handwriting, and taped on the red telephone next to her single bed. I had studied the number many times while she was reading a long passage, and after a while I could not get it out of my mind.

There is no one I could call, I said when Lieutenant Wei pressed me again. She studied my face as if trying to decide if I was lying out of defiance. She retrieved a file folder from a drawer, and pages rustled under her impatient fingers. I looked out the window at the evergreen trees, wishing to be one of them. I loved trees more than I loved people; I still do. Few creatures are crueler than human beings, Professor Shan had said once; we had been standing side by side next to her fifth-floor window, looking down at people busy with their late-afternoon lives. I can guarantee you, Professor Shan said, pointing to the weeping willows by the roadside, every one of those trees is more worthwhile than the people you'll get to know in life; isn't it a good thing that once you are bored by people you still have trees to watch?

"Your father's work unit? Can you call him there?" Lieutenant Wei said. "But of course we'll have to arrange for you to call during the weekdays to catch him at work."

She was reading my registration form, where I had put down "service" for my father's occupation, along with the name of the department store where he worked night shifts. I wondered if she was calculating my parents' ages, as the registration form asked for their birth information, too.

There was no need to call him, I replied. My parents were not the type who would begrudge the army for not giving them sufficient information about my well-being.

Lieutenant Wei seemed not to notice the hostility of my words. "Your mother—what kind of illness does she have?"

When I had entered elementary school I had been instructed by my father to put down "retired early from illness" for my mother's occupation. What kind of illness? the teachers would ask. What did she do before she became ill? At first I did not know how to answer, but by middle school I became an expert in dealing with people's curiosity—she was a bookkeeper, I would say, the most tedious and lonely job I could come up with for her; lupus was what had been troubling her, I would explain, the name of the disease learned in fifth grade when a classmate's mother had died from it. I thought about what kind of tale would stop Lieutenant Wei from pursuing the topic. In the end I said that I did not know what had caused her disability.

The earliest I could remember people commenting on her illness was when I was four. I was standing in a long line waiting for our monthly egg ration when my father crossed the street to buy rice. What kind of parents would leave a child that small to hold a place in line? asked someone who must have been new to the neighborhood, and a woman, not far behind me, replied that my mother was a mental case. *Nymphomania* was the word Professor Shan had used, and it was from her that I had learned the story of my parents' marriage: At nineteen, my mother had fallen in love with a married man who had recently moved into the neighborhood, and when the man claimed that he had nothing to do with her fantasy, she ran into the street calling his name and telling people she had aborted three babies for him. They would have locked her up permanently had it not been for my father's marriage proposal. My father, who people had thought would remain a bachelor for life, came to my mother's parents and asked to take the burden off their hands. Which would you have chosen for your daughter had you been a mother, Professor Shan asked me, an asylum or an old man? She'd told me the story not long after I had become a regular visitor to her flat. I had stammered, not knowing how to pass the test. Professor Shan said that it was my mother's good fortune that her parents had given her up to a man who loved her rather than to an asylum; love makes a man blind, she added, and I wondered if my father's misfortune was transparent to the world.

Later I would realize that my family—my father's reticence, my mother's craziness, and my existence as part of their pretense of being a normal married couple—must have been gossip for the neighborhood, and their story, sooner or later, would have reached me, but when I left Professor Shan's flat that day, I resented her heartlessness. We were only fifty pages into *David Copperfield*, and I could have easily found an excuse not to go to her flat again, but what good would it have done me? I was no longer my parents' birth child, and their marriage, if it could be called a marriage, was no doubt a pitiful one.

Lieutenant Wei closed the file folder. She seemed, all of a sudden, to have lost interest in my case. She looked at her wristwatch and said that since there was still an hour until the end of the day, meaning eleven o'clock, when drills started, I might as well use the time wisely and go water and weed our platoon's vegetable garden.

Today I would give anything for a garden, but the only space I can claim now is my flat. It's on the north side of the building, so the only sunshine I get is slanted light for an hour in the evening. My father used to keep pots of green plants on the windowsill, but they have long since withered and found their way to the trashcans. Today I would give anything for a garden—perhaps not as big as the one we used to have in the army, as it would be pure greed to ask for that, but a small patch of earth. At eighteen, though, I had not the urge to nurture anything. "The garden was weeded and watered yesterday, Lieutenant," I said.

"Are you telling me that I have given you a worthless order? How about the pigs? If you think the vegetables grow without your contribution, maybe you could put some efforts into cleaning the pigsties."

The pigs, not yet fully grown, were kept at the far end of the camp. There were five pigs for each company, and the conscripts in the cooking squad had told us that the pigs were to be butchered at the end of our year for the farewell banquet. Other than the five pigs, we saw little meat. Once in a while Ping would devise an extensive plan to sneak a pig out of the camp, find a willing butcher to kill it, and another willing soul to cook it; the scheme grew more detailed and vivid, but it was only talk, for the sake of passing time.

I said it was not our squad's turn to take care of the pigs. Most shared duties—grounds-keeping around the barracks, gardening, helping the cooking squad prepare meals for the company, feeding the pigs and cleaning the pigsties, cleaning the toilet stalls and the washing room—were rotated among the four squads in the platoon, and apart from the kitchen duties, during which we could sneak extra food to our table, they were dreaded and carried out with aversion.

"I see that you haven't learned the most basic rule about the army," Lieutenant Wei said. "This is not the civilian world, where one can bargain."

FOUR

THE CIVILIAN WORLD slowly crept in on us, in the form of letters from old school friends and packages of chocolates from parents, memories of childhood holidays and teenage expeditions, and, in my case, Professor Shan's voice, reading D. H. Lawrence, her tone unhurried. *Well, Mabel, and what are you going to do with yourself?* When I closed my eyes at the shooting range I could hear her voice, and the question, posed from one character to another, now seemed to request an answer from me. Or else: *To her father, she was The Princess. To her Boston aunts and uncles she was just "Dollie Urquhart, poor little thing."*

The point of a boot kicked my leg, and I opened my eyes. I was not in Professor Shan's flat, released momentarily from responsibility by her voice, but facedown, my elbows on sandbags, my right cheek resting on the wooden stock of a semiautomatic rifle. The late October sunshine was warm on my back, and two hundred yards away the green targets, in the shape of a man's upper body, stood in a long line. Two magpies chattered in a nearby tree, and the last locusts of the season, brown with greenish patterns, sprang past the sandbags and disappeared into the yellowing grass. I shifted my weight and aligned my right eye with the front and rear sights. The training officer did not move, his shadow cast on the sandbags in front of me. I waited, and when the shadow did not leave to check on the next girl, I pulled the trigger. Apart from a crack, nothing happened—it would be another two weeks before we would be given live ammunition.

"Do you think you got a ten there?" asked the training officer.

"Yes, sir," I said, still squinting at the target.

He sighed and said he did not think so. Try again, he said. I held the rifle closer so that the butt was steadied by my right shoulder. I had noticed that people, once put into an army, become two different species of animal—those who were eager to please, like the most loyal, best trained dogs, and those who, like me, acted like the most stubborn donkeys and needed a prod for every move. I looked through the sights and pulled the trigger.

"Much better," the training officer said. "Now remember, the shooting range is not a place to nap."

Shooting practice was one of the few things I enjoyed in the army. Major Tang showed up occasionally to inspect us, but since aiming was one thing we had to practice on our own, he had little patience for staying at the shooting range for hours. The three platoon leaders, including Lieutenant Wei, sat in the shade of ash trees and chatted while two of the shooting officers for the company, who liked to sit with them, told jokes. Our officer, older and more reticent, sat a few steps away and listened with an indulgent smile. The two girls on my right talked in whispers, and now and then I caught a sentence; they were discussing boys, analyses and guesses that I did not bother to follow. On my left, Nan hummed a tune under her breath while maintaining a perfect shooting position. I was amazed at how soldierly she could act, her posture perfect in formation drills, her impeccable bed-making winning her titles in the internal-affairs contest. Anyone could see her mind was elsewhere, but the military life seemed to provide endless amusements for her; she never misbehaved, and she was among the few who hadn't received any public humiliation. I turned my head slightly, still resting my right cheek on the stock but looking at Nan rather than the target. Her uniform cap was low on her eyebrows, and in the shadow of the cap she squinted with a smile, singing in a very low voice.

"The Last Rose of Summer," she told me when I asked her about the song during the break. Nan was a small girl and looked no more than thirteen years old. She had joined a famous children's choir when she was six, and when the other children her age had entered middle school and left the choir, she had remained because she liked to sing, and she could still pass for a young child. When she reached sixteen, the choir changed its name from "children's choir" to "children and young women's choir." She'd laughed when she told us about it. Would she go back to the choir? one of the girls had asked her, and she'd thought for a moment and said that perhaps after the army she would have to find some other hobbies. One could not possibly remain in a children's choir all her life, she'd said, though she seemed to me the kind of person who could get away with anything she set her heart on. I could imagine her still singing at twenty or thirty among a group of children, looking as young and innocent as them—though this I did not tell Nan. We were friendly toward each other, but we were not friends, perhaps the only two in our platoon who hadn't claimed a close friend eight weeks into the military life. I did not see the need to have someone next to me when I took a walk around the drill grounds after dinner for the fifteen minutes of free time; nor did I need to share my night-watch duty with a special friend, so I was often paired with leftover girls from the other platoons—girls like me who had no one to cling to—and it suited me well to spend half a night with someone as quiet as I was in the front room of the barracks, dozing off in two chairs set as far apart as possible.

Nan was a different case. She was friendly with everyone, including the officers and the conscripts in the cooking squad, and was courted by quite a few girls hoping to become her best friend. You could see that she was used to such attention, amused even, but she would not grant anyone that privilege. Even our squad leader, who had become a favorite of the officers with her increasingly militant treatment of us, was unwilling to assign the most dreadful duties—cleaning the toilets, or the pigsties—to Nan. A less gracious person than Nan would have been the target of envy, yet she seemed untouched by any malignancy.

One girl, overhearing our conversation, asked Nan to sing "The Last Rose of Summer." Nan stood up from where we were sitting in a circle and flicked dried grass and leaves from her uniform. Her voice seemed to make breathing hard for those around her; her face, no longer appearing amused, had an ancient, ageless look. I wondered what kind of person Nan was to be able to sing like that—she seemed too aloof to be touched by life, but how could she sing so hauntingly if she had not felt the pain described in those songs?

The shooting range was quiet when Nan finished singing. A bumblebee buzzed and was shooed away, and in the distance, perhaps over the hills where a civilian world could not be seen, a loudspeaker was broadcasting midday news, but we could not hear a word. After a while, a girl from another platoon who had sneaked away from her squad to join our circle begged Nan to tell us something about her trips abroad. Apart from Nan, none of us had traveled abroad—none of us had ever had a legal reason to apply for a passport.

I could not decide if Nan was annoyed or pleased by such requests, but she never failed to tell some tales: singing in front of a Vienna palace, learning tap dancing from an American teenager on a cruise ship, taking a long train ride across Siberia in February on her way back to China from a European tour, the whole time stuck in a carriage with girls eight or nine years younger. She had learned chess from the choir director on that train ride, she said, while the young children sang and clamored, and a doll-like girl, not yet seven, had played violin for hours like an oblivious angel.

"How old is your choir director?" the girl from the other platoon asked.

Nan shrugged and began another tale about the Macedonian folk songs they'd had to learn because of a detour. I noticed that this was her way of not answering questions she found unpleasantly nosy or uninteresting. Even though Nan kept smiling, you could see that the girl who had asked the question was ashamed of her blunder. In fact, there was so much pain and yearning in the girl's face that I turned to look at the officers under the ash trees, Lieutenant Wei massaging the nape of Lieutenant Hong's neck, and the two young shooting officers competing with exaggerated gestures to talk to another platoon leader. From where we sat, twenty meters away, they looked young and ordinary, their laughter distant but their happiness tangible. After a moment the older shooting officer looked at his wristwatch and, almost apologetically, blew the whistle to signal the end of the break.

At night, when I could not sleep, I thought about other people and their pain. I wondered, for instance, what kind of pain could be found in Nan's heart that gave such unbearable sadness to her songs, but she was the most imperturbable person I had met, and if she could be connected to any pain, it would be what she inflicted on others, perhaps against her will. I thought about the girls who vied for her attention, often with open animosity toward each other; they had become transparent in their longing, but I did not know what more they could ask from Nan. She shared her songs and her stories; she treated everyone kindly. Would they be lying in their beds, wondering if Nan had ever known pain? But why would one want to access another person's pain, when there is enough in one's own life? In the barracks there was much love in the air—boys left behind in the civilian world were missed and written long letters; boys met in the camp were discussed, sometimes with giggles, sometimes less gleefully; more subdued was the longing between the girls that manifested itself as a competition to become best friends. *People don't know what they are doing and saying. They chatter-chatter, and they hurt one another, and they hurt themselves very often, till they cry.* At night I tried to remember Professor Shan's voice when she read her favorite story to me, and when I was not sure if I remembered the exact words, I turned on my flashlight and reread the story under the quilt. *But don't take any notice, my little Princess.*

We had spent ten months with *David Copperfield,* slowly at first, two or three pages a day, and later five or six pages. I don't remember at what point I had begun to understand what was read to me, in bits and pieces of course; it must be similar to the moment a child first understands the world in words, when what is spoken to her has not yet taken on a definite meaning, but she becomes more confident each day that there is a message behind those jumbled sounds. I told my parents that I had been visiting Professor Shan, as she had agreed to tutor me with my schoolwork, a lie that my father had not questioned and my mother had not bothered to listen to. I did not tell Professor Shan that I had begun to understand her, but surely she saw the change: Perhaps my eyes wandered less often to the trees outside the window, or perhaps my face betrayed an eagerness where before was only ignorance. In any case, two-thirds into the novel she stopped translating for me. Neither of us talked about this change of routine. I was quiet, still intimidated by her, though I had begun to look forward to the hour spent in her flat. She had not begun to tell me her stories—that would come later. I had not begun to share her attachment to books—that too would come later, much later, perhaps only after I stopped visiting her. Still, her fifth-floor flat, where life did not seem to be lived out in the measuring of rice and flour or the counting of paper bills and coins, at least during the time I was there, became a place that no other place could be: Strangers, closer to my heart than my neighbors and acquaintances, loved tragic and strange loves and died tragic and strange deaths, and Professor Shan's unperturbed voice made it all seem natural. Looking back, I wonder if it was because of my limited understanding of the language that all tragedies became acceptable to me. Perhaps all that time I was imagining a different story than the one read to me.

After *David Copperfield*, we read *Great Expectations*. Then *The Return of the Native* and, later, *Tess of the d'Urbervilles*. It was during *Jude the Obscure* that she began to tell me her story, in fragments I would piece together later. Sometimes the story came at the beginning of the afternoon, sometimes when she took a break from reading the novel to me. She never talked long about herself, and afterward we did not discuss it. I had become less nervous around her; still, I did not talk much about my life at school or at home—intuitively I knew she had little interest in the life I lived outside the hour in her flat. Only once did I ask her advice, about where to go for high school. I was not an excellent student, though decent enough to do well in entrance exams. She asked me my choices of schools, and when I listed them for her, she answered that they were all good schools, and it rather did not matter, in her opinion, where I went. In the end, I chose the school farthest from our neighborhood, a decision that later proved convenient when I had to come up with an excuse to stop visiting Professor Shan.

FIVE

I TURNED OUT to be excellent at shooting. I was one of the few who scored all tens in our first live-ammunition practice, and when we marched back from the shooting range, I was displayed in front of the company along with three other girls with a red ribbon pinned to my chest. Major Tang called the four of us budding sharpshooters and gave a speech that ended with the slogan "My gun follows my orders, and I follow the Communist Party's orders."

"That slogan," said Jie, one of the other sharpshooters. "Don't you think it sounded so . . . off-color?"

"What do you mean?" I asked.

"You're too innocent for this discussion," Jie laughed, but a few days later she sought me out. "Do you read English?"

Apart from the officers and the conscripts in the cooking squad, all of us were able to read some English, since we had studied it in high school, and I said that to Jie. "I know that, of course," she said. "I'm asking you if you could read an English novel for me."

I had never talked to anyone about Professor Shan, and I did not memorize English vocabulary during the free time, as some of the other girls, who had their hearts set on going to America after college, did. I replied vaguely that I could try, and after dinner the next day Jie approached me with a copy of *Lady Chatterley's Lover.* "It was once a banned book," she told me with hushed excitement, and asked me to promise not to let the secret out to anyone. "My boyfriend sent it to me. Don't lose it. He went to great trouble to find a copy."

The book, a poorly Xeroxed copy, was wrapped in an old calendar sheet, the words small and smudged. "Don't look like I'm corrupting you. You're old enough to know these things." In a lower voice Jie told me that there were many colorful passages in the novel, and could I mark all the passages describing sex between the man and the woman for her? I blushed at the words she used—*zuo-ai,* doing love, an innocent yet unfortunate mistranslation of the English phrase *making love.* Jie said she didn't have the patience to read the book herself, and told me if I wanted to I could skip pages as long as I did not fail to mark what she should be reading.

Jie was an outgoing girl, loud and confident, fond of crass jokes. Perhaps the fact that I did not have someone to reveal her secret to was behind her reasoning; or she might have simply pitied me for my naïveté about the world, and thought of me as someone in need of enlightenment. In any case, I did not ask her for an explanation—it was easier to let people have their opinions than to convince them otherwise.

At night I covered my head with the quilt and pointed the light from my flashlight onto the pages. I was sixteen when Professor Shan began to read the stories of D. H. Lawrence to me; it was the fall I entered high school. My favorite author, she said of Lawrence, but did not say more. It became clear to me—and I tried not to show my disappointment—that we would not return to Dickens or Hardy, at least not for a long while. She pointed out the novels she would read to me after we finished with the two volumes of Lawrence's stories: *The White Peacock, Sons and Lovers, The Rainbow, Women in Love*. Her eyes seemed to gleam unusually as she laid out her plan. I wonder whether she had been waiting for that moment ever since I had begun visiting her. Were Dickens and Hardy only a preparation for Lawrence? Was she waiting for me to grow older, or to become better with English, so that I could understand Lawrence?

That fall, milk was no longer rationed, but our family could not afford it, as I needed lunch money for the high school canteen. Every day I rode out of the school gate at quarter to four, the earliest possible time, and cycled across a district and a half to get to Professor Shan's flat at quarter after five. I did not go home to report to my parents first. My father, on a longer night shift now, would leave for work around five, and it mattered little to my mother when I returned home—my father left a cooked meal for us, which my mother rarely touched. She was becoming even thinner, ghostly hollows around her cheeks, and she lay in her bed and read ancient romance novels for hours.

There was a woman who was beautiful, who started with all the advantages, yet she had no luck. She married for love, and the love turned to dust. Professor Shan began reading to me as soon as I arrived. Sometimes she would lay snacks on the table—a few biscuits, half an orange, a handful of roasted chestnuts—but she herself never ate anything when I was around, so I did not touch the food either.

I did not like Lawrence, and my mind began to wander to other things. I had enjoyed Dickens, who talked to me at times in a wordy manner as I imagined a grandparent would. I had never met my father's parents, and my mother's parents had washed their hands of her, so I was only a stranger to them. I had loved Hardy, and had dreamed of the countryside in his books—black-and-white dreams in which everything looked slanted as if in a woodcut print—but this may have had more to do with the joy of finding myself able to understand English. I dared not show that I was annoyed by Lawrence. I had lived with a mad mother all my life and had found madness, which seemed prevalent in the stories read to me now, the most uninteresting topic. I tried to suppress a yawn and let my mind wander to a man whose name I did not know and whose face had begun to haunt me. The man lived on the second floor of Professor Shan's building and had a young daughter named Nini. "Nini's Papa" was how I greeted him. He did not use my name—he had never asked me for it, so perhaps he did not know mine either—and he called me Nini's Sister, as if I were connected to his daughter by blood.

I now know his name, as he has become one of the most renowned flutists in the nation. I have seen his face on posters, and read in newspapers and magazines the story of his success after years of hardship, about his childhood spent as an orphan with distant relatives, serving in his teens as an apprentice to a blind folk musician whom he then had buried while traveling across south China, about his years of playing in the street for small change, his failed marriage and estranged daughter. The articles called him "a figure of inspiration." He has not aged much in twenty-five years, though he looks less melancholy, more at ease with the world. I imagine his students in the conservatory having youthful crushes on him, love that has long been due him. Sometimes I wonder if he still remembers me, but the moment the thought occurs to me, I laugh at myself. Why should he think about someone who is a reminder of his humiliation? Only those who live in the past have space in their hearts for people from the past; the man surely has enough success to savor only the present, with many people to occupy his heart, perhaps far too many.

Nini's father had married into the flat on the second floor. Having no place of his own and, worse, no job, made him a laughingstock, or, rather, his wife. It was said that she had fallen in love with him when she saw him play his flute in the park, a near beggar who, the neighbors used to say, "must have a short circuit in his brain to think of himself as an artist." Much to her parents' chagrin, she made up her mind to marry him and support him while he tried his luck getting into the National Conservatory. A year later they had a daughter, and his in-laws, with whom he and his wife shared the two-bedroom flat on the second floor, refused—unlike most grandparents—to take care of the baby. Nini's mother worked as a clerk in a government agency, and while she was away, Nini's father could be seen walking the baby around the neighborhood. It must have been disheartening for a man, once homeless, to be made homeless again, during the daytime, along with his child, but as a young girl I did not sense the agony of his situation. Rather, I was envious of his freedom, not belonging to a school or a work unit, and I wished to be his companion during his long hours of aimless wandering.

Nini was just learning to speak when I first began to visit Professor Shan. I was not the kind of well-raised child who knew to compliment a woman on her new dress or a father on his adorable daughter, but whenever I saw Nini and her father in the late afternoons, often playing in the small garden across the narrow lane from Professor Shan's building, I would greet them. I praised the girl for the stick she held in her hand, or the pebbles she gathered into a pile. Her father thanked me, speaking on her behalf, and it became a habit for both of us to speak through his daughter. "Nini, have you had a good day with your *baba*?" I would ask her. "Tell your sister that we've had a good day," her father would reply, and even later, when Nini was older and chose not to acknowledge either of our existences, we would still use the girl as an intermediary to exchange words.

I never saw Nini's father play the flute. He had a gaunt look by the time I entered high school: Where there had once been a smile, there was now only a distracted look, his hair gray before its time, his back beginning to stoop. He spent less time with Nini then—the girl must have been accepted by her grandparents, as a few times I saw them walk her to a preschool. I wondered what he would do with his time now that Nini was in school. When I walked past their flat on the way to Professor Shan's, I studied the green wooden door, the paint peeling off at the edge, a child's doodle by the doorknob. I imagined the world behind the door, what Nini's father, when he unlocked the door, would have to brace himself to face. At night I tried to remember his face and his voice, but hard as I tried, I was never able to recall enough details to make him a real person.

On an early November afternoon, when I was locking my bicycle in front of Professor Shan's building, Nini's father appeared quietly from around the corner.

"How are you, Nini's Papa?" I said when he did not speak. "Did Nini have a good day?"

An old woman exited the building and gave a meaningful glance toward him before calling out to her grandchildren to come in and do homework. In a low voice, Nini's papa asked if he could talk with me for a few minutes.

I followed him to the small garden. It was one of those mild autumn days, the last before the harsh winter would begin. The sun, half setting, was pinkish orange in the cloudless western sky, which was warm orange and pink and magenta.

The man stopped by a trellis of wisteria, the flowers long gone, the last leaves hanging on to the vine. "I want to let you know that I will be leaving the neighborhood tomorrow."

I nodded, as if I had known it all along and was not surprised by the news. The streetlights, whitest blue, blinked to life with a collective buzzing.

"Nini's mama and I signed the divorce papers today," he said.

I had known Nini's mother for as long as I could remember. She was fifteen years older, ordinary in all ways but for her marriage. She was too old to be part of my generation, but not old enough to become one of those ubiquitous women we called "auntie," who claimed the right to yell at any child from the neighborhood, so our paths had never crossed. It occurred to me that I had never, despite all the time I spent imagining his life, thought of her as someone dear to him. I wondered if she had been forced to divorce him by her parents, or if she had, at long last, joined the world in condemning him as a useless man.

"I was waiting for you to come back from school," he said. "You've always been kind to me, and I want to have a proper farewell."

"Where will you be tomorrow?"

He looked lost at the question, and then said that there were ways for a man to manage.

"Will you still try to get into the conservatory?"

Perhaps he would, he said, but such things were not up to him. One should not give up, I said eagerly, quoting an old saying about fate allowing what is allowed, but it is one's responsibility to fight for what one wants before it's decided by fate. He smiled, and I recognized the derision. I must have sounded childish to him, but when he spoke, his derision was directed at himself. He had fought more than his share of fights against fate, he said; perhaps he should be a warrior rather than a flutist.

I tried to find other words of comfort, but it was enough of an effort to hold back my tears. He was about to say something when a sanitation worker, sweeping a pebble path nearby, began to whistle a love song from a Romanian film from the fifties. We both turned to look at the man. I wondered, for a moment, if my father, mopping the floor of the empty department store in the middle of the night, hummed old love songs to himself.

"Will you let me know when you get into the conservatory?" I asked after the sweeper had moved on.

Nini's father raised his eyes as if startled by the question. Professor Shan is waiting to tutor me, I said.

He hesitated and held out a hand to shake mine. I wished I had more to say to him, and he to me. I took his hand; as soon as our fingers touched we both let go. "Farewell, Nini's Sister," he said.

"Farewell, Nini's Papa," I said.

Neither of us moved. A bicycle bell chimed and was followed by other chimes, none of them urgent—a child must have been walking past the bicycle shed and felt the urge to test all the bells. "Farewell, Nini's Papa," I said again.

He looked at me, and I wondered if he would come closer, and if I should push him away if he did. I wanted to ask him if he would miss me as I would him; I wanted to ask him if away from this sad neighborhood we could see each other again. But the love that was not yet love, the questions that were not asked thus never answered—in retrospect, I wonder if it was all mere fantasy in a lonely teenager's heart. But there were things to be accounted for: the farewell that a man thought necessary for a girl he barely knew, the silence while listening to a stranger's whistling, the hand that was raised to wipe my tears but that had paused midair and then patted my head. Be good, he said, and walked away into the dark shadows of the trees.

I was no more than ten minutes late when I got to Professor Shan's flat. She opened the door before I knocked and looked at me quizzically. There was a traffic accident in Peace Road, I said, and she led me into the flat without acknowledging my lie. When she turned the pages to the place we had ended the day before, I stared at the yellow tassel on the bookmark. The man's fingers had been cold to the touch; I clasped my hands together, and my palms felt feverish.

Professor Shan stopped reading. "You seem to have trouble focusing today," she said, and replaced the bookmark in the book, putting it back where it belonged on top of a leather trunk.

I mumbled, but she waved in dismissal and told me to help myself to the fruits and biscuits she had laid out on the table. She walked to the only window in the room and parted the curtains. I wondered if she spent her days, when I was not around, studying the world from her fifth-floor window; and if she had caught me talking to Nini's papa, on that day or previously.

"When one is young, one thinks of love as the most important thing," Professor Shan said, still facing the window. "It's natural if you think so, though I do hope you've learned a few things from the books I've read to you. One could waste one's life pursuing a flower in the mirror, a moon in the river, but that is not what I want to see happen to you."

I looked at the back of her head, the impeccable bun that was pulled a little higher than an old woman's, so that she looked like a ballerina, with her straight back and long pale neck, and when she turned around, for a moment her face looked cold and marble-like in the light. "The moment you admit someone into your heart you make yourself a fool," she said. "When you desire nothing, nothing will defeat you. Do you understand, Moyan?"

SIX

I WAS CAUGHT by Lieutenant Wei one night reading *Lady Chatterley's Lover.* I was close to finishing the novel; perhaps one more night would do. I had bracketed every sex scene and marked it with an arrow in the margin of the page, though I was not enjoying the novel myself. Duty propelled me to continue reading and, on top of that, curiosity about what Professor Shan might say about each of the characters. Toward the end I was overtaken by fatigue. Perhaps that was what made me less alert to the creaking of the barracks door. When Lieutenant Wei lifted the quilt from my head, I had barely enough time to hide the book under the makeshift pillow of bundled clothes.

"What are you hiding from me?" Lieutenant Wei asked in a low voice.

The early December night air was cold on my warm face, which must have looked flushed in the glare of her flashlight. I fumbled under the bundled clothes without lifting my head from the pillow. When I found the right book I raised it to the light. Lieutenant Wei grabbed it and told me to get dressed and report to her room in two minutes.

When I was certain that she had gone back to her room, I checked under the clothes again. Jie's book was safe there, and I decided that I would smuggle it back to her first thing in the morning.

The confiscated book—a collection of Lawrence's short stories—was lying open on Lieutenant Wei's desk when I entered her room. She signaled for me to sit down on her chair. "What's the book about?" she asked.

"A lot of things, Lieutenant."

"Like what?"

"Men and women, Lieutenant," I said. "And children."

"What about them?"

What about them? I thought about the question and wondered what kind of punishment Lieutenant Wei would give me. The only time I had come to her notice was when I scored perfect marks during shooting practice. It was one of those useless talents you don't ask for in life. Still, at practice I aimed and pulled the trigger with the utmost concentration, my mind calm; the care-taking of the rifle—disassembling it and laying the parts at perfect angles on a sheet of newspaper, then cleaning them with a soft rag and putting them back together with precision, all while the training officer timed us on his stopwatch—gave me immense satisfaction.

"Are they romantic stories?" Lieutenant Wei asked.

I would not call them romantic, I replied. What would you call them, then? she asked, and I said they were stories about mad people.

"Are they worth breaking the rule of internal affairs?"

"Not really, Lieutenant."

"Are you lying?"

"No, Lieutenant," I said.

Lieutenant Wei picked up the book, ready to tear the pages. I wished I could plead with her that the book was a present from a dear friend, but the truth was, I had always known that I would be punished for having it: Apart from the volumes of *Essential English,* which I had little interest in reading, Professor Shan had never allowed me to take a book away from her flat; I had stolen the stories of Lawrence when I decided not to go back.

"I can see you're lying," Lieutenant Wei said. She closed the book and studied the cover. "Do you want the book back?"

"No, Lieutenant."

"Why not?"

"They are unworthy stories, Lieutenant," I said.

She stared at me, and I tried to look as blank as I imagined I had in front of Professor Shan when I told her, a few days after the departure of Nini's father, that my schoolwork no longer allowed me to spend time with her. For the briefest moment Professor Shan had looked disappointed, or perhaps even hurt. One has to do what she thinks suits her best, she'd said, and I mumbled that the coursework was heavier than I'd expected. I had wished to leave her with the impression that I would return once the summer holidays began, but she must have seen through me. She told me to wait and then left the room. I still cannot understand what I did next; I quietly took one of the story collections of Lawrence—the one we had just finished—and slipped it into my book satchel. A moment later, Professor Shan returned with a bar of Lux soap, which had just begun to be imported, the most expensive and most luxurious soap. It was wrapped in a piece of peach-colored paper with a beautiful woman printed on it, and I recognized the fragrance that I had always connected with her flat. Be good to yourself, she said, and before I could think of words of gratitude or apology, she waved for me to leave and told me to close the door behind me.

The soap and the book had traveled with me to the army. At night I slept with them, sometimes opening the book to a random page and imagining Professor Shan's voice reading it. I had seen her around the neighborhood a few times after that, and she acted as if we had never known each other. I wondered then—and wondered again in the army—why she did not confront me about the stolen book. Could it be that she had stopped reading the stories after I left, so never realized her loss?

When Lieutenant Wei asked me if I was certain that I did not need the book, I replied that as far as I cared, the book could be tossed into the garbage can at this very moment.

Lieutenant Wei said that in that case, she would keep the book for herself. I wanted to remind her that she did not read English. "Who knows? Maybe one day I can learn English, too, so I can read the book myself," she said, as if she had read my mind. "What do you think? Will I be able to read the book after I learn English?"

"I don't know, Lieutenant," I said.

"How long did you study English before you could read the book?"

The digital clock on her desk said quarter to midnight. I wondered how long she would keep me. A few years, I said, and shifted in the chair.

"A few years is not that long," Lieutenant Wei said. "Maybe you can start teaching me now. Will I be able to read a little English by the time you leave?"

I did not know what kind of trap she was setting. A few of the girls from the platoon had become friendly with Lieutenant Wei, but I did not see the point of befriending an officer.

"I've had reports that you have received letters from your parents, is that right?" Lieutenant Wei asked.

"Yes, Lieutenant," I replied. My father had written twice, both letters brief, saying that he and my mother were well and that they hoped I was, too.

"Why are you unhappy?"

"Unhappy, Lieutenant?"

"What's bothering you?"

"I don't understand the question, Lieutenant."

"Did you break up with your boyfriend?" Lieutenant Wei said.

"I have never had a boyfriend, Lieutenant," I said. I would rather she had ripped my book and sent me back to the barracks with a week of cleaning duty at the pigsties.

"When I enlisted," Lieutenant Wei said, "my boyfriend saw me off at the train station and then sent a letter to the training camp to break up with me. The first letter I got in the camp. I was much younger than you are now. I was fourteen and a half. He was eighteen, and he did not have the courage to say it to my face. You think it's the end of the world, but it is not. The army is a good place to sort these things out."

I wondered if other girls, for different misdemeanors, were kept hostage at odd hours in this room and informed of the love history of Lieutenant Wei. It was ludicrous of her, I decided, to think that any unhappiness could be explained by a breakup; more ludicrous if she thought she could, by recounting her own story of triumph over heartbreak, lessen other people's pain.

"Apparently you have no interest in this discussion about feelings," Lieutenant Wei said.

"I do my best to summarize my feelings in my ideological reports, Lieutenant," I said. Every Sunday night, we read our weekly reports at the squad meeting. I always began mine that in the past week I had kept up my faith in Communism and my love of our motherland; I filled the rest of the page with military and political slogans that not even Major Tang could find fault with. I had been criticized by our squad leader for being insincere in my reports, so I learned to add personal touches. "In the past week I have continued my efforts to understand the invincibility of Marxism," and "In the coming week I will work on *The Communist Manifesto.*"

Lieutenant Wei sighed. "I'm not talking about the feelings in your ideological reports."

"I don't have much feeling about most people, Lieutenant," I said. There had not been a boyfriend and perhaps there never would be one—the man who had not wiped away my tears under the wisteria trellis had later done so, repeatedly, when my memories were revised into dreams, and he who had chosen not to claim the love had left no space for others to claim it: In high school there had been a boy or two, like there is a boy or two for most girls during those years, but I had returned their letters in new envelopes, never adding a line, thinking that would be enough to end what should not have been started.

Without a word Lieutenant Wei put the book in her drawer. I wondered how Professor Shan would have felt had she known that her beloved book had fallen into the hands of someone who, in her mind, was ill-educated. I felt a slight, vindictive joy, directed both at Professor Shan and at myself.

I saluted Lieutenant Wei's back when I was dismissed, but before I opened her door she told me in an urgent tone to come back. We stood in front of her window, huge flakes of snow falling in the windless night. In a hushed voice, as if it were a secret that we needed to keep between us, she said without turning to me, "You know, I've never seen real snow."

SEVEN

THE SNOW CONTINUED falling the next morning, bringing a festive mood to the camp. It was the first snow many of the locals had ever seen, and the weatherman had forecast a record storm, more snow than in one hundred and twenty years, if not longer. The officers' orders came as though from a faraway land, their shrill whistles marking our military routines muffled. At formation drill, we marched with less resolve, the ground becoming more and more plush by the hour. A huge snowman was erected in front of the mess hall by the cooking squad, his straw hat almost touching the eaves; a squad of smaller snowmen were installed next to the pigsties, in perfect formation.

The wind picked up in the evening, and by the next day the snow was more of a concern than a marvel. It did not stop until the end of the third day. The temperature had fallen sharply. There was no heating in the camp, and most of the pipes were frozen. The cooking squad, who kept the big stove burning, managed to have running water in the kitchen, and each of us was rationed a basin of water. In the mornings we broke the ice on the surface to clean our faces.

Ping was the first in our squad to develop frostbite, which in a day or two affected all of us, on our cheeks and ears, hands and feet. None of us, after days of marching in the snow, had dry shoes or socks.

The snowstorm had turned us quiet; talking seemed to require extra energy that we did not possess. On the evening of the third day, while we were waiting for the dinner whistle, Ping reread her father's letter from the previous week—the snowstorm had stopped the post, and the weekly letter from Ping's father, precise as clockwork, had not come—and announced that she was not crying not because there was nothing to cry about, but because tears would do more damage to her already swollen cheeks. Nan smiled, then sang us a folk song in which a girl named Little Cabbage loses her mother during her infancy and goes on to suffer a long and painful life under the reign of a cruel stepmother and spoiled half brother.

"We Little Cabbages should unite and take our fates into our own hands," Ping said after Nan finished the song. "I have an idea: We should pair up and share beds at night."

The most miserable time of the past few days had been crawling under the ice-cold quilt. Most of us went to bed wearing layers of clothes. Still, a small shift in position would cause one's arm or leg to come into contact with the cold sheet; we dared not move in our sleep, and as a result woke up with cramped muscles.

Ping began telling a story that she said she had read in *Reader's Digest*. A priest, having arrived in the Canadian wilderness, was assigned a young local girl as a guide for his journey to his post, and when the two were stranded in a shed by a snowstorm, the girl discovered that she had forgotten to bring a flint and tinder. At night, it was so cold that they were in danger of freezing to death, so the girl suggested that they sleep together to keep each other warm. "Of course the priest, who had never been close to a young woman, fell in love when the girl wrapped them up together in a blanket. He never reached his destination but married the girl. Years later, she told him that she had lied—a local girl, she would never have forgotten the flint and tinder," Ping said, for a moment looking alive and happy. "Imagine that!"

Lieutenant Wei might not allow us to share beds, our squad leader said. Why not? Ping asked, and said that Lieutenant Hong had begun sleeping in Lieutenant Wei's bed. "They're cold, too."

"How did this discovery occur?" Nan asked, and winked at me as if she and I had access to some secret knowledge that was denied Ping. She was on the way to the restroom a couple of nights ago, Ping said, when she saw Lieutenant Hong sneak into

Lieutenant Wei's room. "They didn't see me, of course," Ping said. "But think about it. It makes sense, no? Two bodies are better than one in this cold weather."

Two girls whose beds were across the aisle nodded at each other and asked the squad leader to pair them up. The squad leader said that she would have to report to Lieutenant Wei, and five minutes later returned with the official permission. Should we draw lots every night? Ping asked, becoming more excited about her idea. We could spend the day guessing who we would sleep with at night, she said; suspense would make the time go faster.

Nan watched the squad with amusement. I waited, and when she did not say anything, I said that I could not bed with another person.

"Why?" asked Ping.

I would not be able to sleep, I said.

"But think about how warm it would be," Ping said. "One can't possibly sleep well in this cold."

I shook my head, and said that under no condition would I share a bed with another person.

"You're aware"—the squad leader looked at the other girls before turning to me—"that if we've made the decision collectively, you should honor it."

I could feel the other girls' animosity. I had made myself into a hedgehog, with its many arrows, which could neither protect itself nor frighten its enemies, sticking out ridiculously.

"I'll sleep alone, then, too," Nan said.

"But it's not fair," Ping said. "I don't understand why some people feel they have the right to be special."

People make fools of themselves in this or that way—

Professor Shan's words came back to me later that night, when I tried to stay still under the ice-cold quilt; *neither you nor I are exempt,* she had said, *but we do our best, do you understand*?

The snow stopped the next day. The city, having no means to deal with the snow, had been paralyzed by the storm. The afternoon drills were called off, and when we arrived at the city center, with shovels and pickaxes, most of the roads were covered by frozen snow that had been packed hard by wheels and feet. "Soldiers," announced a general who drove past us in a Jeep with Major Tang, speaking through a megaphone. "You've been fed by the army, and now it's time to prove your value to the army."

The city, where proprietors of small shops called out to passersby for business, and peddlers fought to sell fruits and other goods, as I had found out during my only Sunday visit, was vacant. The streetlamps were scarcely lit, perhaps to conserve energy. A few early stars flickered in the sky, which was a smooth dome of deep blue. Once in a while a bus, empty and lit dimly from inside, rattled past us, and we would stop our pickaxes and shovels to watch the wheels leave hard tracks in the newly loosened snow.

"What do you mean you can't finish?" Major Tang yelled at Lieutenant Wei, when she reported to him, an hour into cleaning, that she worried we had been assigned too much. The night wind cut into our cheeks as if with a thin blade, but more dispiriting than the pain was the endless road. "The word *impossible* does not exist in the military dictionary. Now, Lieutenant, do you and your soldiers have the courage to face the challenge from nature?"

"Yes, Major," Lieutenant Wei replied.

Major Tang told us that dinner would be ready only when the road was cleared. "Now let's sing a song to boost our morale," he said, and ordered us to sing "The Marching Song of the Red Women's Warriors."

An hour and then two hours later, the platoon still saw no hope of finishing the road. Ping threw her shovel onto the hard snow and began to cry. Our squad leader tried to hush her, but halfway through her sentence, she was choked by tears, too. I leaned on the handle of the pickax and watched a few of my squad mates join in the crying, their world complicated only by the most superficial dilemmas.

Lieutenant Wei came toward our squad, and without a word grabbed the pickax from my hands and lifted it over her head. The ground shook when the pickax hit the hard snow, and more girls stopped shoveling. Lieutenant Wei looked possessed, her jaws tight, her arms brandishing the pickax with mad force. Ping stopped crying and, shivering, hid behind another girl. Nan shook her head before picking up the shovel again, trying to pry loose the snow that Lieutenant Wei's pickax had cracked.

It was after midnight when we returned to the barracks. Nan said that she had changed her mind, and she wanted a bedmate too. "I won't do it," I said when my squad mates looked at me, and I said it again to Lieutenant Wei. The lights-out bugle blew, the drawn-out tune seeming to take forever to reach the end. *She had no great desire to live,* I remembered from one of Lawrence's stories, underlined twice with red pen by Professor Shan. I wondered if she had thought that she, too, lacked a great desire to live, but that must not be the case: People who do not cling to life perish, one way or another. As far as I could see, Professor Shan would live forever in her flat, watching with all-seeing eyes those who peopled her books; perhaps she was thinking of me at this very moment, shaking her head at my follies.

I climbed into bed before Lieutenant Wei left the barracks, and turned my back to my squad.

EIGHT

IN LATE JANUARY, three days after the Lunar New Year, I left home to return to the army. I did not tell my parents that there was still another week until the holiday leave ended, nor did I inform anyone at the camp of my decision to return early.

"Would you like me to see you off at the train station?" my mother asked when I came into her bedroom to say goodbye. She was leaning against a stack of pillows on her bed, an old novel, its pages yellow and fragile, resting on her chest as if her hands were no longer strong enough to lift the book. She had become less careful with her looks, strands of hair going astray, pajamas worn all day long where before she had always dressed herself at dawn; she looked frailer, too. On the day I returned from the army, she had seemed happy to see me.

There was no need, I replied. My father, standing in the doorway with a duffel bag in his hand, waited for us to finish our farewell. In the duffel bag he had packed, heads to ends, two dozen pickled eggs, wrapped up neatly in four columns of newspaper. I had told him not to bother with the eggs, but he had insisted that I looked ill-fed.

"So, you are doing well in the army?" my mother asked.

I said that all was well. I had noticed, upon returning, that my mother would sometimes make an effort to chat with me, but her interest was fleeting, and she was easily tired or bored by me; so eventually we settled into the old mode, conversations between us polite and formal. My father, too, seemed to cling to my presence more than before: In the mornings when he returned home from the night shift, he would pick up two pieces of fried bread from the street peddler and watch me eat them before they turned cold. The previous day he insisted on accompanying me when I went to the stores to buy a few things for the camp, looking away when I asked the clerk for sanitary napkins.

Had they missed me while I was gone? I could not tell. My parents had always been quiet around each other, simple household communications transmitted not by words: My father, upon returning from work in the morning, would brew the tea and then hand a cup to my mother, who would by then have groomed and dressed herself; when breakfast was ready, he'd place her plate first on the table, and she would join us without having to be reminded, though she rarely touched the food. My father would nap from mid-morning to early afternoon, and my mother left the flat when he slept. I never knew where she went, but she always came back and rested in bed when my father got up to finish the day's chores. When she became weaker, she no longer took long walks when my father napped. They must have talked to each other, but mostly there was silence between them, a comfort more than a reason for resentment. I believe, to this day, that despite its cruelty, fate granted them the best companions they could have asked for in a marriage: They knew what they needed from each other, and they did not request what they could not have.

My mother told me to come closer to her bed. My father nodded at me in a pleading way, and she told me to bend over so she could have a good look at my face. She touched my cheeks where the frostbitten skin was now puffy and tender, with a yellowish hue, which gave my face the look of a rotten apple. "Look what they did to you," my mother said, as if she had noticed it for the first time.

The frostbite is getting better, I said, and then asked my father if it was time for us to go.

"Things get better. Or else they get worse," my mother said. "You should learn to take care of your face. You are prettier than you let yourself believe."

I don't mind looking ugly, I said.

"You should know that you can't possibly be ugly, because you are my daughter." She was almost inaudible.

Later I wondered if she meant that she would not have adopted a homely-looking baby, or if, perhaps, on a whim, she wanted to claim my blood connection to her. She seemed to have other things to say, but I said goodbye, and she only laughed lightly. Typical for a young girl to be in a hurry, she said, and then waved for my father and me to leave her alone.

Neither my father nor I talked on the bus ride to the train station. He looked older, moving more slowly than I remembered. Men his age should be thinking about retirement, but I knew he could not retire before I could support them. I felt guilty about escaping home and leaving the burden of my mother to him. How was he managing while I was not home? I asked him as we waited in the long line at the boarding entrance. He seemed surprised by my question. Nothing much to manage, he replied, and said that things were as they always were. This talk, neither here nor there, left us embarrassed, and I could see his relief when we finally boarded the train. He lifted my suitcase to the luggage rack and carefully stored the duffel bag with the eggs under my seat. Be well, then, he said, shaking my hand, again solemnly. I told him not to wait for the departure of the train, knowing he would not obey my wish. When the whistle blew, he stepped off the train and waved behind the gray and grimy window when the train inched forward, and I waved back once, thinking perhaps we were the loneliest family in the world because we were meant to be that way.

No one questioned my lie when I arrived. The camp was empty, no rushing steps on the staircase for the early morning training, no singing contest before meals so that Major Tang could determine which platoon would enter the mess hall first. The senior officers, who had families at the compound across the street, showed up once a day, and only when they were present did the junior officers—Lieutenant Wei and the other two platoon leaders, the company supply officer, and the clerk—assume a military appearance.

I began to eat with the cooking squad in the kitchen so that the officers would not be reminded of my presence. The conscripts, boys my age or younger, had joined the army to seek a future that was otherwise not available to them. I knew there were girls who were particularly close to the cooking squad—whether for friendship or an extra bite or two I could not decide. Before, I had talked to the conscripts only when our squad was on cooking duty, so I worried that they would resent a stranger, but they seemed happy that I—or perhaps any girl for that matter—chose to eat with them. They told jokes, making fun of people that I had never met, or of one another, and I tried my best to smile, since I knew they were doing it for my sake.

After each meal, I followed the two conscripts on duty to the pigsties, and then to the vegetable garden, which did not require a lot of work at this time of the year. None of us had things to rush to, so we made the outings last as long as we could. The boys took turns pushing the handcart, slowly so the slopping swill would not spill out of the buckets; at the beginning I asked to help, but they were gallant and never let me. Their jokes continued on these trips, but soon bits and pieces of their secrets surfaced. It did not take me long to figure out that each of them was in love with a girl from the company, but theirs was the most hopeless kind of love, as they would continue their lives in the army, and we would be gone by summer. When the boys began to confess, I did not ask questions or make comments; all they needed was someone not in their position to listen to them, so I did. None of the girls being dreamed about was me, though the conscripts did not seem to sense any awkwardness in confessing to a girl they had collectively dismissed as undesirable.

I wished this life could go on forever. When the swill was poured into the trough, white steam rose into the chilly air, and the pigs, already snorting with impatience, pushed against one another—but sooner or later, satisfied by a good meal, they would calm down. The conscripts cleaned the trough and then the sties, and the pigs found their favorite spots to lie in the sun. The pigs' needs were simple, their happiness easily granted; the boys were in pain, but still they joked, their dreams laughable to their companions and themselves alike. If I climbed atop the low brick wall of the pigsties, I could see the shooting range, and the hill beyond that was turning yellowish green. The earth in the vegetable garden softened every day, and soon another planting season would begin, but when harvest time came, we girls would be back in the civilian world. If I focused on the joyful squeals of the pigs, I could pretend my parents did not exist; in the sun-filled vegetable garden, who were Professor Shan and Nini's father but phantoms in one's fantasies?

The night before the other girls returned from leave, Lieutenant Wei found me in the barracks. Apart from brief greetings, she had left me alone the past few days, and I wondered if my early return was an inconvenience. Sometimes I could hear, from the hallway, her voice along with the other officers. One night a few male officers from the boys' companies had visited, and their laughing and singing had not ended until after midnight.

"So, I see you're getting yourself ready ahead of time," Lieutenant Wei said. She examined the barracks, which I had been cleaning daily.

"Yes, Lieutenant."

"Did you have a good leave? Was your family well?"

"Yes, Lieutenant."

"Why did you come back early, then?"

"I misremembered the date, Lieutenant," I said.

Perhaps I was disappointing her with my insistence, but disappointment can occur only where there is something to hope for in the first place. I had no hope to offer her.

"I see that you've spent a lot of time with the cooking squad," she said.

"They are kind to let me help, Lieutenant."

"But I want to remind you to keep things simple regarding them."

"I don't understand, Lieutenant."

"Of course you do," she said. "Don't you know that you do a bad job acting dumb?"

"I consider my behavior soldierly around the cooking squad, Lieutenant."

"You don't have much feeling toward those poor boys, is that what you're saying? To tell you the truth, you're not my concern. You could suffer the most horrible thing and I wouldn't give a damn. But have you ever thought about the boys? They won't have your future. When you're back in the city they will still be here. You don't mess with other people's lives and then disappear. But how can you understand other people's pain, you city girl, full of yourself?"

We had been polite around each other since the snowstorm, and I thought we would go on maintaining that formality. If the boys of the cooking squad were in pain, I was not the one who'd caused it, I wanted to defend myself, but I knew Lieutenant Wei was talking about herself more than the conscripts. I did not give my future much thought, though other girls made it obvious, with their talk about college life and occasionally about going abroad, that we girls had futures worthy of our suffering in the army. I wondered if I could make Lieutenant Wei feel better by telling her about my parents, whom I had run away from, or about Professor Shan, whom I longed to visit again but for reasons I did not understand could not allow myself to, or Nini's father, whom I would never see again. But animosity is easier to live with than sympathy, and indifference leaves less damage in the long run.

NINE

IN EARLY APRIL we set out on a month-long march across Mount Dabie, hailed by Major Tang as the revolutionary cradle of our Communist nation. The expedition, planned to boost our Communist morale, was nevertheless a welcome alternative to our daily drills, and to the long hours we spent sitting in ideological seminars.

Never would I have a more memorable time than the month I spent in the mountains, though I wonder, when I say this, if it appears so only because it is our nature to make a heaven out of places to which we can never return. But if I close my eyes and hum the songs that we sang on the road—"The Red Azaleas," "The Warsaw Marching Song," "The Song of the Communist Youth," "Under the Shining North Star"—I can see us again, lining up on the first day at the drill grounds, waiting for the lorries to arrive and transport us from the camp to an army depot in the mountains. *Don't we look like giant snails bearing our homes on our backs?* I remember Ping's comment—each of us carried, bundled tightly in a plastic sheet, a bedroll and a set of uniforms for changing, a heavy raincoat, two pairs of shoes, a satchel with towels, a cup, a toothbrush and toothpaste, and a canteen, all arranged as compactly as possible so the items would not become more of a burden than they were. Turtles, Nan corrected Ping, and went on to tell a joke about turtles, though hard as I try now, I can remember only the laughter around her after she finished the joke.

We were jostled in the covered lorries, for hours it seemed, on the winding mountain road, and our excitement was slowly replaced by exhaustion. On a particularly uneven stretch of road, Nan stood up from where she was sitting on her bedroll, and worked loose the rope that bound the two roof tarps together. Lieutenant Wei, who was sitting at the other end, ordered her to sit down. Nan looked out the gap for a long moment and then retied the tarps as best she could. "If the lorry missed a turn, we would die together," she said to no one in particular, and began to sing in English: *If you miss the train I'm on, you will know that I am gone. You can hear the whistle blow a hundred miles.*

Her voice was more sorrowful than ever, though there was a smile on her face. Lieutenant Wei seemed to be as stricken as we were, even though she could not understand what Nan was singing. When the song ended, we listened to the tree branches scratching the tarp and pebbles bumping off the wheels of the lorry. I wondered why sadness seemed to roll off Nan as raindrops roll off a lotus leaf, without leaving any trace; I wondered how one could acquire as unaffected a soul as she had.

We stayed in the army depot that night, the last time during the journey we would be sleeping in bunk beds—later we would sleep on the unpaved dirt floors of village schools, and in the meeting halls of People's Communes from the fifties that were no longer in use, and in the field, our whole squad squeezed together in a small patch of space. I would soon learn to let my defenses down, but on that first night, when the mountain air chilled our bones and made our teeth chatter, I again refused to share a bed with a squad mate.

At three o'clock in the morning, I was shaken awake for my night-watch duty. I wrapped myself in a quilt and went into the yard, and took my position under the brick wall. The night was clear and cold, the stars so close that one could almost reach them by raising a hand. An owl hooted and was answered by another, and I remembered the story—one of the few my father had told me—about the owls that carried the message of death: They would spend each night counting the hairs in a person's eyebrows, and when they finished counting at daybreak, that person would die. When the owl hooted again, I shivered and rubbed my eyebrows, as my father had done for me when I was little, so the owls cannot count your eyebrows, he had said, his gentle touch on my eyebrows a comfort.

Jie, the other girl on night duty, shone her flashlight at me from where she was sitting at the foot of a tree. I clicked on my flashlight and waved back. A minute later she trotted over. "Are you cold?" she said.

"Yes."

"Are you afraid?"

"No."

"Are you lonely?"

Jie arranged her quilt around her and said she would sit with me, and I did not remind her that, if we were discovered, we would both get into trouble. We sat back to back, leaning onto each other, both huddled with our machine guns, though we had not been supplied with ammunition. Jie had behaved casually around me since the winter, and I wondered if it was natural for friendship to be formed out of shared secrets; she was the closest friend I had ever had.

"If some bad guys came, we could do nothing," Jie said.

"We'd whistle and then run," I said, searching my quilt for the whistle I had been supplied along with the gun.

Jie laughed lightly and asked me if I realized the irony of our hugging guns that would not shoot. I don't understand, I said, though I did; Jie was fond of telling me off-color jokes, as if my reading *Lady Chatterley's Lover* for her had qualified me to hear all the secrets she said she could not share with the others.

"Have you ever been in love?" Jie said.

"No," I said.

"Sometimes you miss someone so much that all of a sudden you can't remember how he looks or sounds," she said, and asked if I had ever experienced that.

I thought about Nini's father, whose face I could call up if I wanted to, though I rarely did; I thought about Professor Shan, whose voice came more easily to me than her face.

"My boyfriend and I—we did it in the winter."

"Like they did in the novel?" I asked.

Jie told me not to believe anything I'd read in that book. "You think you will remember every moment, every detail, but the truth is, I can't remember much about it. Can't even remember how long we were at it."

How could one forget such things? I could recall many details of the afternoons in Professor Shan's flat, the last sunshine of the day slanting in from the window, her fingers slowly turning the pages, a cricket chirping from under one of the old trunks; I had not forgotten a single word that Nini's father had said to me on the night of his divorce.

"Let me ask you—if two people love each other, doesn't it mean that every minute of one's life matters to the other?"

I had never loved someone, I said, so I would not know. Jie said that in that case, she was asking for directions from a blind person. Her boyfriend was not interested in her life in the army; he saw it as a nuisance that kept them apart for a year. "But won't you remember tonight fifty years from now?" Jie asked. "I wish he'd remember these things with me. Two heads are better than one."

"In bed," I said. Jie laughed and said she did not know I could be naughty. It was a pity that I was in his place, I said, and Jie told me not to make fun of her. I was sad that she did not understand I meant it: She and I would drift apart once we left the army; we were not close, not even real friends. I would not be the one to carry the memory of tonight for her.

I wished her boyfriend were here; I wished too that someone other than Jie were next to me, someone who one day would share the memory of the mountains with me. The wish, illogical as it was, persisted into the following days when we marched in the mountains. It was sunny in those days, the sky blue, red azaleas wild on the cliffs. If one looked up, one could see the long line of green figures ahead, disappearing and then reappearing along with the winding road, and when one quieted her steps momentarily, the singing of the companies behind would drift uphill. In the valleys, there were creeks, and sometimes a river, and there was always a lone fisherman sitting in the shade of his wide-brimmed straw hat, and a long-legged white egret nearby, neither disturbing the other. When the mountains were replaced by rolling hills we knew that we were approaching a village: First came the fields of purple milk vetch that unfolded like giant rugs, white and yellow butterflies busying themselves in and out of the lavender blossoms; closer to the village, there were rice paddies, and water buffaloes with bare-footed boys sitting astride them; once in a while a sow would spread herself across the narrow road that led into the village, a litter of piglets pushing against her. Small children chased after us, calling us Auntie Soldiers and begging for candies. Even the youngest ones knew not to eat them right away—they gingerly licked the candies and then wrapped them up so they would last days, perhaps even weeks. Feeling guiltily privileged compared to the children, we competed to offer them treats, but sooner or later we would leave them behind and march on until dusk fell, when smoke could be seen rising from the field kitchen in the valley.

Walking comforted me. I marched alone and did not join the chorus when the platoon was singing; here in the mountains, walking was the only thing required of me, and for hours I would be left undisturbed, my mind empty of troubling thoughts. Never before had I loved the world as I did then, the sunshine and the spring blossoms, the new trees in the woods, and the lizards in the grass. Even the daily ritual of blister popping—in our satchel each of us carried a sewing needle, and in the evenings the brigade doctor would pass out cotton balls soaked in alcohol so we could sanitize the needle and pop the blisters on our feet—brought me an odd sense of liberation. There was a joy in knowing the realness of one's body: the sting when a blister was pierced; the heaviness in one's arms where the blood was pulled down by its own weight after a day of marching; the exhaustion in one's limbs lying down on the floor of a village school; the moment of uncontrollable shivering when one left the cluster of warm bodies for night-watch duty, the coldness seeping in.

TEN

WE ARRIVED AT a town called Seven-Mile Plain after one of the longest marching days, covering thirty-two kilometers—across two rivers, over mountains, and through valleys. It was the fifteenth day, halfway through our journey, and when we limped into the town's only elementary school, the full moon was already in the eastern sky, golden with a red hue. The cooking squad had set out in the school yard one of the most extravagant meals we would have on our journey: stir-fried eels, marinated pork with snow peas, tofu and vegetable soup, and, to our surprise, a bottle of local beer for each of us.

In a very long toast, Major Tang summarized every day of the journey, squinting at times, trying to read the map he held. Is he already drunk? Ping mumbled, eyeing the basins of food on the ground that would soon have a layer of fat congealing on their surfaces.

A free night was announced after dinner, and we were told that bedtime would be called an hour later. That generosity, along with the beer from dinner, created a festive mood. Girls walked in twos and threes in the schoolyard, which was a sizable plot that went uphill until it reached a fence. Locust trees, decades old, surrounded it, with clusters of cream-colored blossoms hanging heavily between branches, their sweet fragrance growing more intense as the night progressed. Under one of the oldest trees a group of girls sang a love song from an old movie.

I walked to the school gate and was disappointed to discover that it was padlocked. Before I turned around, someone stepped from the dark shadow of the high wall and called to me.

It was a boy in uniform, and he asked me if I knew Nan. I thought of denying it, but he said he had seen me at drills and knew that I was in Nan's squad. He told me his name and which company he was from, and then asked me if I could pass a letter to Nan.

"Where are you staying?" I asked, and the boy said that his company was stationed for the night in the middle school across the street.

"And you can leave the schoolyard freely?" I said.

The boy smiled and said he had jumped the wall. I thought about him outside the school gate, waiting to catch a glimpse of Nan. When he asked me again if I could pass on his letter, I said that Nan had too many admirers to care about a letter from a stranger. The boy appeared crestfallen, and I refrained from asking him why he had never imagined other people falling in love with the girl of his dreams. "Here," he said, passing a green bottle through the gap in the metal gate. "You can have this if you help me."

He had put a bottle of local yam liquor in my hand. Under the crudely drawn trademark of a phoenix was a line that proclaimed it the fiercest drink west of the Huai River, with a 65 percent alcohol concentration.

"I only drank a little," said the boy eagerly. "It's almost full to the top."

"What do I do with it? Pour it on my blisters?"

He seemed perplexed at my joke, and I wondered if his courage had come from the drink, which had made him as much a fool as his love had. I did not know why I had accepted his present. I had given my ration of beer to a conscript in the cooking squad—I had never touched alcohol in my life, nor had I ever seen it around our flat. I took a stroll around the schoolyard, and when I couldn't locate Nan, I sat down in the farthest corner of the yard, under an old locust tree, its bulging root the perfect seat. *What dissolves one's sorrow but a good drink?* It was one of my mother's favorite quotations from an ancient poem, even though she had never touched a drop. I uncapped the bottle, wiped its mouth carefully, took a gulp, and was immediately choked to tears.

After the burning sensation in my chest became less of a torture, I took another mouthful, all the while aware of my intention to pour the liquid out and discard the bottle, though I never did gather the resolution. When Lieutenant Wei approached me, much later it seemed, I recognized her footsteps. I hesitated, and did not stand up to salute her.

"What are you doing here?" she asked. "You missed the bedtime whistle."

It occurred to me that I had heard some muffled steps, and later that the schoolyard had become quiet, but I had not once thought of my obligation to report to the classroom for bedtime. I did not hear the whistle, I replied. I wondered if the officers were conducting a search for me; and perhaps in my daring confusion I even asked the question aloud, since Lieutenant Wei snatched the bottle from my hand and said I should be grateful that she did not report me missing. "What would happen if you reported me?" I asked. I stood up, trying to steady myself by leaning onto the tree trunk. The world seemed sharper, as if a hand had retraced the edge of everything: the moon, the dark shadows of the trees, Lieutenant Wei's frown, my bottle in her hand. "Would I be punished in any way that you think would make me repent?"

"You're drunk."

Perhaps so, I said.

"Is anything the matter?" she asked, her voice softening. "Can I help you?"

Anything the matter? I laughed and said that the trouble was, I did not know a single thing that could be called *the matter.* How do you unravel a mess of yarn when you don't even see the yarn? I said, realizing that I must sound ridiculous.

Lieutenant Wei asked if she could have a drink. I nodded. She took a sip of the liquor, then passed the bottle to me. Let us drink like good friends, she said. I took a gulp and poured the rest of the liquid on the root of the locust tree. "We are not meant to be friends," I said to Lieutenant Wei.

"Not for once?" she asked.

I could not tell if her tone was a pleading one. "I was not yet given a life when you were born; when I was born you were old already," I said.

"I don't understand," Lieutenant Wei said.

Of course she would not understand. When I was in elementary school, I had once discovered a handmade bookmark in one of my mother's old novels, a few lines of an ancient folk song written in my mother's neat handwriting: *I was not yet given a life when you were born; when I was born you were old already. How I wish I had not come this late, but death has placed moun-*

tains and seas between you and me. I had thought, at twelve, that my mother had written out the lines for my father, and I had cried then for them, thinking that she was right, that one day death would come for my father long before it was her time. Later I realized that it was not for my father but for a married man that she had written those lines out; I did not know who the other man was, but I knew he must be younger than my father. Still, with a wife and children, and without any affection to spare for my mother, he must have been as unreachable as death would have made him.

"Why are you unhappy?" Lieutenant Wei said when I did not speak. Placing a finger under my chin, she lifted my face slightly toward the moon. "Tell me, how can we make you happy?"

I now know that it was out of innocent confidence that Lieutenant Wei asked those questions. She was twenty-four then, a sensible and happy person. There are people, I now know, who have been granted happiness as their birthright, and who, believing that every mystery in life can be solved and every pain salved, reach out with a savior's hand. I wish I had replied differently, but at eighteen, I was as blind to her kindness as she was to my revulsion at any gesture of affection. "Why don't you give me a happiness drill right at this moment?" I said. "There is nothing we can't achieve in the army, isn't that right, Lieutenant?"

The rainy season began the next day, and it rained on and off for the rest of our journey. The mountain road was muddy, and the bedrolls on our backs, despite our heavy raincoats, inevitably got damper each day, "good for nothing but cultivating mushrooms," as Nan drily observed one night. Wildflowers by the roadside drooped in the storms, but even if they had not, we would not have regained the impulse to decorate our buttonholes with them. The officers stopped ordering us to sing, and sometimes we walked for an hour or two without talking, the only noise coming from the rustling of our raincoats, the rain falling on the tree leaves, and our footsteps in the soft mud.

I avoided Lieutenant Wei as much as she avoided me, though strangely, when we sat down in an open field at breaks, I would watch the rain fall off my visor, and hope for the chance to talk to her again. Stop being an idiot, I scolded myself; still, I found myself involuntarily searching for her when we set up camp in the evenings.

The rain stopped on May Day, and the sky lit up, the purest blue I had ever seen. We ended the marching early, at midday, and stationed ourselves in a place called Da-Wu—*nirvana*—an unusual name for an impoverished mountain town. There were only two days left in our journey, but before we returned to the camp, there was to be a field exercise that night. Da-Wu, once a model town, which had spent more than it could afford building intricate air-raid shelters and tunnels outside of town as preparation for the Sino-Soviet war, provided the perfect site.

We set out at eight, the third platoon to use the training site. On the way there we met the other platoon of girls, marching and singing as if returning from a most exhilarating game. The assignment was simple—two squads were to face each other in a meeting engagement, and the squad leaders were to lead their soldiers to annihilate the enemies. Each of us got two rounds of ten blanks, and when we reached the entrance to a network of tunnels, Lieutenant Wei whistled, the signal to begin.

The musty tunnel, unused but by the most adventurous children perhaps, smelled sulfuric from the encounters of the previous platoons. We stumbled our way through, the flashlight of the squad leader the only light. Someone giggled when she bumped into the person ahead of her, and Ping, in a loud whisper, wondered if there were rats or bats rushing to find shelter from us. It was as if we were returned to our childhood for a war game in the schoolyard, and the machine guns only added to the excitement, since as children the most we could do was use a tree branch as a weapon, or shape our hands into pistols.

After fifteen minutes, we exited the tunnel and stepped into a long trench. Across the dark field we heard rustling, so our squad leader ordered us to find shooting positions in the trench. No more than five minutes later we had emptied our rounds of ammunition into the emptiness between us and our enemies, the metallic explosions shrieking in our ears and lighting up the field just long enough for us to see the smoke dispersing. What a fun game! a girl shouted before she fired the last bullet. There was clapping on the other side of the battleground in reply.

When we gathered again, Lieutenant Wei asked us to report on the battle. I killed ten and injured five, Ping yelled out, and soon it became a boisterous competition. When the clamor quieted down, Lieutenant Wei said let me show you something, and led the platoon down a different road back to town.

We stopped at a trench on the other side of the battleground. Hundreds, perhaps thousands of fireflies twinkled, lighting up the tall, slender grasses in the trench. No one spoke. We had killed as many times as we had been killed, yet we had never been as alive as we were on that beautiful night in May.

"In memory of tonight, I'm going to ask someone to sing a song for us," Lieutenant Wei said. Many girls turned to Nan, and she handed her machine gun to the girl standing next to her. Lieutenant Wei shook her head at Nan and turned to me. "Can you sing a song for the platoon?"

I could not read Lieutenant Wei's face. "I'm not good at singing, Lieutenant," I replied.

"That is not a problem for us," Lieutenant Wei said. "All we need is for you to step up and sing."

Some of the girls gazed at me sympathetically, others were perplexed. They must have been wondering what wrong I'd committed to earn myself this punishment. When I still did not move, Lieutenant Wei raised her voice and ordered me to step out of the formation, her voice no longer patient.

At eighteen I entered the army fresh and young, and the fire-red stars on my epaulets shone onto my blossoming youth, I sang flatly. It was the first marching song we had been taught back in the fall. Lieutenant Wei ordered me to stop. "Sing us a civilian song," she said.

"I don't know any civilian songs, Lieutenant."

"Do you need me to find someone to teach you a song at this very moment, Comrade Moyan?" Lieutenant Wei said.

"I am a slow learner, Lieutenant."

"There is nothing we can't achieve in the army," Lieutenant Wei said. "We'll stay here all night waiting for you to learn a song and sing it for us, if that has to be the case."

When I began to sing again there was a ripple of unease. "It Is a Shame to Be a Lonely Person" was the song, called by Major Tang the product of a corrupt and lost generation. Halfway through I saw Jie roll her eyes, unimpressed by my foolish stubbornness; Nan watched me, puzzled. What would Professor Shan have said if she had seen me then, singing and crying in front of people who deserved neither my song nor my tears? *One's fate is determined by what she is not allowed to have, rather than what she possesses:* Professor Shan's words came to me then, her only comment after reading me a Lawrence story called "The Fox."

ELEVEN

A MILITARY JEEP was waiting for me when we returned to the meeting hall where we had set up camp for the night. Major Tang, who was exchanging small talk with the driver, informed me that I was to leave immediately for the train station at the county seat. Three hours earlier a telegram had arrived at the camp, which the driver now produced from his pocket, the thin green slip of paper smelling of cigarette smoke. *Mother passed away please return,* sent by someone whose name I did not recognize. My father, unable to leave my mother alone, must have sent someone to the post office in his place. I imagined the stranger spelling out the message; when words of condolence were offered he must have said, thank heaven it was not his daughter who would be getting the telegram.

I brought only my satchel with me. There was no time to say farewell to anyone, as the driver had orders to make sure I caught the last night train to Beijing. We arrived just as the train was leaving the station, so the driver, ignoring my suggestion that I could spend the night in the station and catch the first train in the morning, sped down a country road that for the most part ran parallel to the train tracks until his Jeep overtook the puffing engine. At the next station, a small one with neither a waiting area nor a ticket booth, the driver insisted on waiting with me and seeing me board the train safely. The only other passenger on the platform was a dozing old man, leaning on a thick tree branch he used as a walking stick; at his feet were two heavy nylon bags and a bamboo basket. He stirred when he heard our steps. The driver asked him where he was going, but the old man, not understanding the question or perhaps too deaf to hear it, mumbled something in some local dialect before dozing off again. Soon the train arrived, and the driver helped the old man up the steps and then passed him his bags. I went for the basket, and only then did I discover the small child, wrapped in an old blanket and sleeping inside, one finger curled under her smiling face.

I lifted the basket gingerly, and the child shifted her head, heaved a sigh, but did not wake. Someone—a conductor perhaps—took the basket from me. The driver said something about "the poor child," but I did not hear him clearly enough to reply. Once I boarded the train, the driver pulled the metal door and closed it behind me. When I looked at him from the window in the door, he saluted me and waited until the train began to move before putting down his hand.

I waved at him. I did not know if he could see me through the dark night and smoky window, though he did not move, standing straight and watching the train leave. When I could no longer see him I leaned against the cold metal door, the loneliness I had learned to live with all of a sudden unbearable. I did not know the driver's name, nor had I gotten a close look at his face—but for years to come I would think of his salute, a stranger's kindness always remembered because a stranger's kindness, like time itself, heals our wounds in the end.

My father looked like a very old man, his eyes hollow, his hands shaking constantly, the grief too heavy. He had turned seventy the day before my mother's death—a suicide, I had guessed at once, though he did not tell me what she had done. It was from neighbors that I found out—she had hanged herself in the bedroom. Anybody else would have broken that curtain rod with her weight, but of course your mother was so skinny, an old woman said to me, as if my mother's only misfortune was that she had never become a nicely plump woman.

"Your mother was the kindest woman in the world," my father said the night before her cremation. He was lying in bed, his head propped up by the stack of pillows my mother had used when she read. I told him to eat a little and then rest, but the noodle soup I had made for him remained untouched, and he insisted on watching me pack up my mother's side of the bedroom. Her clothes—many of them from her youth—were to be cremated with her; her collection of novels and ancient poetry I was to put into boxes and move out to the foyer. My father, like uneducated people in his generation, revered anything in print; he told me to keep the books, that I should use them as I continue my education. "She was never happy to be married to an old man, but she kept her promise."

I examined each book, hoping to find the handmade bookmark that I had once discovered. I did not know what promise my father was talking about, but I knew I need not press him for an explanation. In the past two days, he had talked more than he had for years. Stories of my mother's childhood and youth—of being the middle daughter sandwiched between many siblings and feeling neglected by her parents, of her loving books despite her parents' decision to send her to a factory as an apprentice at fifteen, of her favorite three-legged cat named Sansan, of her delight in painting her fingernails with the petals of balsams every spring, red or pink or lavender, depending on which color was blooming in her best friend's garden—all this was related to me. I wondered if my mother had told my father these stories in the early years of their marriage—but she had already been a madwoman then, so how could he have been certain that she was not

I had not been to Professor Shan's flat since I had left her, ye
from the look of things, time had stopped in her world.

"I heard about your mother's passing," Professor Shan saic and signaled me to sit down on her bed. "Is your father doing al right?"

A few days earlier my father had asked me if I thought he hac been responsible for my mother's death—would she have had a longer life if he had not married her? he asked me, and I assured him that my mother, despite her unhappiness, loved him as she never loved anyone else. My father looked at me sadly and did not speak—he must have been thinking of the married man who had never returned my mother's love, so I showed him the bookmark I had saved from her books. What does the poem mean? he asked after reading the lines many times, and I said it was a love song from a younger woman to an older man.

"Love leaves one in debt," Professor Shan said. I nodded, though I wondered whether she meant that my father was forever paying back his debt to my mother because of his love for her, or that being loved and unable to love back had made her indebted to him. "Best if you start free from all that, do you understand?"

I had read enough love stories to be interested in one more, I said, and Professor Shan seemed satisfied by my answer. After that I resumed my daily visit to her flat, and I continued for the next twelve years. At the beginning she read to me, and later, when her eyesight deteriorated, I took over, though she was always the one to tell me which book to read. She never asked me about my life in the army, and she showed little interest in the civilian life I'd led in college, and later as a schoolteacher. When I reached marriageable age, people began to press me,

just making up tales the same way she had made up her love story with a married man?

"She asked me if twenty years was enough," my father said after a moment. "Twenty years was a long time for an older man like me, I told her. So she said let's be husband and wife for twenty years. People said I was out of my mind to marry a madwoman, but you see, she was only unhappy. She did not break her promise."

I placed a romance novel on top of a pile quietly. I wondered if my mother had calculated it all out—an older man in love with her was better than an asylum or the reign of her disgraced parents and siblings—but no matter, she had returned his kindness with twenty years of a life she had no desire to live.

"Of course it's not fair for you, Moyan," my father said. "I thought twenty years enough time to bring up a child together. She did not want you at first."

"Why did she agree?"

"A child gives a marriage a future. That was what people told me. I thought when we had you she would forget that foolish deal of twenty years," my father said, his voice so low I could barely hear him. "I am sorry we haven't had much to offer you as parents."

I turned my back to my father, pretending to pick at another stack of books so he would not see my tears. Neither he nor I, in the end, had given her more reason to live than the obligation to fulfill a simple promise, though even in her maddest years, she hadn't given up the pretense that she was my birth mother. I wished Professor Shan had never told me about my adoption.

The next day my father and I saw my mother off at the funeral home. There was no memorial service for her, nor did any of her siblings come and acknowledge her departure. My father insisted on waiting by the furnace alone, so I wandered into one of the meeting halls and sat through a memorial service for a stranger whose children and grandchildren wailed when it was time for the man to go to the furnace.

On the bus ride home, my father carried the wooden box, inside of which was an ivory-colored silk bag that contained what was left of my mother. I had tried to convince him to bury her in the municipal cemetery, but he had refused. He wanted to be buried with her on the same day, he explained to me. Not right next to her, he said, since she had fulfilled her promise and he should fulfill his of leaving her alone—but also not too far from her, he added after a moment. "I'm sorry we have to burden you," my father said when I said nothing about his request. I knew that he had guessed by then that I had found out about my adoption, as one's birth father would not have to apologize for his own last request. "You deserve a better life, but this is all we could do for you."

TWELVE

THE PIGS would continue lying in the sunshine after meals until they were butchered for the farewell banquet in late July. The new grass at the shooting range would soon be tall enough for small children to play hide-and-seek in, though no children would ever know the place, where bronze bullet shells that would otherwise have made thrilling toys remained undisturbed. At the exhibition drill, on an extremely hot August day, several girls fainted from standing in the sun and listening to the speeches of a general and several senior officers. Lieutenant Wei, along with other junior officers, stood in formation and saluted by the camp

entrance until the last lorry carrying boys and girls e
home had left for the train station. While the cook
cleaned up the mess hall after the banquet, they sip
liquor, and when they became drunk they cried and la
among themselves. At night Lieutenant Wei walked th
barracks and picked up a few items left behind—a stam
point pen almost out of ink, an army-issue tiepin, golden
with a red star at one end. There were other things for
member, details I had not seen with my eyes yet neverth
become part of my memory, some gathered from a chat
in college, others imagined.

I did not report back to the army after my mother'
tion. On the last day of my five-day leave I sent a telegra
camp, addressing no one and giving mental breakdow
reason for not being able to return. I did not know wha
happen to me—if, without the last two months of tra
would still be qualified to go to college in September—a
not care enough to worry about it. My father had be
shaky old man, and the department store where he had
for thirty years had to let him go, apologetically granting h
his salary as his pension and an expensive-looking gilded c
a retirement present. We talked a lot at the beginning, ab
mother and sometimes my childhood, but these convers
wore us out, as neither of us was used to talking, and in t
my father replaced my mother in their bedroom, lying in b
day long; I wandered my days away till sunset as my mothe
once done.

A few weeks after I had come home, I was standing b
roadside and watching workers brush the trunks of elm
with white paint mixed with pesticide when Professor Shan
proached me. "I see that you're back," she said. "Come with

subtly at first and later less so, saying that a young woman's best years were brief, saying that I was becoming less desirable by the day, like a fresh lychee that had not found a buyer in time. Professor Shan must have suspected all this talk but, as always, she refused to let the mundane into her flat. Instead, we read other people's stories, more real than our own; after all, inadequate makers of our own lives, we were no match for those masters.

My father died less than a year after my mother, and against his wish I buried their urns next to each other. I visit them every year on my birthday, my only trip outside the district where I live and teach. My mother fell in love at an early age, my father late; they both fell for someone who would not return their love, yet in the end their story is the only love story I can claim, and I live as proof of that story, of one man's offering to a woman from his meager existence, and of her returning it with her entire adult life.

I think of visiting Professor Shan's grave in Shanghai, too, but I know I will never do it, as the location is kept from me by her children. In the last days of her life they came back from America to arrange the funeral and the sale of her flat. They were alarmed by my friendship with their mother, and before she was transferred from the geriatric ward to the morgue they told me that I was wrong if I thought they would give me a share of the inheritance.

I laughed and said that had never been my intention, though I could see they did not believe me. Why would they, when life to them was a simple transaction between those who owe and those who own? Before she entered the hospital, Professor Shan had watched me pack up her books. Take them home before my children sell them to the recycling station, she told me, and I packed them all, including the book of D. H. Lawrence's stories that I had once stolen from her. The summer after I left the army, Lieutenant Wei had mailed it to me, along with my half-empty suitcase, with the bar of Lux soap wrapped in my civilian clothes, and a letter expressing her condolences. "I wish we had met under different circumstances," the letter concluded.

I did not write to thank Lieutenant Wei for sending the suitcase, nor did I reply, a few months later, when she sent another letter, saying that she and the other two platoon officers had been officially invited to visit my college, and she would love to see me in my city. After that there was one more letter, and then a wedding invitation, and now, twenty years later, a funeral notice. Professor Shan would have approved of my silence, though I wonder if she was wrong to think that without love one can be free. What was not understood when I was younger is understood now. Lieutenant Wei's persistence in seeking my friendship came from the same desire as Professor Shan's to make me a disciple. Both women had set their hearts on making a new person, though, unlike Professor Shan, Lieutenant Wei was too curious and too respectful to be a successful hijacker of other people's lives. Sometimes I wonder if I would have become her friend had I not met Professor Shan. Perhaps I would have subjected myself to her will as I had Professor Shan's, and I would have become a happier person, falling in love with a suitable man, because that is what Lieutenant Wei would have considered happiness. But what is the point of talking about the past in this haphazard way? Kindness binds one to the past as obstinately as love does, and no matter what you think of Professor Shan or Lieutenant Wei, it is their kindness that makes me indebted to them. For that reason, I know Lieutenant Wei will continue coming to me in my dreams, just making up tales the same way she had made up her love story with a married man?

"She asked me if twenty years was enough," my father said after a moment. "Twenty years was a long time for an older man like me, I told her. So she said let's be husband and wife for twenty years. People said I was out of my mind to marry a madwoman, but you see, she was only unhappy. She did not break her promise."

I placed a romance novel on top of a pile quietly. I wondered if my mother had calculated it all out—an older man in love with her was better than an asylum or the reign of her disgraced parents and siblings—but no matter, she had returned his kindness with twenty years of a life she had no desire to live.

"Of course it's not fair for you, Moyan," my father said. "I thought twenty years enough time to bring up a child together. She did not want you at first."

"Why did she agree?"

"A child gives a marriage a future. That was what people told me. I thought when we had you she would forget that foolish deal of twenty years," my father said, his voice so low I could barely hear him. "I am sorry we haven't had much to offer you as parents."

I turned my back to my father, pretending to pick at another stack of books so he would not see my tears. Neither he nor I, in the end, had given her more reason to live than the obligation to fulfill a simple promise, though even in her maddest years, she hadn't given up the pretense that she was my birth mother. I wished Professor Shan had never told me about my adoption.

The next day my father and I saw my mother off at the funeral home. There was no memorial service for her, nor did any of her siblings come and acknowledge her departure. My father insisted on waiting by the furnace alone, so I wandered into one of the meeting halls and sat through a memorial service for a stranger whose children and grandchildren wailed when it was time for the man to go to the furnace.

On the bus ride home, my father carried the wooden box, inside of which was an ivory-colored silk bag that contained what was left of my mother. I had tried to convince him to bury her in the municipal cemetery, but he had refused. He wanted to be buried with her on the same day, he explained to me. Not right next to her, he said, since she had fulfilled her promise and he should fulfill his of leaving her alone—but also not too far from her, he added after a moment. "I'm sorry we have to burden you," my father said when I said nothing about his request. I knew that he had guessed by then that I had found out about my adoption, as one's birth father would not have to apologize for his own last request. "You deserve a better life, but this is all we could do for you."

TWELVE

THE PIGS would continue lying in the sunshine after meals until they were butchered for the farewell banquet in late July. The new grass at the shooting range would soon be tall enough for small children to play hide-and-seek in, though no children would ever know the place, where bronze bullet shells that would otherwise have made thrilling toys remained undisturbed. At the exhibition drill, on an extremely hot August day, several girls fainted from standing in the sun and listening to the speeches of a general and several senior officers. Lieutenant Wei, along with other junior officers, stood in formation and saluted by the camp entrance until the last lorry carrying boys and girls eager to go home had left for the train station. While the cooking squad cleaned up the mess hall after the banquet, they sipped cheap liquor, and when they became drunk they cried and later fought among themselves. At night Lieutenant Wei walked through the barracks and picked up a few items left behind—a stamp, a ballpoint pen almost out of ink, an army-issue tiepin, golden-colored, with a red star at one end. There were other things for me to remember, details I had not seen with my eyes yet nevertheless had become part of my memory, some gathered from a chat with Nan in college, others imagined.

I did not report back to the army after my mother's cremation. On the last day of my five-day leave I sent a telegram to the camp, addressing no one and giving mental breakdown as the reason for not being able to return. I did not know what would happen to me—if, without the last two months of training, I would still be qualified to go to college in September—and I did not care enough to worry about it. My father had become a shaky old man, and the department store where he had worked for thirty years had to let him go, apologetically granting him half his salary as his pension and an expensive-looking gilded clock as a retirement present. We talked a lot at the beginning, about my mother and sometimes my childhood, but these conversations wore us out, as neither of us was used to talking, and in the end my father replaced my mother in their bedroom, lying in bed all day long; I wandered my days away till sunset as my mother had once done.

A few weeks after I had come home, I was standing by the roadside and watching workers brush the trunks of elm trees with white paint mixed with pesticide when Professor Shan approached me. "I see that you're back," she said. "Come with me."

I had not been to Professor Shan's flat since I had left her, yet from the look of things, time had stopped in her world.

"I heard about your mother's passing," Professor Shan said and signaled me to sit down on her bed. "Is your father doing all right?"

A few days earlier my father had asked me if I thought he had been responsible for my mother's death—would she have had a longer life if he had not married her? he asked me, and I assured him that my mother, despite her unhappiness, loved him as she never loved anyone else. My father looked at me sadly and did not speak—he must have been thinking of the married man who had never returned my mother's love, so I showed him the bookmark I had saved from her books. What does the poem mean? he asked after reading the lines many times, and I said it was a love song from a younger woman to an older man.

"Love leaves one in debt," Professor Shan said. I nodded, though I wondered whether she meant that my father was forever paying back his debt to my mother because of his love for her, or that being loved and unable to love back had made her indebted to him. "Best if you start free from all that, do you understand?"

I had read enough love stories to be interested in one more, I said, and Professor Shan seemed satisfied by my answer. After that I resumed my daily visit to her flat, and I continued for the next twelve years. At the beginning she read to me, and later, when her eyesight deteriorated, I took over, though she was always the one to tell me which book to read. She never asked me about my life in the army, and she showed little interest in the civilian life I'd led in college, and later as a schoolteacher. When I reached marriageable age, people began to press me, subtly at first and later less so, saying that a young woman's best years were brief, saying that I was becoming less desirable by the day, like a fresh lychee that had not found a buyer in time. Professor Shan must have suspected all this talk but, as always, she refused to let the mundane into her flat. Instead, we read other people's stories, more real than our own; after all, inadequate makers of our own lives, we were no match for those masters.

My father died less than a year after my mother, and against his wish I buried their urns next to each other. I visit them every year on my birthday, my only trip outside the district where I live and teach. My mother fell in love at an early age, my father late; they both fell for someone who would not return their love, yet in the end their story is the only love story I can claim, and I live as proof of that story, of one man's offering to a woman from his meager existence, and of her returning it with her entire adult life.

I think of visiting Professor Shan's grave in Shanghai, too, but I know I will never do it, as the location is kept from me by her children. In the last days of her life they came back from America to arrange the funeral and the sale of her flat. They were alarmed by my friendship with their mother, and before she was transferred from the geriatric ward to the morgue they told me that I was wrong if I thought they would give me a share of the inheritance.

I laughed and said that had never been my intention, though I could see they did not believe me. Why would they, when life to them was a simple transaction between those who owe and those who own? Before she entered the hospital, Professor Shan had watched me pack up her books. Take them home before my children sell them to the recycling station, she told me, and I packed them all, including the book of D. H. Lawrence's stories that I had once stolen from her. The summer after I left the army, Lieutenant Wei had mailed it to me, along with my half-empty suitcase, with the bar of Lux soap wrapped in my civilian clothes, and a letter expressing her condolences. "I wish we had met under different circumstances," the letter concluded.

I did not write to thank Lieutenant Wei for sending the suitcase, nor did I reply, a few months later, when she sent another letter, saying that she and the other two platoon officers had been officially invited to visit my college, and she would love to see me in my city. After that there was one more letter, and then a wedding invitation, and now, twenty years later, a funeral notice. Professor Shan would have approved of my silence, though I wonder if she was wrong to think that without love one can be free. What was not understood when I was younger is understood now. Lieutenant Wei's persistence in seeking my friendship came from the same desire as Professor Shan's to make me a disciple. Both women had set their hearts on making a new person, though, unlike Professor Shan, Lieutenant Wei was too curious and too respectful to be a successful hijacker of other people's lives. Sometimes I wonder if I would have become her friend had I not met Professor Shan. Perhaps I would have subjected myself to her will as I had Professor Shan's, and I would have become a happier person, falling in love with a suitable man, because that is what Lieutenant Wei would have considered happiness. But what is the point of talking about the past in this haphazard way? Kindness binds one to the past as obstinately as love does, and no matter what you think of Professor Shan or Lieutenant Wei, it is their kindness that makes me indebted to them. For that reason, I know Lieutenant Wei will continue coming to me in my dreams, as Professor Shan's voice still reads to me when I sit in my flat with one of her books in hand.

I now memorize ancient poems from my mother's books. I reread the romantic stories and never tire of them. They are terrible stories, terribly written, yet they are about fate, a kinder fate that unites one with her lover despite hardships and improbability—and they never fail to give me a momentary hope, as they must have given my mother years ago, as if all will be well in the end.

But it is Professor Shan's collection that I truly live with, Dickens and Hardy and Lawrence, who once saw me as a young girl and who will one day see me as an old woman. The people who live out their lives in those books, like their creators, are not my people, and I wonder if it is this irrelevance that makes it easy for me to wander among them, the same way that my not being related to my parents by blood makes it easy for me to claim their love story as mine.

The girls I served with in the army must be mothers and wives by now. I imagine them continuing with their daily lives, unaware of Lieutenant Wei's death: Ping, in a warm cocoon, once provided by her father, now by her husband; Jie, married but perhaps keeping a lover from time to time; and our squad leader, the most militant eighteen-year-old of us all, providing a warm home for her family, for even a militant girl could turn out to be a loving wife and mother. I have never forgotten any person who has come into my life. As I am on my way to work this morning, I see Nan's face on a TV screen in a shop window. I watch her through the glass pane—I cannot hear what the program is saying, but by the way she smiles and talks, you can tell she is an important person. I study her, still petite and beautiful, still able to pass for a young woman in a choir. For a moment my heart mourns for the passing of time as it has never mourned the deaths of my parents, or Professor Shan, or Lieutenant Wei. If I close my eyes I can hear again Nan's beautiful voice, singing "The Last Rose of Summer" at the shooting range, a random act of kindness that will continue living on in the memory of someone who is a stranger to her now.

A Man Like Him

THE GIRL, UNLIKE most people photographed for fashion magazines, was not beautiful. Moreover, she had no desire to appear beautiful, as anyone looking at her could tell, and for that reason Teacher Fei stopped turning the pages and studied her. She had short, unruly hair and wide-set eyes that glared at the camera in a close-up shot. In another photo, she stood in front of a bedroom door, her back to the camera, her hand pushing the door ajar. A bed and its pink sheet were artfully blurred. Her black T-shirt, in sharp focus, displayed a line of white printed characters: MY FATHER IS LESS OF A CREATURE THAN A PIG OR A DOG BECAUSE HE IS AN ADULTERER.

The girl was nineteen, Teacher Fei learned from the article. Her parents had divorced three years earlier, and she suspected that another woman, a second cousin of her father's, had seduced him. On her eighteenth birthday, the first day permitted by law, the daughter had filed a lawsuit against him. As she explained to the reporter, he was a member of the Communist Party, and he should be punished for abandoning his family, and for the immoral act of having taken a mistress in the first place. When the effort to imprison her father failed, the girl started a blog and called it A Declaration of War on Unfaithful Husbands.

"What is it that this crazy girl wants?" Teacher Fei asked out loud before reaching the girl's answer. She wanted her father to lose his job, she told the reporter, along with his social status, his freedom, if possible, and his mistress for sure; she wanted him to beg her and her mother to take him back. She would support him for the rest of his life as the most filial daughter, but he had to repent—and, before that, to suffer as much as she and her mother had.

What malice, Teacher Fei thought. He flung the magazine across the room, knocking a picture frame from the bookcase and surprising himself with this sudden burst of anger. At sixty-six, Teacher Fei had seen enough of the world to consider himself beyond the trap of pointless emotions. Was it the milkman, his mother asked from the living room. Milkmen had long ago ceased to exist in Beijing, milk being sold abundantly in stores now; still, approaching ninety, she was snatched from time to time by the old fear that a neighbor or a passerby would swipe their two rationed bottles. Remember how they had twice been fined for lost bottles, she asked as Teacher Fei entered the living room, where she sat in the old armchair that had been his father's favorite spot in his last years. Teacher Fei hadn't listened closely, but it was a question he knew by heart, and he said yes, he had remembered to pick up the bottles the moment they were delivered. Be sure to leave them in a basin of cold water so the milk does not turn, she urged. He stood before her and patted her hands, folded in her lap, and reassured her that there was no need to worry. She grabbed him then, curling her thin fingers around his. "I have nothing to say about this world," she said slowly.

"I know," Teacher Fei said. He bent down and placed her hands back in her lap. "Should I warm some milk?" he asked, though he could see that already she was slipping away into her usual reverie, one that would momentarily wash her mind clean. Sometimes he made an effort, coaxing her to walk with baby steps to exercise her shrinking muscles. A few years ago, the limit of her world had been the park two blocks down the street, and later the stone bench across the street from their flat; now it was their fifth-floor balcony. Teacher Fei knew that in time he would let his mother die in peace in this flat. She disliked strangers, and he couldn't imagine her in a cold bed in a crowded hospital ward.

Teacher Fei withdrew to the study, which had been his father's domain until his death. His mother had long ago stopped visiting this room, so Teacher Fei was the one who took care of the books on the shelves, airing the yellowing pages twice a year on the balcony, but inevitably some of the books had become too old to rescue, making way for the fashion magazines that Teacher Fei now purchased.

The black-clad girl taunted him from the magazine lying open on the floor. He picked her up and carefully set her on the desk, then fumbled in the drawer for an inkpot. Much of the ink in the bottle had evaporated from lack of use, and few of the brushes in the bamboo container were in good shape now. Still, with a fine brush pen and just enough ink on the tip, he was able to sketch, in the margin of the page, a scorpion, its pincers stabbing toward the girl's eyes. It had been six years since he retired as an art teacher, nearly forty since he last painted out of free will. Teacher Fei looked at the drawing. His hand was far from a shaking old man's. He could have made the scorpion an arthropod version of the girl, but such an act would have been beneath his standards. Teacher Fei had never cursed at a woman, either in words or in any other form of expression, and he certainly did not want to begin with a young girl.

LATER, WHEN MRS. Luo, a neighbor in her late forties who had been laid off by the local electronics factory, came to sit with Teacher Fei's mother, he went to a nearby Internet café. It was a little after two, a slow time for the business, and the manager was dozing off in the warm sunshine. A few middle school students, not much older than twelve or thirteen, were gathered around a computer, talking in tones of hushed excitement, periodically breaking into giggles. Teacher Fei knew these types of kids. They pooled their pocket money in order to spend a few truant hours in a chat room, impersonating people much older than themselves and carrying on affairs with other human beings who could be equally fraudulent. In his school days, Teacher Fei had skipped his share of classes to frolic with friends in the spring meadow or to take long walks in the autumn woods, and he wondered if, in fifty years, the children around the computer would have to base their nostalgia on a fabricated world that existed only in a machine. But who could blame them for paying little attention to the beautiful April afternoon? Teacher Fei had originally hired Mrs. Luo for an hour a day so that he could take a walk; ever since he had discovered the Internet, Mrs. Luo's hours had been increased: Most days now she spent three hours in the afternoon taking care of Teacher Fei's mother and cooking a meal for both of them. The manager of the Internet café had once suggested that Teacher Fei purchase a computer of his own; the man had even volunteered to set it up, saying that he would be happy to see a good customer save money, even if it meant that he would lose some business. Teacher Fei rejected the generous offer—despite his mother's increasing loss of her grip on reality, he could not bring himself to perform any act of dishonesty in her presence.

Teacher Fei located the girl's blog without a problem. There were more pictures of her there, some with her mother. Anyone could see the older woman's unease in front of the camera. In her prime she would have been more attractive than her daughter was now, but perhaps it was the diffidence in her face that had softened some of the features which in her daughter's case were accentuated by rage. Under the heading "Happier Time," Teacher Fei found a black-and-white photo of the family. The girl, age three or four, sat on a high stool, and her parents stood on either side. On the wall behind them was a garden, painted by someone without much artistic taste, Teacher Fei could tell right away. The girl laughed with a mouthful of teeth, and the mother smiled demurely, as befitting a married woman in front of a photographer. The father was handsome, with perfectly shaped cheekbones and deep-set eyes not often found in a Chinese face, but the strain in his smile and the tiredness in those eyes seemed to indicate little of the happiness the daughter believed had existed in her parents' marriage.

Teacher Fei shook his head and scribbled on a scrap of paper the man's name and address and home phone number, as well as the address and number of his work unit, which were all listed by the girl. A scanned image of his resident's ID was displayed, too. Teacher Fei calculated the man's age, forty-six, and noted that on the paper. When he went to the message board on the girl's website, Teacher Fei read a few of the most recent posts, left by sympathetic women claiming to have been similarly hurt by unfaithful husbands or absent fathers. "Dearest Child," one message started, from a woman calling herself "Another Betrayed Wife," who praised the young girl as an angel of justice and courage. Teacher Fei imagined these women dialing the father's number at night, or showing up in front of his work unit to brandish cardboard signs covered with words of condemnation. "To all who support this young woman's mission," he typed in the box at the bottom of the Web page, "the world will be a better place when one learns to see through to the truth instead of making hasty and unfounded accusations."

"A Concerned Man," Teacher Fei signed his message. A different opinion was not what these women would want to hear, but any man with a brain had to accept his responsibility to make the truth known. A girl among the group of middle schoolers glanced at Teacher Fei and then whispered to a companion, who looked up at him with a snicker before letting herself be absorbed again by the screen. An old man with wrinkles and without hair. Teacher Fei assessed himself through the girls' eyes: bored and boring, no doubt undesirable in any sense, but who could guarantee the girls that the flirtatious young man online who made their hearts speed was not being impersonated by an equally disgraceful old man?

LATER THAT EVENING, when Teacher Fei had wrung a warm towel to the perfect stage of moistness and passed it to his mother, who sat on another towel on her bed, a curtain separating her partly undressed body from him, he thought about the two girls and their youthful indifference. One day, if they were fortunate enough to survive all the disappointments life had in store for them, they would have to settle into their no longer young bodies.

"Do you remember Carpenter Chang?" Teacher Fei's mother asked from the other side of the curtain. Three times a week, Mrs. Luo bathed Teacher Fei's mother, and on the other evenings Teacher Fei and his mother had to make do with the curtain as he assisted her with her sponge bath and listened to her reminisce about men and women long dead. Half an hour, and sometimes an hour, would pass, his mother washing and talking on one side of the curtain, him listening and sometimes pressing for details on the other side. This was the time of day they talked the most, when Teacher Fei knew that although his mother's body was frail and her mind tangled by memories, she was still the same graceful woman who, with her unhurried storytelling, knew how to take the awkwardness out of a situation in which she had to be cared for by a grown son who had remained a bachelor all his life.

Having his mother as his only companion in old age was not how Teacher Fei had envisioned his life, but he had accepted this with little grievance. He enjoyed conversations with her, for whom things long forgotten by the world were as present as the air she shallowly breathed: two apprentices pulling a giant paper fan back and forth in a barbershop to refresh the sweating customers, the younger one winking at her while her grandfather snored on the bench, waiting for his daily shave; the machine her father had installed in the front hall of their house, operated by a pedaling servant, which cut a long tube of warm, soft toffee into small neat cubes that, once hardened, were wrapped in squares of cellophane by her and her four sisters; the cousins and second cousins who had once been playmates, fed and clothed and schooled alongside her and her sisters when they were young, but who later claimed to have been exploited as child laborers by her capitalist father; her wedding to Teacher Fei's father, attended by the best-known scholars of the day and lamented by most of her relatives, her mother included, as a bad match.

Teacher Fei's father had been the oldest and poorest of his mother's suitors. Twenty years her senior, he had worked as a part-time teacher in the elite high school that she and her sisters attended, and when she rejected him a renowned scholar wrote to her on his behalf, assuring the sixteen-year-old girl of what was beyond her understanding at the time: that Teacher Fei's father would become one of the most important philosophers in the nation and, more than that, would be a devoted husband who would love her till death parted them.

Teacher Fei had always suspected that his mother had agreed to see his father only to appease the scholar, but within a year the two had married, and afterward, before Teacher Fei's father found a university position, his mother used her dowry to help her husband support his parents and siblings in the countryside. Unable to become pregnant, she adopted a boy—Teacher Fei—from the long line of nephews and nieces who lived in close quarters in her husband's family compound, which had been built and rebuilt in the course of four generations. She had never hidden this fact from Teacher Fei, and he remembered being saddened after a holiday in his father's home village when he was eight and finally understood that he alone had been plucked from his siblings and cousins. His relatives, birth parents included, treated him with respect and even awe. It was his good fortune, his mother had said, comforting him, to have two pairs of parents and two worlds.

Poor man, she said now, and for a moment, lost in his reverie, Teacher Fei wondered if he had told her about the avenging daughter. Then he realized that his mother was still talking about the carpenter, who had once carved five coffins for his children, all killed by typhoid within a week. The carpenter's wife, who had been hired as a wet nurse for Teacher Fei when he first left his birth mother, had returned to the house years later with the news. Even as a ten-year-old, Teacher Fei could see that the woman had been driven out of her mind and would go on telling the story to any willing ears until her death.

It's the innocent ones who are often preyed upon by life's cruelty, Teacher Fei replied, and when his mother did not speak he recounted the girl's story from the magazine. He paused as his mother, dressed in her pajamas, pulled the curtain aside. All set for the dreamland, she said. He did not know if she had heard him, but when he tucked her in she looked up. "You should not feel upset by the girl," she said.

He was not, Teacher Fei replied; it was just that he found the girl's hatred extraordinary. His mother shook her head slightly on the pillow, looking past his face at the ceiling, as if she did not want to embarrass him by confronting his lie. "The weak-minded choose to hate," she said. "It's the least painful thing to do, isn't it?"

She closed her eyes as if exhausted. Rarely did she stay in a conversation with him with such clarity these days, and he wondered whether she had chosen to neglect the world simply because it no longer interested her. He waited, and when she did not open her eyes he wished her a night of good sleep and clicked off the bedside lamp.

"The weak-minded choose to hate," Teacher Fei wrote in his journal later that night. For years, he'd had the habit of taking notes of his mother's words. "I have nothing to say about this world," he wrote, the line most often repeated in the journal. Twenty-five years ago, his father, after a long day of musing in his armchair, had said the same thing, his final verdict before he swallowed a bottle's worth of sleeping pills. Teacher Fei's mother had not sounded out of sorts when she had called him that evening to report his father's words, nor had she cried the following morning on the phone with the news of his father's death. Teacher Fei suspected that if his mother had not been an active accomplice, she had, at the least, been informed of the suicide plan; either way it made no difference, for the border between husband and wife had long been obscured in his parents' marriage. What surprised Teacher Fei was his mother's willingness to live on. He visited her daily after his father's death and, within a year, moved in with her. He recorded and analyzed every meaningful sentence of hers, looking for hints that the words were her farewell to the world. He was intentionally careless about his pills, and hers, too, as he believed she must have been in his father's final days—they had always been a family of insomniacs—but by the fifth anniversary of his father's death, Teacher Fei stopped waiting. She had nothing to say about the world, his mother told him that day, more out of amusement than resignation, and he knew then that she would not choose to end her life.

THE MESSAGE THAT Teacher Fei had left on the girl's website was not there when he checked the next day at the Internet café. Why was he surprised? Still, his hands shook as he composed another message, calling the girl "a manipulative liar." A young couple, seventeen or eighteen at most, cast disapproving glances at Teacher Fei from another computer, seemingly alarmed by his vehement treatment of the keyboard.

The chat rooms he normally frequented held little attraction for him today. He was leaving on a business trip abroad, he told a friend in one chat room who called herself "Perfume Beauty," and then repeated the news to similarly named women in other chat rooms, knowing that they would find other idling men to flirt with. The night before, he had imagined the reaction of the girl and her female allies to his message, and had composed an eloquent retort to throw at these petty-minded women. But no doubt the girl would again erase his comment, and he could not stop her, nor could he expose her dishonesty. Teacher Fei logged off the computer and watched the boy sneak a hand under the girl's sweater and wiggle it around, perhaps trying to unhook her troublesome bra. The girl looked at the screen with a straight face, but her body, moving slightly in cooperation, betrayed her enjoyment.

The girl noticed Teacher Fei's attention first and signaled to her boyfriend to stop. Without withdrawing his hand, he mouthed a threat at Teacher Fei, who lifted his arms as if surrendering and stood up to leave. When he walked past the couple, he raised a thumb and gave the boy a smile, as though they were conspiring comrades; the boy, caught off guard, grinned disarmingly before turning his face away.

Teacher Fei had never cupped his hands around a woman's breasts, and for an instant he wished that he possessed the magic to make the boy disappear and take his place next to the girl. What stupidity, Teacher Fei chided himself, after he had gulped down a can of ice-cold soda water at a roadside stand. It was that angry girl and her fraudulence—that was what was depriving him of his peace. He wished that he had been his mother's birth son, that he had her noble and calm blood running through his veins, guarding him against the ugliness of the world.

The good fortune that his mother had once assured him of had not lasted long. At eighteen, he had been an ambitious art student about to enter the nation's top art institute, but within a year, his father, an exemplary member of the reactionary intellectuals, was demoted from professor to toilet cleaner, and Teacher Fei's education was terminated. For the next twenty years, Teacher Fei's mother accompanied his father from building to building, one hand carrying a bucket of cleaning tools and the other holding her husband's arm, as if they were on their way to a banquet. Yet, in the end, even she could not save her husband from despair. Teacher Fei's father had killed himself two years after he was restored to his position at the university.

The next day, Teacher Fei saw that his second message to the girl had also been confiscated by the cyberworld. A different message, left by a woman who hailed the girl as a guardian of the morality of modern China, taunted Teacher Fei in bold type.

He hastily composed another post, and then spent twenty minutes rephrasing it in a calmer tone, but a day later, when that message had also been deleted, his rage erupted. He called her "a scorpion girl" in a new message, saying that he hoped no man would make the mistake of his life by marrying her and succumbing to her poison; he took great pity on her father, since an evil daughter like her would make any father live in a hell.

Her father . . . Teacher Fei paused in his typing as the man's unhappy face in the photo came back to him. He decided to call the man's work unit, an institute affiliated with the Ministry of Propaganda, from a phone booth in the street. A woman answered, and when Teacher Fei asked for the man by name she inquired about the nature of his business. An old school friend who had lost touch, he said, apologizing that he did not have another number for him and so had to make the initial contact through the work unit.

The woman hesitated and then told him to wait. When the phone was picked up again, Teacher Fei was surprised by the voice, which sounded as though it belonged to a much older man. It didn't matter what his name was, Teacher Fei replied when the girl's father asked for it; he was merely calling as a man who was sympathetic to a fellow man's situation. He then asked if there was a chance that they could meet in person. The line clicked dead while he was in mid-sentence.

WHEN MRS. LUO came the next day, Teacher Fei begged her to stay till later in the evening. He would pay her double for the extra hours, he said, and Mrs. Luo, after complaining about the inconvenience, agreed, adding that a man like Teacher Fei indeed deserved an occasional break from caring for an elderly woman. Mrs. Luo had not lowered her voice, and Teacher Fei glanced at his mother, who sat in the armchair with her eyes fixed on a square of afternoon sunshine on the floor. She was obedient and quiet in front of Mrs. Luo, who, like everybody else, believed that Teacher Fei's mother had long been lost in her own world of dementia.

A man like him. In the street, Teacher Fei pondered Mrs. Luo's words. What did that mean—a man like him—a bachelor without a son to carry on his blood, a retired art teacher whose name most of his students had forgotten the moment they graduated from elementary school, a disgraceful old man who purchased fashion magazines at the newsstand and wasted his afternoons alongside teenagers in a cyberworld, making up names and stories and sending out romantic lies? What did he deserve but this aimless walk in a world where the only reason for him to live was so that his mother could die in her own bed? There must be places for a man like him to go, inexpensive foot-massage shops where, behind an unwashed curtain, a jaded young woman from the countryside would run her hands where he directed her while she chatted with a companion behind another curtain. Or, if he was willing to spend more—and he could, for he had few expenditures beyond his magazines and the Internet café, and had long ago stopped buying expensive brushes and paper and pretending to be an artist—one of the bathing palaces would welcome him into its warmth, with a private room and a woman of his choice to wait on him.

—

IT WAS A few minutes after five when Teacher Fei arrived at the institute, betting that the girl's father was not the type to leave work early, since there would be little reason for him to hurry home. While Teacher Fei waited for a guard to inform the man of his arrival, he studied the plaque at the entrance to the institute. THE ASSOCIATION OF MARXIST DIALECTICAL MATERIALISM, it said, and it occurred to Teacher Fei that had his father been alive he would have said that it was the parasites in these institutes who had ended hope for Chinese philosophers.

"Please don't get me wrong. I am a serious man," Teacher Fei said to the girl's father when he appeared. "A man most sympathetic to your situation."

"I don't know you," the man said. Had Teacher Fei not known his age, he would have guessed him to be older than sixty; his hair was more gray than black, and his back was stooped with timidity. A man closer to death than most men his age, Teacher Fei thought. But perhaps he would have more peace to look forward to in death.

A stranger could be one's best friend just as one's wife and daughter could be one's deadly enemies, Teacher Fei replied, and he suggested that they go out for tea or a quick drink. A small group of workers, on their way from the institute to the bus stop across the street, passed the pair of men; two women looked back at them and then talked in whispers to the group. The girl's father recoiled, and Teacher Fei wondered if the daughter knew that her father already lived in a prison cell, its bars invisible to the people in the street.

They could go to the man's office for a chat, Teacher Fei offered, knowing that this was the last thing he would want. The father hurriedly agreed to go to a nearby diner instead. He was the kind of man who was easily bullied by the world, Teacher Fei thought, realizing with satisfaction that he had not sought out the wrong person.

At the diner the girl's father chose a table in the corner farthest from the entrance, and in the dim light he squinted at the bench, wiping off some grease before he sat down. When the waitress came, Teacher Fei asked for a bottle of rice liquor and a plate of assorted cold cuts. He was not a drinker, nor had he ever touched marinated pig liver or tongue, but he imagined that a friendship between two men should start over harsh liquor and variety meats.

Neither spoke for a moment. When their order arrived, Teacher Fei poured some liquor for the girl's father. A good drink wipes out all pain for a man, Teacher Fei said, and then poured a glass for himself, but it soon became clear that neither of them would touch the drink or the meat, the man apparently feeling as out of place in the dingy diner as Teacher Fei did.

"What are you going to do?" Teacher Fei asked when the silence between them began to attract prying glances from the diner's middle-aged proprietress, who sat behind the counter and studied the few occupied tables.

The man shook his head. "I don't understand the question," he said.

"I think you should sue your daughter," Teacher Fei said, and immediately saw the man freeze with hostility. Perhaps someone had approached him with a similar proposition already. Or perhaps that was why the young girl had sued her father in the first place, egged on by an attorney, a manipulative man using her rage for his own gain.

Not that he could offer any legal help, Teacher Fei explained. He had been an art teacher in an elementary school before his retirement. He was in no position to do anything to hurt the girl's father, nor did he have the power to help him in his situation. It was only that he had followed his daughter's story in the media, and when he had seen the family picture he had known that he needed to do something for the girl's father. " 'How many people in this world would understand this man's pain?' I asked myself when I saw your picture."

The girl's father flinched. "I am not the kind of man you think I am," he said.

"What?" Teacher Fei asked, failing to understand his meaning. He was not into other men, the girl's father said, so could Teacher Fei please stop this talk of friendship? The proprietress, who had been loitering around the nearby tables checking on the soy sauce bottles, perked up despite the man's hushed voice.

It took Teacher Fei a moment to grasp what the man was hinting at. Nor am I who you think I am, he thought of protesting, but why should he, when he had long ago made the decision not to defend himself against this ridiculous world?

The proprietress approached the table and asked about the quality of the food and drink. When the man did not reply, Teacher Fei said that they were very fine. The woman chatted for a moment about the weather and returned to her counter. Only then did the man insist that it was time for him to go home.

"Who is waiting at home?" Teacher Fei asked, and the man, taken aback, stood up and said he really needed to leave.

"Please," Teacher Fei said, looking up at the man. "Could you stay for just a minute?" If he sounded pathetic, he did not care. "You and I . . . ," he said slowly, glancing over at the entrance to the diner, where a pair of college students, a girl and a boy, were studying the menu on the wall. "We are the kind of men who would not kick our feet or flail our arms if someone came to strangle us to death. Most people would assume that we must be guilty if we don't fight back. A few would think us crazy or stupid. A very few would perhaps consider us men with dignity. But you and I alone know that they are all wrong, don't we?"

The man, who was about to leave some money on the table, tightened his fingers around the bills. Teacher Fei watched the college students take window seats, the boy covering the girl's hands with his own on the table. When the man sat back down, Teacher Fei nodded gratefully. He did not want to look up, for fear that the man would see his moist eyes. "When I was twenty-four, I was accused of falling in love with a girl student," he said. "Pedophile" had been the word used in the file at the school, the crime insinuated in the conversations taking place behind his back. The girl was ten and a half, an ordinary student, neither excelling among her classmates nor falling behind; one often encountered children like her in teaching, faces that blended into one another, names mis-recalled from time to time, but there was something in the girl's face, a quietness that did not originate from shyness or absentmindedness, as it usually did in children of her age, that intrigued Teacher Fei. He envisioned her at different ages—fifteen, twenty, thirty—but there was little desire in that imagining other than the desire to understand a face that had moved him as no other face had. "No, don't ask any questions, just as I won't ask whether you indeed kept a mistress while being married to your wife. It doesn't matter what happened between your cousin and you, or my girl student and me. You see, these accusations exist for the sake of those who feel the need to accuse. If it wasn't your cousin, there would have been another woman to account for your not loving your wife enough, no?"

The man took a sip from his glass, spilling the liquor when he put it down. He apologized for his clumsiness.

"My mother used to say that people in this country were very good at inventing crimes, but, better still, we were good at inventing punishments to go with them," Teacher Fei said.

When he and his cousin were young, they had vowed to marry each other, the man said; a children's game mostly, for when the time came they had drifted apart. She was widowed when they met again, and he tried to help her find a job in the city, but she was never his mistress.

"You don't have to explain these things to me," Teacher Fei said. "Had I not known to trust you, I would not have looked for you." The man could say a thousand things to defend himself, but people, his own daughter among them, would just laugh in his face and call him a liar. The crime that Teacher Fei had been accused of amounted to nothing more than a few moments of gazing, but one of the other students, a precocious eleven-year-old, had told her parents of the inappropriate attention the young teacher had paid to her classmate; later, when other girls were questioned, they seemed to be caught easily in the contagious imagining. He had just been curious, Teacher Fei said when he was approached by the principal. About what, he was pressed, but he could not explain how a face could contain so many mysteries visible only to those who knew what to look for. His reticence, more than anything, caused fury among the parents and his fellow teachers. In the end, he chose to be called the name that had been put in the file: A man's dirty desire was all his accusers could grasp.

"One should never hope for the unseeing to see the truth," Teacher Fei said now. "I could've denied all the accusations, but what difference would it have made?"

"So there was no . . . proof of any kind?" the man said, looking interested for the first time.

"Nothing to put me in jail for," Teacher Fei said.

"And someone just reported you?"

"We can't blame a young girl's imagination, can we?" Teacher Fei said.

The man met Teacher Fei's eyes. It was just the kind of thing his daughter would have done, the man said. "She'd have made sure you lost your job," he added with a bitter smile, surprising Teacher Fei with his humor. "Count yourself a lucky person."

Teacher Fei nodded. He had won the district mural contest for the school every year, his ambition and training in art making him a craftsman in the end, but shouldn't he consider it good fortune that his ability to paint the best portrait of Chairman Mao in the district had saved him from losing his job? The time to think about marriage had come and then gone, his reputation such that no matchmaker wanted to bet a girl's future on him. Still, his parents had treated him with gentle respect, never once questioning him. But as cleaners of public toilets they could do little to comfort him other than to leave him undisturbed in his solitude. Indeed, he was a lucky man, Teacher Fei said now; he had never married, so no one could accuse him of being an unfaithful husband or a bad father.

"Unwise of me to start a family, wasn't it?" the girl's father said. "Before my divorce, my daughter said there were three things she would do. First, she would sue me and put me in prison. If that failed, she would find a way to let the whole world know my crime. And if that didn't make me go back to her mother she would come with rat poison. Let me tell you—now that she has done the first two things, I am waiting every day for her to fulfill her promise, and I count it as my good fortune to have little suspense left in my life."

Teacher Fei looked at the college students paying at the

counter, the boy counting money for the proprietress and the girl scanning the restaurant, her eyes passing over Teacher Fei and his companion without seeing them. "I have nothing to say about this world," Teacher Fei said.

Neither did he, the man replied, and they sat for a long time in silence till the proprietress approached again and asked if they needed more food. Both men brought out their wallets. "Let me," Teacher Fei said, and though the man hesitated for a moment, he did not argue.

In the dusk, a thin mist hung in the air. The two men shook hands as they parted. There was little more for them to say to each other, and Teacher Fei watched the man walk down the street, knowing that nothing would be changed by their brief meeting. He thought about his mother, who would be eager to see him return, though she would not show her anxiety to Mrs. Luo. He thought about his girl student: Fifty-two she would be now, no doubt a wife and mother herself, and he hoped that he had not been mistaken and she had grown into a woman like his mother. She—the girl student, whom he had never seen again—would outlive him, just as his mother had outlived his father, their beauty and wisdom the saving grace for a man like him, a man like his father. But for the other man, who would be watching the night fall around the orange halo of the streetlamps with neither longing nor dread, what did the future offer but the comfort of knowing that he would, when it was time for his daughter to carry out her plan of revenge, cooperate with a gentle willingness?

Prison

YILAN'S DAUGHTER DIED at sixteen and a half on a rainy Saturday in May, six months after getting her driver's license. She had been driving to a nearby town for a debate when she had lost control. The car traveled over the median and ran into a semi. The local newspapers put her school picture side by side with the pictures from the site of the accident, the totaled black Nissan and the badly dented semi, the driver standing nearby and examining the damage to his truck, his back to the camera. The article talked about Jade's success as an immigrant's daughter—the same old story of hard work and triumph—how she had come to America four years earlier knowing no English, and had since then excelled in school and become the captain of the debate team. It also quoted Jade's best friend saying that Jade dreamed of going to Harvard, a dream shared by Yilan and her husband, Luo; and that she loved Emily Dickinson, which was news to Yilan. She wished she had known everything about Jade so she could fill the remaining years of her life with memories of her only daughter. At forty-seven, Yilan could not help but think that the important and meaningful part of her life was over; she was now closer to the end than the beginning, and within a blink of the eyes, death would ferry her to the other side of the world.

The year following Jade's accident, however, stretched itself into a long tunnel, thin-aired and never-ending. Yilan watched Luo age in his grief and knew she did the same in his eyes. He had been a doctor in China for twenty years; they had hoped he would pass the board exam to become an American doctor, but, too old to learn to speak good English, he now worked in a cardiology lab as a research assistant and conducted open-heart surgery on dogs twice a week. Still, they had thought that the sacrifice of both their careers—Yilan had been an editor of an herbal medicine journal—was worthwhile if Jade could get a better education.

The decision to immigrate turned out to be the most fatal mistake they had made. At night Yilan and Luo held hands in bed and wept. The fact that they were in love still, despite twenty years of marriage, the death of their only child, and a future with little to look forward to, was almost unbearable in itself; sometimes Yilan wondered whether it would be a comfort if they could mourn in solitude, their backs turned to each other.

It was during the daytime, when Luo was at work, that Yilan had such thoughts, which she felt ashamed of when he came home. It was time to do something before she was torn in half into a nighttime self and a crazier daytime self, and before the latter one took over. After a few weeks of consideration, she brought up, at dinner, the idea of adopting a baby girl from China. They would get a daughter for sure, she said, for nobody would be willing to give up a son.

Luo was silent for a long moment before he said, "Why?"

"All these stories about American parents wanting their adopted girls to learn Chinese and understand Chinese culture—

we could do at least as much," Yilan said, her voice falsely positive.

Luo did not reply and his chopsticks remained still over his rice bowl. Perhaps they were only strangers living an illusion of love; perhaps this idea would be the gravedigger of their marriage. "Another person's unwanted child won't replace her," Luo said finally.

Even though his voice was gentle, Yilan could not help but feel a slap that made her blush. How could she expect that a girl not of their blood—a small bandage on a deep, bleeding wound—would make a difference? "Such nonsense I was talking," she said.

But a few days later, when they retreated to bed early, as they had done since Jade's death, Luo asked her in the darkness if she still wanted a child.

"Adopt a baby?" Yilan asked.

"No, our own child," Luo said.

They had not made love since Jade's death. Even if pregnancy was possible at her age, Yilan did not believe that her body was capable of nurturing another life. A man could make a child as long as he wanted to, but the best years of a woman passed quickly. Yilan imagined what would become of her if her husband left her for a younger, more fertile woman. It seemed almost alluring to Yilan: She could go back to China and find some peace and solace in her solitude; Luo, as loving a father as he was, would have a child of his blood.

"I'm too old. Why don't I make room for a younger wife so you can have another child?" Yilan said, trying hard to remain still and not to turn her back to him. She would not mind getting letters and pictures from time to time; she would send presents—jade bracelets and gold pendants—so the child would grow up with an extra share of love. The more Yilan thought about it, the more it seemed a solution to their sad marriage.

Luo grabbed her hand, his fingernails hurting her palm. "Are you crazy to talk like this?" he said. "How can you be so irresponsible?"

It was a proposal of love, and Yilan was disappointed that he did not understand it. Still, his fury moved her. She withdrew her hand from his grasp to pat his arm. "Ignore my nonsense," she said.

"Silly woman," Luo said, and explained his plan. They could find a young woman to be a surrogate mother for their fertilized egg, he said. Considering potential legal problems that might arise in America, the best way was to go back to China for the procedure. Not that the practice was legal in China, he said—in fact, it had been banned since 2001—but they knew the country well enough to know that its laws were breakable, with money and connections. His classmates in medical school would come in handy. His income, forty thousand dollars a year, while insufficient for carrying out the plan in America, was rich for the standard in China. Besides, if they brought the baby back to America, there would be less worry about the surrogate mother later wanting to be part of the baby's life, as had happened to an American couple.

Yilan listened. Luo had been a surgeon in an emergency medical center in China, and it did not surprise her that he could find the best solution for any problem in a short time, but the fact that he had done his research and then presented it in such a quiet yet hopeful way made her heartbeat quicken. Could a new baby rejuvenate their hearts? What if they became old before the child grew up? Who would look after her when they were too frail to do so? An adopted child would be a mere passerby in their life—Yilan could easily imagine caring for such a child for as long as they were allowed and sending her back to the world when they were no longer capable—but a child of their own was different. "It must be difficult," Yilan said hesitantly, "to find someone if it's illegal."

Luo replied that it was not a worry as long as they had enough money to pay for such a service. They had little savings, and Yilan knew that he was thinking of the small amount of money they had got from Jade's insurance settlement. He suggested that they try Yilan's aunt, who lived in a remote region in a southern province, and he talked about a medical-school classmate who lived in the provincial capital and would have the connections to help them. He said that they did not have much time to waste; he did not say "menopause" but Yilan knew he was thinking about it, as she was. Indeed it was their last chance.

Yilan found it hard to argue against the plan, because she had never disagreed with Luo in their marriage. Besides, what was wrong with a man wanting a child of his own? She should consider herself lucky that Luo, with a practical mind and a methodical approach to every problem in life, was willing to take such a risk out of his love and respect for her as a wife.

YILAN WAS SURPRISED, when she arrived at her aunt's house in a small mountain town, by the number of women her aunt had arranged for her to consider. She had asked her aunt to find two or three healthy and trustworthy young women from nearby villages for her to choose from, but twenty thousand yuan was too big a sum for her aunt to make a decision. What she did, instead, was to go to a few matchmakers and collect a pile of pictures of women, with their names, ages, heights, and weights written on the back. Some pictures were even marked with big, unmistakable characters about their virginity, which made Yilan wonder how much these women, or her aunt and the matchmakers, understood the situation. Even she herself felt doubtful now that she saw all these faces from which she had to pick a hostess for her child. What was she to look for in these women?

"No virgins, of course, or first-time mothers," Luo said when she called collect and told him of the complications they had not expected. He was waiting for his flight, two months later than Yilan's, to the provincial capital, where, with the help of his classmate, Yilan would have already finished her hormone therapy for the ovulation. It would have been great if he could have accompanied her to pick out the surrogate mother, and to the treatment before the in vitro fertilization, but he had only a few weeks of vacation to spare, and he decided that he would wait till the last minute to travel to China, in case the procedure failed and he needed to spend extra time for another try.

"You mean we want to pick someone who has already had a child?" Yilan said.

"If we have options, yes. A second-time pregnancy will be better for our child," he said.

Luo had arranged to rent a flat for a year in the provincial capital, where Yilan and the surrogate mother would spend the whole pregnancy together. They had to be certain, he said, that the baby they got in the end was theirs—he could easily imagine them being cheated: an unreported miscarriage and then a scheme to substitute another baby, for instance, or a swapping of a baby girl for a baby boy. It surprised Yilan that Luo had so little trust in other people, but she did not say anything. After all, it was hard for her to imagine leaving her child to a stranger for nine months and coming back only for the harvest; she wanted to be with her child, to see her grow and feel her kick and welcome her to the world.

Yilan had expected a young widow perhaps, or a childless divorcée, someone who had little to her name but a body ready for rent. A mother would make the situation more complicated. "We can't separate a mother from her child for a year," she said finally.

"Perhaps it's not up to us to worry about it if someone is willing," Luo said. "We're buying a service."

Yilan shuddered at the cold truth. She looked out the telephone booth—the four telephone booths in the main street, in the shape of fat mushrooms and colored bright orange, were the only objects of modern technology and art in this mountain town, and to protect them from vandalism as well as probing curiosity, the booths were circled by a metal fence, and one had to pay the watchperson a fee to enter. The watchperson on duty, a middle-aged man, was dozing off in his chair, his chin buried deeply in his chest. A cigarette peddler across the street sat by his cart with his eyes turned to the sky. A teenager strolled past and kicked a napping dog, and it stirred and disappeared among a row of low houses, behind which, in the far background, were the mountains, green against the misty sky.

"Are you there?"

"I'm wondering." Yilan took a deep breath and said, "Why don't we move back to China?" Perhaps that was what they needed, the unhurried life of a dormant town, where big tragedies and small losses could all be part of a timeless dream.

Luo was silent for a moment and said, "It's like a game of chess. You can't undo a move. Besides, we want our child to have the best life possible."

Our child, she thought. Was that reason enough to make another child motherless for a year?

"Yilan, please," Luo said in a pleading tone, when she did not talk. "I can't afford to lose you."

Shocked by the weakness in his tone, Yilan apologized and promised that she would follow his instructions and choose the best possible woman. It saddened her that Luo insisted on holding on to her as if they had started to share some vital organs during their twenty years of marriage. She wondered if this was a sign of old age, of losing hope and the courage for changes. She herself could easily picture vanishing from their shared life, but then perhaps it was a sign of aging on her part, a desire for loneliness that would eventually make death a relief.

The next day, when Yilan brought up her worries about depriving a child of her mother, Yilan's aunt laughed at her absurdity. "Twenty thousand yuan for only one year!" her aunt said. "Believe me, the family that gets picked must have done a thousand good deeds in their last life to deserve such good fortune."

Yilan had no choice but to adopt her aunt's belief that she and Luo were not merely renting a woman's womb—they were granting her and her family opportunities of which they would not dare to dream. Yilan picked five women from the pile—the first pot of dumplings, as her aunt called it—to interview, all of them mothers of young children, according to the matchmakers. Yilan and her aunt rented a room at the only teahouse in town, and the five women arrived in their best clothes, their hands scrubbed clean, free of the odor of the pigsties or the chicken coops, their faces over-powdered to cover the skin chapped from laboring in the field.

Despite her sympathy for these women, Yilan could not help but compare them to one another and find imperfections in each. The first one brought the household register card that said she was twenty-five, but she already had sagging breasts under the thin layers of her shirt and undershirt. It did not surprise Yilan that the village women did not wear bras, luxuries they did not believe in and could not afford, but she had to avert her eyes when she saw the long, heavy breasts pulled downward by their own weight. She imagined the woman's son—two and a half, old enough to be away from his mama for a year, the woman guaranteed Yilan—dangling from his mother's breasts in a sling and uncovering her breasts whenever he felt like it. It made Yilan uncomfortable to imagine her own child sharing something with the greedy boy.

The next woman was robust, almost mannish. The following woman looked slow and unresponsive when Yilan's aunt asked her questions about her family. The fourth woman was tidy and rather good-looking, but when she talked, Yilan noticed the slyness in her eyes. The fifth woman was on the verge of tears when she begged Yilan to choose her. She listed reasons for her urgent need of money—husband paralyzed from an accident in a nearby mine, aging parents and in-laws, two children growing fast and needing more food than she could put in their mouths, a mud-and-straw house ready to collapse in the rainy season. Yilan thought about all the worries that would distract the woman from nourishing the baby. Yilan was ashamed of her selfishness, but she did not want her child to be exposed so early to the unhappiness of the world. Not yet.

At the end of the morning, Yilan decided to look at more women instead of choosing one from the first batch. Even though Luo had explained to her that the baby would be entirely their own—they were the providers of her genes and the surrogate mother would only function as a biological incubator—Yilan worried that the baby would take up some unwanted traits from a less than perfect pregnancy.

When Yilan and her aunt exited the teahouse, a woman sitting on the roadside curb stood up and came to them. "Auntie, are you the one looking for someone to bear your child?" she said to Yilan.

Yilan blushed. Indeed the young woman looked not much older than Jade. Her slim body in a light-green blouse reminded Yilan of watercress; her face was not beautiful in any striking way but there was not the slightest mistake in how the eyes and nose and mouth were positioned in the face. "We're looking for someone who has had a child before," Yilan said apologetically.

"I have a child," the woman said. From a small cloth bag she wore around her neck with an elastic band, she brought out a birth certificate and a household register card. The birth certificate was her son's, four years old now, and on the register card she pointed out her name, which matched the mother's name on the birth certificate.

Yilan studied the papers. Fusang was the woman's name, and she was twenty-two, according to the register card, married to a man twenty years older. Yilan looked up at Fusang. Unlike the other married women, who wore their hair short or in a bun, Fusang's hair was plaited into one long braid, still in the style of a maiden.

"Young girl, nobody's recommended you to us," Yilan's aunt said.

"That's because I didn't have the money to pay the matchmakers," Fusang said. "They refused to tell you about me."

"Why do you want to do it?" Yilan said, and then realized that the answer was obvious. "Where's your son?" she asked.

"Gone," Fusang said.

Yilan flinched at the answer, but Fusang seemed to have only stated a fact. Her eyes did not leave Yilan's face while they were talking.

"What do you mean 'gone'?" Yilan's aunt asked.

"It means he's no longer living with me."

"Where is he? Is he dead?" Yilan's aunt said.

For a moment Fusang looked lost, as if confused by the relevance of the question. "I don't know," she said finally. "I hope he's not dead."

Yilan felt her aunt pull her sleeve, a warning about the young woman's credibility or her mental state. "Does your husband know you're coming to see us?" Yilan said.

Fusang smiled. "My husband—he doesn't know his own age."

Yilan and her aunt exchanged a look. Despite the disapproval in her aunt's eyes, Yilan asked Fusang to come and see them again the next day. By then she would have an answer, Yilan explained. Fusang seemed unconvinced. "Why can't you tell me now? I don't want to walk all the way here again tomorrow."

"Which village are you from?" Yilan's aunt asked.

Fusang said the village name. It had taken her two and a half hours to walk to town. Yilan took out a ten-yuan bill and said, "You can take the bus tomorrow."

"But why do you need to think about it?"

Unable to look at Fusang's eyes, Yilan turned to her aunt for help. "Because we need to find out if you're lying," Yilan's aunt said.

"But I'm not. Go ask people," Fusang said, and put the money carefully into the bag dangling from her neck.

FUSANG HAD BEEN sold to her in-laws at the price of two thousand yuan. Their only son was a dimwit whom nobody wanted to marry, and they had to buy a young girl from a passing trader, one of those moving from province to province and making money by selling stolen children and abducted young women. Luckily for the old couple, Fusang was docile and did not resist at all when they made her the dimwit's wife. When asked about her previous life, however, her only answer was that she had forgotten. The in-laws, for fear she would run away and they would lose their investment, kept her a prisoner for a year, but the girl never showed any sign of restlessness. The second year of the marriage, she gave birth to a son who, to the ecstasy of the grandparents, was not a dimwit. They started to treat her more like a daughter-in-law, granting her some freedom. One day, when the boy was two, Fusang took him to play outside the village, and later came home and reported that he was missing. The villagers' search turned up nothing. How could a mother lose her son? her enraged in-laws asked her. If not for her dimwit husband, who had enough sense to protect Fusang from his parents' stick and fists, she would have been beaten to death. In the two years following the boy's disappearance, both in-laws had died, and now Fusang lived with her husband on the small patch of rice field his parents had left them.

This was the story of Fusang that Yilan's aunt had found out for her. "Not a reliable person, if you ask me," her aunt said.

"Why? I don't see anything wrong."

"She lost her own son and did not shed one drop of tear," Yilan's aunt said. After a pause, she sighed. "Of course, you may need someone like that," she said. "It's your money, so I shouldn't be putting my nose in your business."

Yilan found it hard to explain to her aunt why she liked Fusang. She was different from the other village women, their eyes dull compared to Fusang's. Young and mindlessly strong, Fusang seemed untouched by her tragic life, which would make it easier for her to part with the baby—after all, it was not only a service Yilan was purchasing but also a part of Fusang's life that she was going to take with her.

The next day, when Fusang came again, Yilan asked her to sign the paper, a simple one-paragraph contract about an illegal act. Fusang looked at the contract and asked Yilan to read it to her. Yilan explained that Fusang would stay with her through the pregnancy, and Yilan would cover all her living and medical expenses; there was not any form of advance, only the final payment that Fusang would get right before Yilan and the baby left for America. "Do you understand the contract?" Yilan asked when she finished explaining it.

Fusang nodded. Yilan showed Fusang her name, and Fusang put her index finger in the red ink paste and then pressed it down below her name.

"Have you had any schooling?" Yilan asked.

"I went to elementary school for three years," Fusang said.

"What happened after the third grade?"

Fusang thought about the question. "I wasn't in the third grade," she said with a smile, as if she was happy to surprise Yilan. "I repeated the first grade three times."

LUO ARRIVED TWO days before the appointment for the in vitro fertilization. When he saw Yilan waiting at the railway station, he came close and hugged her, a Western gesture that made people stop and snicker. Yilan pushed him gently away. He looked jet-lagged but excited, and suddenly she worried that Fusang might not arrive for the implantation of the embryo. It had been two months since they had talked, and Yilan wondered if the young woman would change her mind, or simply forget the contract. The nagging worry kept her awake at night, but she found it hard to talk to Luo about it. He did not know Fusang's story; he had approved of her only because she was young and healthy and her body was primed for pregnancy and childbirth.

Fusang showed up with a small battered suitcase and a ready smile, as if coming for a long-awaited vacation. When Yilan introduced her to Luo, she joked with him and asked if it would be hard for him to be separated from his wife for a year. It was an awkward joke, to which Luo responded with a tolerant smile. He acted deferential but aloof toward Fusang, the right way for a good husband to be, and soon Fusang was frightened into a quieter, more alert person by his unsmiling presence.

The procedure went well, and after two weeks of anxious waiting, the pregnancy was confirmed. Fusang seemed as happy as Yilan and Luo.

"Keep an eye on her," Luo said in English to Yilan when they walked to the railway station for his departing train.

Yilan turned to look at Fusang, who was trailing two steps behind, like a small child. Luo had insisted that Fusang come with them. "Of course," Yilan replied in English. "I won't let our child starve. I'll make sure Fusang gets enough nutrition and sleep."

"Beyond that, don't let her out of your sight," Luo said.

"Why?"

"She has our child in her," Luo said.

Yilan looked again at Fusang, who waved back with a smile. "It's not like she'll run away," Yilan said. "She needs the money."

"You trust people too easily," Luo said. "Don't you understand that we can't make any mistakes?"

Shocked by his stern tone, Yilan thought of pointing out that she could not possibly imprison Fusang for the whole pregnancy, but they did not need an argument as a farewell. She agreed to be careful.

"Be very vigilant, all right?" Luo said.

Yilan looked at him strangely.

"It's our child I'm worrying about," Luo said, as if explaining himself. And after a moment, he added with a bitter smile, "Of course, for a loser like me, there's nothing else to live for but a child."

Yilan thought about the patients he had once saved, most of them victims of traffic accidents, when he served at the emergency center that belonged to the traffic department. They used to make him happy—since when had he lost faith in saving other people's lives? "We can still think of coming back to China," Yilan said tentatively. "You were a good surgeon."

"It doesn't mean anything to me now," Luo said, and waved his hand as if to drive away the gloom that had fallen. "All I want now is a child and that we give her a good life."

THE FIRST FEW days after Luo left, Yilan and Fusang seemed at a loss for what to do with each other's company. Yilan made small talk but not too often—they were still at the stage where she had to measure every word coming out of her mouth. The only meaningful thing, besides waiting, was to make the flat more comfortable for the waiting. A shabbily furnished two-bedroom unit in a gray building indistinguishable from many similar buildings in a residential area, it reminded Yilan of their first home in America, with furniture bought at the local Goodwill store and a few pieces hauled in from the dumpster. Jade, twelve and a half then, had been the one to make the home their own, decorating the walls with her paintings, framed in cheap frames bought at the dollar store; Jade had always been good at drawing and painting, which baffled Yilan, as neither she nor Luo had any artistic talent.

Yilan had brought with her a few books of paintings that Jade had loved, and now, when the stay in the flat was confirmed, she took them out of her luggage and put them on a rickety bookcase in the living room. "I brought these for you," Yilan said to Fusang, who stood by the living room door, watching Yilan work. Clueless like a newborn duckling, Fusang had taken on the habit of following Yilan around until Yilan told her that she could go back to her own bedroom and rest. "When you are free," Yilan said, and then paused at her poor choice of words. "When you're not tired, spend some time looking at these paintings."

Fusang came closer and wiped her hands on the back of her pants. She then picked up the book on top, paintings by Jade's favorite artist, Modigliani. Fusang flipped the pages and placed a hand over her mouth to hide a giggle. "These people, they look funny," she said when she realized Yilan was watching her.

Yilan looked at the paintings that she had tried hard to like because of Jade's love for them. "They are paintings by a famous artist," she said. "You don't have to understand them, but you should look at them so the baby will get a good fetal education."

"Fetal education?"

"A baby needs more than just nutrients for her body. She needs stimuli for her brain, too."

Fusang looked perplexed. Yilan thought about Fusang's illiterate mind. Would it be an obstacle between the baby and the intelligence of the outside world? Yilan did not know the answer, but it did not prevent her from playing classical music and reading poems from the Tang dynasty to Fusang and the baby. Sometimes Yilan looked at the paintings with Fusang, who was always compliant, but Yilan could see that her mind was elsewhere. What did a young woman like Fusang think about? Jade used to write in journals that she had not thought to hide from Yilan, so Yilan at least got to know the things Jade had written down. Fusang, however, seemed to have no way of expressing herself. She talked less and less when the increasing hormones made her sicker. She spent several hours a day lying in bed and then rushing to the bathroom with horrible gagging sounds. Yilan tried to remember her own pregnancy; Jade had been a good baby from the beginning, and Yilan had not experienced much sickness at all. She wondered how much it had to do with a mother's reception, or rejection, of the growing existence within her body. She knew it was unfair of her to think so, but Fusang's reaction seemed unusually intense. Yilan could not help but think that Fusang's body, without any affection for the baby, was suffering intentionally. Would the baby feel the alienation, too?

Such thoughts nagged Yilan. No matter how carefully she prepared the meals, with little salt or oil or spice, Fusang would rush to the bathroom. Yilan tasted the dishes—tofu and fish and mushroom and green-leafed vegetables—which were perfectly bland; she did not see why Fusang would not eat.

"You have to force her," Luo said over the phone. "You're too softhearted."

"How do you force a grown-up to eat when she doesn't want to?" Yilan said in a frustrated voice. She had told Fusang to take a nap in her bedroom when she picked up Luo's phone call, but now she hoped that Fusang would hear the conversation and understand their displeasure.

"There should be a clause somewhere in the contract. You could tell her that we will not pay her the full sum if she doesn't cooperate."

"You know the contract doesn't protect anyone on either side," Yilan said.

"She doesn't know. You can frighten her a little," Luo said.

"Wouldn't a frightened mother send some toxic signals to our baby?" Yilan said, and then regretted her sarcastic tone. "Sorry," she said. "I don't mean to be so cross with you."

Luo was quiet for a moment. "Think of a way to improve," he said. "I know it's hard for you, but it's harder for me to stay here, doing nothing."

Yilan imagined her husband coming home every night to an empty house, the hope of the reunion with his wife and child the only thing that kept him working hard. She should be more patient with him, she thought. It was not like she herself was pregnant and had a right to throw a tantrum at a helpless husband.

THAT EVENING, WHEN Fusang returned to the table with a hand on her mouth, Yilan said, "You need to try harder, Fusang."

The young woman nodded, her eyes swollen and teary.

"You're a grown-up, so you have to know the baby needs you to eat."

Fusang glanced at Yilan timidly. "Do you think I can eat some really spicy food?"

Yilan sighed. Spice would give the baby too much internal *fire,* and the baby would be prone to rashes, a bad temper, and other problems. Yilan wondered how she could make Fusang understand her responsibility to have a good and balanced diet. "Did you also crave spicy food last time you were pregnant?" Yilan asked.

"Last time? For three months I only ate fried soybeans. People in the village all said I would give birth to a little farting machine," Fusang said, and giggled despite herself.

Yilan watched Fusang's eyes come alive with that quick laugh. It was what had made her choose Fusang the first time they met. Yilan realized she had not seen the same liveliness in the young woman since she moved to the provincial capital. "So," Yilan said, softening her voice, "did you end up having a baby like that?"

"Of course not. Funny thing is—his dad worried so much that he would cry at night and say that people were laughing at our baby. Isn't he a real dimwit, with a brain full of lard?" Fusang said, her voice filled with tenderness.

It was the first time Fusang had talked about her previous life, full of mysteries and tragedies that Yilan had once wanted to know but that had been made unimportant by the baby's existence. Yilan thought that Fusang would just remain a bearer of her child, a biological incubator, but now that Fusang had mentioned her husband with such ease, as if they were only continuing an earlier conversation, Yilan could not hide her curiosity. "How is your husband? Who's taking care of him?"

"Nobody, but don't worry. I asked the neighbors to keep an eye on him. They won't let him starve."

"That's very nice of them," Yilan said.

"Of course," Fusang said. "They're all thinking about my twenty thousand yuan."

Yilan thought of telling Fusang not to underestimate people's kindness, that money was only a small part of a bigger world. She would have said so, had Fusang been her own daughter, but Fusang had lived in a world darker than Yilan could imagine, where a girl could be stolen from her family and sold, and a son could disappear into other people's worlds. "Are you going back to your husband?" Yilan asked.

Fusang studied Yilan for a moment and said, "I'll be honest with you, Auntie, if you don't tell this to others. Of course I'm not going back to him."

"Where will you go, then?"

"There is always someplace to go," Fusang said.

"It would be hard for a young woman like you," Yilan said.

"But I'll have the twenty thousand yuan you pay me, right?"

Fusang said. "Besides, what do I fear? The worst would be to be sold again to another man as a wife, but who could be worse than a dimwit?"

Yilan thought about the husband who had enough feeling and intelligence to save Fusang from his parents. She could easily end up with someone with much more to be feared, and twenty thousand yuan, barely enough to cover two years of rent for a flat such as the one they lived in, was far from granting her anything. Yet Fusang seemed so sure of herself, and so happy in knowing that she had some control of her future, that Yilan had no heart to point out the illusion. She thought about her Chinese friends in America, a few divorced ones who, even though much older than Fusang, could still be a good choice for her. But would it be a wise thing to make that happen, when the best arrangement, as her husband had said, was to conclude the deal after the baby's birth and never have anything to do with Fusang again?

They became closer after the conversation. Fusang seemed more settled in the flat and in her own body, and she no longer followed Yilan around like a frightened child. Despite her husband's phone calls reminding her about nourishing both the baby's body and her brain, Yilan stopped filling every moment of Fusang's life with tasks. They found more comfort in each other's absence. In fact, Yilan enjoyed reading and listening to music and daydreaming alone now, and a few times, in the middle of a long meditation, Yilan heard a small voice from Fusang's bedroom, singing folk songs in a dialect that Yilan did not understand. Fusang's singing voice, low and husky, was much older than her age, and the slow and almost tuneless songs she sang reminded Yilan of an ancient poem that kept coming to her since Jade's death: a lone horse of the Huns running astray at the edge of the desert, its hooves disturbing the old snow and its eyes reflecting the last hopeful light of the sun setting between tall, yellow grasses.

Twice a day, Yilan accompanied Fusang to a nearby park for an hour-long walk. Yilan told strangers who talked to them that Fusang was her niece. Nobody doubted them, Fusang's hand grasping Yilan's arm in a childlike way. Yilan did not let Fusang go with her to the marketplace for groceries—there were many things Yilan wanted to protect Fusang and the baby from: air and noise pollution from the street crowded with cars and tractors, unfriendly elbows in front of the vendors' stands, foul language of vendors arguing with customers when the bargaining did not work out.

FUSANG'S BODY SEEMED to change rapidly within a short time. By the tenth week of the pregnancy, the doctor prescribed an ultrasound, and half an hour later, Yilan and Fusang were both crying and laughing at the news of a pair of twins snuggling in Fusang's womb, their small hearts big on the screen, pumping with powerful beats.

Yilan and Fusang left the hospital arm in arm, and on the taxi ride home, Yilan changed her mind and asked the driver to send them to the restaurant that had the best spicy dishes in town. She ordered more than they could consume, but Fusang had only a few bites of the spicy dishes. "We don't want the twins to get too hot," she said.

"It may not hurt to let them experience every taste before they are born," Yilan said.

Fusang smiled. Still, she would touch only the blander dishes. "I've always wondered what it'd be like to have twins," she said. "To think we'll have two babies that will look just the same."

Yilan hesitated at Fusang's use of "we" and then explained that the twins came from the implantation of multiple embryos and that they would not be identical. They might not be the same gender, either.

"Let's hope for a boy and a girl, then," Fusang said.

Yilan gazed at Fusang. "At my age, I wouldn't want to bargain."

"Auntie, maybe you hate people asking, but why do you want a baby now?"

Yilan looked at Fusang's face, which glowed a soft peach color. The news of the twins seemed to have transformed Fusang into an even more beautiful woman. This was what Yilan was going to miss, a pregnant daughter sitting across the table from her, sharing with her the joy of a new life.

"Are you angry, Auntie? I shouldn't have asked."

"I had a daughter and she died," Yilan said. "She was five years younger than you."

Fusang looked down at her own hands on the table and said after a moment, "It's better now. You'll have more children."

Yilan felt the stinging of the tears that she tried to hold back. "It's not the same," she said. Luo had been right—nobody would be able to replace Jade. For a moment, she wondered why they would want to take pains to get more children, whose presence could be taken away as easily as Jade's; they themselves could disappear from the twins' lives and leave them among the orphans of the world. Weren't they the people in the folktales who drank a poisonous fluid to stop a moment of thirst? But it was too late to regret.

"You should stop thinking about your daughter," Fusang said. "It's not hard at all if you try."

Yilan shook her head and tried hard not to cry in front of the young woman.

"Really, Auntie," Fusang said. "You'll be surprised how easy it is to forget someone. I never think about my son."

"But how can you forget him? He came from your own body," Yilan said.

"It was hard at first, but I just thought of it this way: Whoever took him would give him a better life than his own parents. Then it didn't hurt to think of him, and once it didn't hurt, I forgot to think about him from time to time, and then I just forgot."

Yilan looked at the young woman, her eyes in the shape of new moons, filled with an innocent smile, as if she were not talking about the cruelest truth in life. Illiterate and young as she was, she seemed to have gained more wisdom about life than Yilan and Luo. Yilan studied Fusang: young, beautiful, and pregnant with Luo's children—who could be a better choice to replace her as a wife than Fusang? Such a thought, once formed, became strong.

"Have you ever thought of going to America?" Yilan said.

"No."

"Do you want to?"

"No," Fusang said. "My tongue is straight and I can't speak English."

"English is not hard to learn," Yilan said. "Take me as an example." Take Jade, she thought.

"Are you matchmaking for me, Auntie? If possible, I want someone younger this time," Fusang said, laughing at her own joke.

Yilan could not help but feel disappointed. Indeed Luo was too old for Fusang—her father's age already. It did not feel right,

Yilan thought, to marry someone your daughter's age to your husband. "Where are your parents?" she asked Fusang. "Do you want to go back to them after this?"

"My mother died when I was two. I've never known her."

"What about your father? Do you remember him?"

"He leased me to a beggar couple for ten years so I could support myself by begging with them. They were like my own parents and raised me from the time I was eight. They promised to return me to my father when I was eighteen, with the money I made as my dowry, so he could marry me off, but then they died and I was brought to my husband's village and before I knew it, aha, I was sold."

"Who sold you? Why didn't you report it to the police?"

"The man said he could find me a job, so I went with him. The next thing I knew, I was locked in a bedroom with a dimwit. And when they finally let me free, my son was already born," Fusang said, shaking her head as if intrigued by a story that did not belong to her. "What's the good of reporting then? They would never find the man."

YILAN AND FUSANG left the restaurant and decided to take a long stroll home. They were the reason for each other's existence in this city, and they had no place to rush to. Fusang's hand was on Yilan's arm, but it was no longer a hand clinging for guidance. Their connection was something between friendship and kinship. When they walked past a department store, they went in and Yilan bought a few maternity outfits for Fusang, cotton dresses in soft shades of pink and yellow and blue, with huge butterfly knots on the back. Fusang blushed when the female salesperson complimented her on her cuteness in the dresses. Yilan found it hard not to broadcast the news of the twins. An older woman passing by congratulated Yilan for her good fortune as a grandmother, and neither Yilan nor Fusang corrected her.

When they exited the store, Yilan pointed out a fruit vendor to Fusang. It was the season for new bayberries, and they walked across the street to buy a basket. As they were leaving, a small hand grasped Yilan's pants. "Spare a penny, Granny," a boy dressed in rags said, his upturned face smeared with dirt.

Yilan put the change into the boy's straw basket, which held a few scattered coins and paper notes. The boy let go of Yilan's pants and then grabbed Fusang's sleeve. "Spare a penny, Auntie."

Fusang looked at the boy for a moment and squatted down. "Be careful," Yilan said, but Fusang paid no attention. She put a hand on the boy's forehead and he jerked back, but Fusang dragged him closer and said in a harsh tone, "Let me see your head."

The boy, frightened, did not move. Fusang stroked his hair back and gazed at his forehead for a moment. "What's your name?" she said, shaking the boy by his shoulder. "How old are you? Where are your parents? Where is your home?"

Before the boy could answer, a middle-aged man ran toward them from the street corner. "Hey," he said in a dialect not of the province. "What are you doing to my son?"

"But he's not your son," Fusang said. "He's mine."

The boy recoiled from Fusang, his eyes filled with trepidation. The man pulled the boy away from Fusang and said to Yilan, "Is she your daughter? Can't you see she's scaring my child? Don't think we beggars do not deserve respect and that you can shit on our faces."

Yilan looked at the man, his yellow crooked teeth and big sinewy hands bearing the threat of a lawless wanderer. He could easily hurt the twins with a mean punch to Fusang's belly. Yilan held Fusang back and said in a placating tone, "My niece lost a son, so please understand that she might make a mistake."

"But I'm not mistaken," Fusang said. "My son has a scar here on his forehead, like a new moon, and he has that, too."

Already a group of people had gathered for the free street show. Someone laughed at Fusang's words and said, "Five out of ten boys have a scar somewhere on their heads, haven't they?"

"Hear that?" the man said to Fusang. "How can you prove he's your son?"

"Can you prove he's your son?" Fusang said. "Do you have his birth papers?"

"Beggars don't bother to bring useless things with them," the man said. He picked up the boy and put him on his shoulders. "Brothers and sisters, if you have a penny to spare for me and my boy, please do so. Or we'll leave now so this crazy woman won't bother us."

Fusang grabbed the man's arm, but with a small push he sent Fusang stumbling back a few steps till she sat down on the ground. Yilan's heart quickened.

"If you dare leave now, you will not have a good death," Fusang said, and started to cry. Neither her curse nor her tears stopped the man. The circle scattered to let him and the boy pass, and besides a few idlers who stayed to watch Fusang cry, the others left for their own business.

Yilan imagined the twins in Fusang's womb, shaken by anger and sadness that they did not understand. She did not know how to comfort Fusang, nor could she believe in Fusang's claim of the boy's identity. After a moment, Yilan said, "Are you all right?"

Fusang put a hand on her belly and supported herself with another hand to stand up. "Don't worry, Auntie," she said. "The babies are fine."

"You could've hurt them," Yilan said. Her words sounded cold, and right away she regretted having spoken them.

Fusang did not reply. Yilan called a taxi, and on the ride home they let silence grow and distance them into strangers. When they entered the flat, Yilan told Fusang to take a rest and not to dwell on the incident; Fusang did not reply but followed Yilan to her bedroom.

"You don't believe me, Auntie," Fusang said, standing at the door. "But he's my son. How can a mother make a mistake?"

Yilan shook her head and sat down on her bed. A moon-shaped scar could happen to many boys and it proved nothing. "You told me that wherever your son was, he was having his own life," Yilan said finally. "So don't think about him now."

"I thought he would have a much better life," Fusang said. "I thought people who wanted to buy a boy from a trader would treat him as their own son. I didn't know he would be sold to a beggar."

Yilan had heard stories of people buying or renting children from poor villages and taking them into the cities to beg. The owners made big money from the small children, whom they starved and sometimes hurt intentionally, so that the children, with their hungry eyes and wounded bodies on display, would look sadder and more worthy of charity. She tried to recall the boy's eyes, whether they bore unfathomable pain and sadness unfit for a child his age, but all she could remember was the man's big hand on his small arm when he was taken away from Fusang.

"Had I known this," Fusang said, "I wouldn't have let the trader take him away. I thought any parents would be better than his dimwit father and me."

"Did you give your son away to a trader?" Yilan asked.

"We couldn't give the boy a good life," Fusang said. "Besides, his grandparents deserved it because of what they had done to me."

Yilan was shocked by the venom in Fusang's words, the first time Yilan had detected the young woman's emotion about her past. "How could you make such a mistake?" Yilan said. "You're the birth mother of your son and no one could replace you."

"But if someone could give him a better life—" Fusang said. "Just like you'll take away the twins and I won't say a thing, because you'll give them more than I can."

"The twins are our children," Yilan said, and stood up abruptly. She was stunned by Fusang's illogic. "You can't keep them. We have a contract."

"If they're in my belly, won't they be my children, too?" Fusang said. "But don't worry, Auntie. I won't keep them. All I'm saying is sometimes mothers do give away their children."

"Then stop thinking of getting him back," Yilan said, and then regretted her frustration. "And perhaps he's not your son at all," she added in a softened voice. "Your son may be living a happy life elsewhere."

Fusang shook her head in confusion. "Why is it that no one wants to believe me?" she said. "He is my son."

"But you have no way to prove it," Yilan said.

Fusang thought for a long moment. "Yes, there is a way," she said, and suddenly became excited. "Auntie, can you give me half of my money now? I'll go find the man and offer ten thousand yuan to buy the boy back from him. He won't sell the boy if he's his son, but if he only bought the boy from a trader, he'll surely sell the boy to me, and that will prove that he is my son."

Yilan did not know how to reply. Ten thousand yuan was a big sum and Fusang might be able to buy the boy from the beggar if indeed the man was only the owner of the boy instead of his father, but that did not make the boy Fusang's son. Or did it matter whether he came from her blood or not? She believed him to be her son, and he might as well become her son, but what did Fusang have, except for the rest of the money she would earn from the pregnancy, to bring the child up? Fusang was still a child herself, acting out of wrong reasoning; she herself needed a mother to pass on generations of wisdom to her.

"Auntie, please?" Fusang said, her pleading eyes looking into Yilan's. "I can send him to his father for now if you don't like having him around."

"But you're planning to leave your husband," Yilan said. "Plus, he can't possibly take care of a small child."

"I'll find someone to take care of him in the village," Fusang said. "I'll stay with my husband if you think I shouldn't leave him. Please, Auntie, if we don't hurry, the man may run away with my son."

What would Fusang do with a small child? Yilan thought. She found it hard to imagine Fusang's life without her own presence, but what would Luo say if she told him about the situation and suggested they find a way to help Fusang and her son to America? Luo would probably say there was no clause about an advance or any other form of payment beyond the twenty thousand yuan. How could she persuade him to see that sometimes people without any blood connection could also make a family—and Fusang, wasn't she their kin now, nurturing their twins with her blood?

"Auntie?" Fusang said tentatively, and Yilan realized that she had been gazing at the young woman for a long time.

"Fusang," Yilan said. "Why don't we sit down for a moment? We need to talk."

But Fusang, mistaking Yilan's words as a rejection, stepped

back with disappointment. "You can say no, but remember, your children are here with me. I'll run away and sell your children if I like. I can starve them even if you find a way to keep me here," Fusang said, and before Yilan could stop her, she ran into the kitchen and climbed onto the dinner table. Yilan followed Fusang into the kitchen and looked at Fusang, her small figure all of a sudden a looming danger. "I can jump and jump and jump and make them fall out of my body now," Fusang said. "I don't care if I don't earn your money. I have a husband to go back to. I will have more children if I like, but you won't ever see the twins if you say no to me now."

Fusang's face was no longer glowing with a gentle beauty but with anger and hatred. This was the price they paid for being mothers, Yilan thought, that the love of one's own child made everyone else in the world a potential enemy. Even as she was trying to find reconciling words to convince Fusang that she would do whatever she requested, Yilan knew that the world of trust and love they had built together was crushed, and they would remain each other's prisoners for as long as they stayed under the same roof.

The Proprietress

THE INTERVIEW WITH the young woman reporter from Shanghai did not come as a surprise to Mrs. Jin, the proprietress of the general store across the street from the county jail. It was not the first time a reporter had asked to talk with her since she had taken in Susu and hidden her from the world of curious strangers; but this story was for a famous women's magazine, and Shanghai was different, a much bigger place than the provincial capital or the county seat, let alone Clear Water Town, which, apart from the jail, had nothing to offer as an attraction for out-of-towners. Mrs. Jin imagined people in Shanghai reading about her and her store, even though she was not the reason the reporter was coming.

The bus that carried the reporter into town arrived at three o'clock. Two hours before that, Mrs. Jin had closed her store. She'd wiped all the shelves, dusted every corner, and washed the cement floor twice. The silk blouse and pants she had put on for the day were new; so were the leather shoes, imported from Italy, according to the words printed on the box. A clearheaded businesswoman, Mrs. Jin did not believe the shoe box, but they were nice shoes, better than anyone in town wore, and worth showing off.

The shoes and the outfit were gifts from Mrs. Jin's son, who was a rather successful construction contractor in the provincial capital. When Mrs. Jin had become a widow, two years earlier, her son had asked her to join his family in the city for more comfortable circumstances, rather than wasting her time in the small store, which made as much money in a month or two as he did in a day. Mrs. Jin refused. At the age of sixty-eight, she was strong enough to lift a thirty-kilo box to the store's highest shelf; there was no need for her to live as a dependent of anyone, her son included. Besides, over those two years she had collected several women who now relied on her for their welfare. She would not give them up for a boring life under the reign of her daughter-in-law, whom she had not liked in the first place.

When she finished cleaning, Mrs. Jin sat down with a cup of tea behind the counter. She had put up a sign that said the store would be closed for the rest of the day, but she knew the townspeople would knock on her back door when they needed her. The sign was only for those who came from out of town; so were the price tags. Mrs. Jin believed the old saying that the smartest hare would not eat the grass at the entrance to its own hole, and she charged her townspeople much less, barely enough to make a profit.

She had lived all her life in Clear Water Town and had watched its young children grow up, some leaving, like her son, others staying and marrying to produce the next generation for her to watch; she herself had been watched by older people, though the number of those who remembered her as a young girl with two pigtails, or as a new wife with a plump and desirable body, was dwindling now. In a few years the memory of her youth would be gone with the oldsters, and nobody would contradict her even if she told the wildest lies about her life. Mrs. Jin sighed. She stood up and checked herself in the mirror. Her hair was neatly tucked into a tight bun and her eyebrows newly plucked, and she examined her face as if studying a stranger; after a while she decided that she was still a presentable woman. Not many women could age as beautifully and regally as she had, a fact that Mrs. Jin was proud of, though there was no one to whom she could boast.

The reporter from Shanghai was less beautiful than Mrs. Jin had imagined—fashionable, for sure, but dresses and jewels and makeup would not help her at Mrs. Jin's age. Her eyes were wide apart, which gave her a distracted look; her hair was not thick enough, and by fifty she would have to consider a wig.

"Some women were born with fewer gifts from heaven," Mrs. Jin said with a smile. "Susu is just one such woman."

"Someone from the courthouse told me she lives with you now," the reporter said. "Can I meet her?"

"She's not ready to meet strangers yet," Mrs. Jin said.

"I won't bother her for long. I'll just ask her a few questions," the reporter said.

Mrs. Jin shook her head. Since the execution of Susu's husband, Mrs. Jin had fended off several reporters for Susu. "She's like a daughter to me, so if you have questions, I can answer them for you."

"What does she think of the court's decision to deny her a baby?" the reporter asked.

"It doesn't matter what she thinks," Mrs. Jin said. It had been a crazy idea on Susu's part in the first place. Who would have thought of asking to have a baby with a husband about to be executed? "The judge said no, so she'd better stop thinking about it."

This seemed to take the reporter by surprise. "What do you think of it, Mrs. Jin?"

"I couldn't have been happier," Mrs. Jin said. These reporters all came with the same despicable ambitions, to witness Susu's grief over her dead husband and to analyze her mad notion of bearing his child. Sometimes they talked about the significance of Susu's case—no one had ever made such a request, they said; she raised the question of whether a man on death row had reproductive rights. But such talk was nonsense. For ordinary people like Susu, there was nothing glorious about occupying a page or two in a history book. "Think about it," Mrs. Jin said. "What would it make a jail look like if every wife asked to have a baby by a husband inside? A mating station it would be, no?"

The reporter smiled. "I think what Susu asked for was artificial insemination," she said, and explained the procedure.

"What a horrible invention," Mrs. Jin said. "There're enough men in this world who will jump at the first opportunity to offer the real thing."

The reporter smiled again. Mrs. Jin savored her wittiness, making a young woman from Shanghai laugh, and supposed that she might like the reporter more than she had thought. Perhaps she could reconsider her decision and let the woman see Susu for five minutes—it all depended on how the reporter behaved.

"Trust me, Susu won't remain a widow for long," Mrs. Jin said. "She'll get a chance to have a baby. I'll see to it personally."

"You said she was like a daughter to you," the reporter said. "Are you a relative?"

"No. She came through this door one day to tell me her story. I liked her, so I said, 'Susu, it's a cruel world. Why don't you stay with me for some time until you're ready to go out there again?' She stayed."

Mrs. Jin observed the reporter. People in this world belonged to two groups: those who were curious about others' stories, and those who were not. Mrs. Jin decided that if the reporter did not show a genuine interest in Mrs. Jin herself, she would finish the interview in a few minutes and make the young woman's trip from Shanghai worthless.

The young woman raised her eyebrows. "You just took her in like that, without even knowing her?"

Feeling the reporter's eyes probe her own for answers and stories, Mrs. Jin was satisfied. "Why? How much more does one need to know to lend a hand to a drowning life?" she said. "It's not the first time for me, anyway. You don't close the door to those who need you."

It was true that Susu was not the first woman Mrs. Jin had picked up from the street, nor would she be the last one. These women lived with Mrs. Jin now in the big house she had once shared with her husband. She had been married to him for forty-three years. There was nothing about him to complain of—in fact, if anyone asked Mrs. Jin, she would say that her husband was the best man she could ever have imagined. Unlike many other men in town, who drank and beat their wives and children, Mrs. Jin's husband was strictly obedient; she had been the one to make decisions and he the one to follow them, from the color of the curtains to the naming of their only son.

It had been her idea, too, to buy the almost defunct general store from the township twenty years earlier, when small private businesses ceased to be illegal. What if there came another round of the Cultural Revolution and the cutting of capitalist tails? her husband said; their business would be the biggest tail in town. Mrs. Jin told her husband one could worry himself to death even in bed, and if he would choose to hide from life like a tortoise, he'd better remember that she would not remain a tortoise's wife. It was the harshest thing she had ever said to him, but it shut him up. She bribed officials of all ranks in the jail so that her husband could go inside twice a week to sell, at high prices, cigarettes, matches, toothpaste, towels, poker cards, and other goods to those who did not have visitors. The store blossomed under the couple's hard labor.

The idea of gathering women companions first occurred to Mrs. Jin not because she felt lonely or abandoned after her husband's death. Rather, she saw this as a new stage of her life. She had taken good care of her husband for four decades—her son, too, before he had gone out and made a man of himself—and now it was time for other responsibilities. It was not difficult to find such women—once a week, female visitors were allowed in the jail to see their men. Some stopped by Mrs. Jin's store for last-minute purchases of articles they had forgotten; more came in after the visiting hour for Mrs. Jin's hospitality, the hot tea and freshly baked buns she offered them for free. Sooner or later they started to talk about their men—fathers, sons, brothers, husbands—similar stories in which the women either believed in the innocence of their loved ones or were readier than the rest of the world to forgive them. Mrs. Jin listened, pouring tea and handing them tissues, reminding herself what a lucky woman she was. She shed tears with them, too, and because of the hours she spent sympathizing, she charged these women extra for any purchases. They left with gratitude. Some returned for more tea and talk; others, whose men were sentenced and either transferred or executed, would be replaced by new women with the same stories.

The reporter, who had come for Susu, decided to write a story about Mrs. Jin instead. An impressive story it would be, she told Mrs. Jin, an important one about sisterhood that would reach all the female readers of the magazine. The reporter's talk was like her big-city clothes, fancy but laughable. She called Mrs. Jin's house "a commune," and praised Mrs. Jin's charity as "revolutionary." Such words reminded Mrs. Jin of a past era: Her own father had been the leader of Clear Water People's Commune, when the town had been a village, before the surrounding farmland was sold for mining. Yet, regardless of the reporter's inanities, Mrs. Jin decided that she herself was indeed extraordinary and worth a story, so when the reporter asked to see Mrs. Jin's commune, she agreed.

The reporter took a picture of Mrs. Jin across the street from the jail. The enclosed compound had been the home of a big landlord, she told the reporter, who found this interesting and snapped more pictures and wrote in her notebook. A few townspeople stopped by to watch and congratulated Mrs. Jin when she told them the news of her being featured in the women's magazine.

She smiled and nodded, already feeling important. She led the reporter across town to her house, a good brick one with a big yard. Upon entering the gate, they bumped into a pair of children who were running wild. The reporter dropped her pen. The two girls, identical twins dressed in the same clothes, stopped immediately. One picked up the pen while the other chirped an apology. Mrs. Jin frowned. Many times she had told the twins to behave properly in her home, but the two girls just did not have the brains for useful lessons. "These are my youngest girls," she said, without introducing them. As she sometimes confused the two, she never used their names.

The twins studied the reporter and smiled simultaneously. "Auntie, I like your bag," one said, touching the reporter's leather handbag. The other handed the pen to the reporter and said, "Auntie, are you an actress? You're the prettiest woman I've ever seen."

"What sweet girls," the reporter said. "How old are you?"

"Six," they both said.

Mrs. Jin watched the twins put on their best charming expressions. Their eyes, too big for their small, heart-shaped faces, gave them a look of helpless innocence. Mrs. Jin said to the twins, "Don't bother the guest."

The girls stepped back, still bearing their matching smiles.

"Their father was sentenced to thirty years," Mrs. Jin said to the reporter, "for robbing an old woman and making her die of a heart attack. Their parents of course did not get married before the girls were born, so they had to hide them from the household registrar."

The two girls followed Mrs. Jin and the reporter to the living room and sat by the foot of the couch, as if the discussion had nothing to do with them.

"Are they in school now?" the reporter asked.

"I got them legalized after they came to live here, so they could go to school. You just have to pay a price," Mrs. Jin said, rubbing two fingers together. The girls listened to Mrs. Jin and the reporter, their eyes moving from one person to the other, not blinking.

"Where is their mother?" the reporter asked.

"I found her a job at a county hospital, washing laundry," Mrs. Jin said. "She comes home once a week."

With great interest the two girls watched the reporter take notes. Mrs. Jin stood up and left for the kitchen, knowing the reporter would have questions for the girls. Mrs. Jin thought that it would look better if she were not present when the twins sang her praises, which she trusted they would do to the best effect.

The girls' mother had come to Mrs. Jin just as many other women had, with a story of a hard life and an unfair fate. She and the father of her children had been so poor that they lacked the application fee for a marriage certificate, and had no money to pay the fine for being pregnant without permission from the county's birth control office.

"Their father was optimistic," the twins' mother had said. "He thought when we had more money, we would pay the fine or the bribery. But nobody gets rich selling pickled pigs' ears, and the girls could not go to school unless they were registered soon. So he robbed the old woman. Silly man! I would've never let him. I would've gone to the street to become a whore myself had I known his plan. He thought he could solve the problem by himself, but now who knows when he'll be released."

Mrs. Jin had no hope for the husband, even though he had not set out to kill the old woman. In fact, he had called for help when she had become motionless, but that, as Mrs. Jin had suspected, did not help him much in the courthouse.

Mrs. Jin did not intend to take in the woman and her children at first. The woman's circumstances were hard indeed, but she was a mother, and a mother should never be defeated by circumstances. The second time they came into the store, however, Mrs. Jin caught the twins stealing candies when she stood up to fetch tissues for their sobbing mother. Mrs. Jin pretended not to notice, but when the three of them were about to leave, she brought out some snacks and insisted on putting them into the two girls' pockets herself. She pinched them and made sure the girls knew that she had seen them take what did not belong to them. But they showed no signs of panic. Instead, they gave Mrs. Jin the most candid smiles, as if they knew she would not have the heart to reveal their crime to their mother, who stood by the store entrance, sighing and dabbing her eyes with a corner of her blouse. Where did the girls get such shameless courage? Mrs. Jin studied their mother again—she was a dull woman, foolish-looking; the twins were much prettier, their eyes too smart for children their age. Perhaps they had inherited this from their father. The possibility that they would grow more like him, wasting their gifts on the wrong ideas, troubled Mrs. Jin. His sentence was long, so his influence on the two girls could be minimized; but she worried about the mother's inability to raise them properly.

She decided to take over their upbringing. The mother was overjoyed that someone with power and wealth would think of her own children's welfare; it was not hard to persuade her to accept a job away from them. She talked about saving every penny to pay back Mrs. Jin, but Mrs. Jin made it clear that she had no need for the money. "Save for the future," she told the mother, who was in grateful tears. "I won't always be around to take care of them for you."

When Mrs. Jin returned to the living room with a cup of tea for the reporter, the twins were leaning on the young woman, who was showing them her small tape recorder. Given an opportunity, the girls would try to charm anyone, Mrs. Jin thought with frustration. Six months they had been living under her roof now, and she had been unable to wipe away that smartness from their eyes. Sometimes she wondered if she had enough time to change them into what she wanted them to be, girls with fear and reverence for what was beyond their control in life; what a shame it would be to be defeated by a pair of six-year-olds. Mrs. Jin placed the tea in front of the reporter, and right away both girls looked up.

"Nana," one of them said. "Auntie said she is going to write a story about you so everybody will know what a good person you are."

"And she'll take our picture so everybody can see how lucky we are," the other girl said.

Mrs. Jin smiled tightly, annoyed by the mock she always perceived in their eyes when they sweet-mouthed her. "Did you both finish your homework?" she said.

"Yes," they said.

"Then go practice knitting in your room." She turned to the reporter and said, "There's so much for them to learn. I want them to be prepared as best they can."

The girls left but a minute later returned with their knitting needles and yarn and sat down by the couch. The reporter watched them knit and took a few pictures; in the flash of light, the girls looked serious and engrossed in what they were doing, though they would never have remembered to pick up their knitting needles if Mrs. Jin had not told them to. She sighed. If not for the reporter, she would have told them in a sharp tongue not to put on a show. More and more now she talked to the girls harshly, which seemed to work only for a minute or two before they became their old selves, smiling at her and talking as if they were her beloved grandchildren. Mrs. Jin was happy that they had not come from her blood.

When the reporter put away the camera, Mrs. Jin suggested a tour of the house, and before the girls could make a move, she told them not to follow.

The house, two-storied, had two bedrooms on the first floor and three more on the second. Mrs. Jin led the reporter upstairs and showed her the two small rooms at the end of the hallway. Standing in each was a single bed, neatly made by Mrs. Jin herself. "These belong to the two older girls," she said. "They come home only on weekends, like the twins' mother." Strictly speaking, it was not a lie, as Mrs. Jin still hoped for the girls to return to her house. They had come at different times but left together. The older one, twenty-one and slightly beautiful, had no place to live after her boyfriend, a small-scale drug dealer, got a sentence of seventeen years. The younger one was nineteen and had told Mrs. Jin stories about her stepfather, who had repeatedly raped an eight-year-old girl, and her mother, who had helped to bait the young girl into their house. Mrs. Jin did not know if she believed the girl's tales, but both would certainly benefit from her supervision.

For a while both girls worked in Mrs. Jin's store, though she could handle the business herself perfectly. She thought she would teach them how to make a living with their hands before sending them out to the real world, but one day they left a note for her, explaining they had *borrowed* her money to go to Shanghai. They promised to come back to see her and return the money when they found good manual jobs, but Mrs. Jin was certain they would fall into the hands of drug dealers and pimps. It was upsetting that they had left without Mrs. Jin's assent, but she knew that soon she would find two more girls to fill the vacancies; the next time she would have to choose carefully so she would not be disappointed.

Returning downstairs, Mrs. Jin entered the hallway and knocked on the first door before pushing it ajar and saying, "Granny, it's me."

There was no answer in the room, as she had expected. Granny, who'd lived in the house for more than a year, was eighty-one and suffered from dementia. As was common, she was not alone—sitting beside her on the single bed was a slender young woman, her hand grasped tightly by Granny's thin, chicken-claw fingers.

"Granny is telling me stories about her husband," the woman said with an apologetic look, and wiggled her hand out of Granny's clasp.

Mrs. Jin nodded. All that Granny remembered and talked about was her dead husband. "I've told you not to waste your time with Granny," Mrs. Jin said. "You've heard enough of her stories."

The woman looked down at the tips of her shoes. "I don't mind," she said. "Granny likes to tell the stories."

"We have a guest in the house," Mrs. Jin said.

"I'll get dinner ready," the woman said. She nodded to the reporter and left the room without making a sound. The reporter watched her close the door.

"Who is she?" she asked.

Mrs. Jin hesitated and replied, "Susu."

"She's beautiful," the reporter said.

"Indeed," Mrs. Jin said. They were silent, as if still entranced by her beauty. It was not healthy for Susu to listen to the old woman's tales about a husband executed fifty years earlier, but Mrs. Jin had not wanted to remind Susu of this in front of the reporter.

After a moment, Mrs. Jin pointed to Granny, who looked lost now that nobody was listening to her stories. "Remember I told you that the jail used to be the landlord's compound? The landlord was Granny's husband. She was his fifth wife." Then, grabbing Granny's hand, Mrs. Jin raised her voice and said, "Granny, tell us about your Mister."

"Mister liked to eat duck gizzards with mustard," Granny said. This was new for Mrs. Jin. On other days she heard the same stories repeatedly about Mister, how before he settled down he had made enough money traveling with an acrobatic troupe to become the biggest landowner in the region.

"Where is he now? What happened to him?" Mrs. Jin said.

Granny thought for a moment and twitched her mouth as if she was crying, though her eyes remained dry. "They took him away," she said.

"Where did they take him?" Mrs. Jin said.

"To the river. Do you know where the river is? They took him there and drowned him, my poor Mister," Granny said, slapping the blanket on her knees, like a wife newly bereft.

Mrs. Jin waited for a moment and said, "Granny, I heard you were his favorite wife."

Granny calmed down. "Mister says I'm the most beautiful woman in the world," she said, her wrinkled face blushing like a bashful young girl's.

Mrs. Jin stepped back and said to the reporter, not lowering her voice, "What a sad thing for her to live for a man who's been dead fifty years."

"Was he really drowned?" the reporter asked.

"Executed beside the river in '51," Mrs. Jin said. "He was thirty years older than she."

The reporter looked at Granny and did not speak for a while. Mrs. Jin walked to the window to straighten the curtain and to give the reporter a moment to absorb the story of Granny. Mrs. Jin did not usually take in old women—their fates were already written out for them, and there was no room for her to make a difference. Granny was an exception. She had come when the last of her husband's other four wives died; the five wives had all refused to remarry and had remained a close family until their passings.

"How long has she stayed here?" the reporter asked.

"Since her last relative died," Mrs. Jin said. "About a year now."

"Did you know her before that?"

"Yes," Mrs. Jin said. "I've known her almost all my life." It was not a lie—she had first seen Granny as a bride sixty years earlier. Mrs. Jin had been eight years old then, a poor peasant's daughter standing in the crowd to witness Granny being married off to the richest man in the village. The new wife was so beautiful that Mrs. Jin, young as she was, wished she could become part of the woman's life one day, but when she asked to be sold to the landlord's family as a handmaiden, her father said it was the stupidest idea she'd ever had.

Not long afterward, however, their lives intersected when Granny's husband was sentenced in a public meeting as an enemy of the new proletarian regime: Mrs. Jin's father was one of the two militiamen who had pushed the convict down to the riverbank and put a bullet into his head. Nobody remembered such old stories except Mrs. Jin. She had waited all these years to become part of Granny's life. Mrs. Jin's lifelong loyalty, however, went unnoticed by Granny, who never recognized her as the eight-year-old admirer, or the daughter of the poor peasant who became a power figure after the revolution.

"Are Susu and Granny friends?" the reporter asked.

"I wish they weren't," Mrs. Jin said. Granny was a bad influence, a woman who let the memory of a short marriage become the only life she knew. Who would be around to take care of Susu if she let herself grow old like that?

"Do you think I can ask Susu a few questions?" the reporter said.

It was hard to refuse someone who had promised to write a story about her, Mrs. Jin thought. Besides, she felt a little tired. She had worked so hard to make a haven for Susu, who still refused to open her eyes to the future. All those reports about her request to the court for a baby must have made her believe she was justified in her grief, but it was wrong to mourn for any man like that, her husband especially, a useless, replaceable person.

Mrs. Jin had read about the case in the newspapers. The young man, twenty-three and newly wedded to his childhood sweetheart, was in an argument with his woman boss. He confessed to the police that she had slapped him a couple of times, and that made him lose his temper; she was found strangled to death in her office with him weeping under her desk, unable to move when the police ordered him to come out.

Mrs. Jin had not connected Susu with the man in the newspapers when she had first come into the store. Unlike the other women, Susu did not talk about what had brought her to the jail, even when Mrs. Jin asked. Mrs. Jin studied Susu; her accent was not local but from the next province, her hips narrow and her eyes clear, still like a maiden. She was beautiful in an unhealthy way, her skin bloodless, almost transparent. Mrs. Jin imagined caring for Susu as her own daughter, filling her bony frame with more flesh and putting color in her cheeks. The more Mrs. Jin thought about it, the less willing she was to let the girl slip away. She offered Susu a free room in her house, so that the young wife would not have to rent cheap accommodations in town while waiting for the trial. Mrs. Jin cooked homemade sausages for Susu to bring to the jail on visiting days and did not ask whom they were for. Eventually, Susu started to talk. She showed her wedding album to Mrs. Jin; in the pictures the husband, slim and tall in a boyish way, did not look like a murderer.

He got a death sentence; when the appeal failed, Mrs. Jin thought the worst was over and it was time to reconstruct the young woman. Her sadness did not bother Mrs. Jin, and when

Susu mentioned her hope to have a baby with her husband before his execution, Mrs. Jin was only slightly alert. Susu would come to her senses, Mrs. Jin decided; it was only the whim of a young woman struck by grief. But when Susu asked to borrow money from Mrs. Jin to hire a lawyer for the request, Mrs. Jin became scared. She had not anticipated the determination in that frail body. Susu was wrong to bet all her future, and the future of a child, on the love of a man who had made the stupidest mistake in life. Mrs. Jin would do anything to prevent that. In the end, however, she gave the money to Susu, not ready to oppose the girl's wish in any way and thus lose her.

Mrs. Jin was relieved when the request was denied; without a child binding Susu to her dead husband, her future was a blank sheet again, full of possibilities. Mrs. Jin persuaded Susu to continue living in the house—she needed some time to recover, after all. The money Mrs. Jin had lent Susu was, in retrospect, a smart move; Susu was not a person who could ever say no to a generous and sympathetic soul.

Mrs. Jin showed the reporter the rest of the house before they came to the kitchen. Susu looked up from the cutting board, where she was chopping vegetables for dumpling fillings. "Susu, this reporter wants to talk to you," Mrs. Jin said.

"Dead is dead. There's nothing to talk about now," Susu said, without acknowledging the reporter.

"She came all the way from Shanghai for you," Mrs. Jin said, "so maybe we'll just answer a few questions for her?"

Susu glanced at the reporter. "I've never been to Shanghai," she said.

"When you feel better, we'll take a trip to Shanghai together," Mrs. Jin said.

Susu looked at the chopper in her hand for a moment and said, "We thought of going there for our honeymoon, but it was too expensive."

Mrs. Jin watched Susu, whose mind was elsewhere. It was the first time she had mentioned her life with her husband since his execution a month before. Mrs. Jin wondered if Susu would, like Granny, start to tell stories so she could remember him—Mrs. Jin wondered what she would have to do to battle against another dead man.

"I'm sorry about your husband," the reporter said. When Susu did not reply, the reporter smiled apologetically at Mrs. Jin and then said, "Your request to have a baby with someone on death row—have you realized that it has sparked a national discussion about the legal as well as the moral and social significance of your case? Can you talk a little about what you think of the discussion?"

Susu looked up at the reporter. "I don't understand your questions," she said.

"Some picture you as a challenger to the present judicial system; some think of you as a victim of the old patriarchal society in which a wife's foremost responsibility is to ensure the continuity of the husband's blood; and some—pardon me—think you were using the petition to draw undue attention to your husband's case—"

"He's dead, isn't he?" Susu said.

"Of course I'm not saying I agree with some, or any, of these views," the reporter said. "I'm curious what you think of these reactions."

Susu looked at the chopper in her hand. "I have nothing to say," she said. "I'm sorry."

The reporter nodded and thanked her. Mrs. Jin was relieved.

After all, Susu would remain a minor character in the reporter's story; Mrs. Jin herself would be the heroine.

The twins sneaked into the kitchen like two kittens drawn by the warmth of the hearth. One of them picked up the teapot and poured tea in two cups, and the other brought them for Mrs. Jin and the reporter. "Auntie, are you going to take our picture?" the girls asked.

"Ah yes," the reporter said.

"Will you send us our picture when you go back to Shanghai?" one of the twins begged, and the other added, "We want to show the picture to our dad so he knows he doesn't have to worry about us."

The reporter promised that she would, and Mrs. Jin watched the two girls clap as if they did not doubt the woman's sincerity at all. They would never miss a chance to put on such a show, to make their presence known to the world. Mrs. Jin looked at them and then at Susu, who watched the girls with hazy eyes. None of the women had reformed for her, and Mrs. Jin wondered how long it would take her to make that happen, and whether she still had time. The thought exhausted her, and she turned to the reporter and asked brusquely if she would like to stay in the house for the night, as the last bus was leaving town in less than an hour.

The reporter hesitated and said she would rather catch the bus. Could she take a picture of them all in the yard? she asked.

The twins were the first ones to get ready. They put on the princess outfits and patent leather shoes that Mrs. Jin had bought for their first performance in school. After a while, Granny walked out of the house, supported by Susu. Granny was dressed in a black satin blouse and pants embroidered with golden chrysanthemums, the outfit that she had ordered long before for her own burial. Mrs. Jin frowned. She did not know if it was an unintentional mistake, but regardless, it was a bad omen. She patted some rouge onto Granny's hollow cheeks, adding color for good luck and hoping no harm would be done to her. She led Granny to a cushioned chair in the middle of the yard and then directed Susu to stand behind the old woman. The twins stood close to Susu, each clinging to an arm. Mrs. Jin studied the group, young and old; all their sufferings came from the men they had been wrongly assigned by heaven. She herself could have been one of them if fate had not been lenient and given her an easier life: a father who, though born into a peasant's family, had risen to the right position through revolution; a husband who had never made a stupid mistake; and a good son who would not leave her to die in the hands of unsympathetic nurses in the old people's home.

The reporter looked through the camera and asked Mrs. Jin to join the group. She walked over and stood straight, an arm's length away from the rest. The light from the setting sun blinded her, but she did not squint. She imagined, in twenty years, the twins, Susu, and all the other women who were not in the picture but who had or would come to this house at one time or another—she imagined them looking at the picture in an old magazine and telling each other how Mrs. Jin had changed their lives. She would be happily watching over them then from the otherworld, where Granny would finally recognize her as the most loyal soul in the world.

House Fire

THEY CALLED THEMSELVES saviors of burning houses, though none of the six women, their ages ranging from mid-fifties to early seventies, had had much experience outside the worlds of their employment before retirement: small cubicles behind barred windows for the two bank tellers; large offices shared by too many people for the three secretaries; and a front room in a six-storied university building, where for many years Mrs. Lu had guarded the door to a girls' dorm.

The six women, friends and comrades for about two years now, had first met at a local park, where mothers, anxious for their children's marriages, met other equally fretful mothers. Between them the six women had four sons and four daughters, all of them unhurried by the ticking of the clock that kept their mothers sleepless at night. Shortly after they befriended one another, the women made ingenious plans in the hope that some of them would become connected by marriage and then by shared grandchildren. Meetings of their children were arranged, coerced in some cases. In the end, none of the matches produced any fruitful results. Still, the six women remained close, and when

Mrs. Fan, the youngest among them, realized that her husband was having an affair with a woman whose identity he refused to reveal, the other five women, enraged by the audacity of the husband, who was approaching sixty yet behaving like a foolish boy without a heart or a brain, appointed themselves detectives to find out the truth.

Their success in uncovering the mistress's name, address, and work unit did little to save Mrs. Fan's marriage. "An old man in love is like an old house on fire, which burns easily and burns down fast," went a popular joke that circulated as a text message from one cellphone to another around the city. The joke must have been made up by some young, carefree soul, but how sadly true it was. Mrs. Fan was taken aback by the intensity of the fire that engulfed her marriage: Three decades of trivial arguments and unimportant disagreements turned out to be flammable material. More appalling was the simple procedure for divorce. In the old days, the employers of both parties, the neighborhood association, the local workers' union, and the women's union would all be involved in the mediation, and the court, as the last resort, would not grant the divorce without making a lengthy effort of its own to save the marriage. After all, any assistance in breaking up a marriage was more sinful than destroying seven temples. But such a belief no longer held in the new era: An application speedily granted by the district courthouse soon left Mrs. Fan a single woman and released her husband to become the bridegroom of an immoral intruder.

The six friends declared war against love outside marriage. They did not need to look far before they found another woman suspecting a cheating husband, and with their previous experience, and a talent that seemed to come naturally to them, they identified the mistress within two weeks. It dawned upon Mrs.

Guan, whose son was a recent graduate from a top MBA program in America, that they could turn their skills into a business, and soon, through word of mouth, their clientele expanded. As agreed by the six friends, they would work for the principle of cleansing society and fighting against deteriorating morals, so they charged less than other firms and accepted only cases in which wives were endangered by disloyal husbands and conniving mistresses. Saviors of burning houses, they called themselves, their belief being that, discovered early enough, a fire could be put out before more harm was done.

THE STORY OF six older women working as successful private investigators was, against their will and without their consent, reported by a local newspaper in a gossipy column called "Odd People at This Unique Time." What transgressor would have thought that an old granny in the street had a mini-walkie-talkie hidden in her palm, or that her most innocent conversation with one's acquaintances would reveal one's secrets? The story was soon picked up by a women's magazine, and when the city TV channel proposed a short documentary on them as part of a month-long series on family values in the new era, the six friends decided to welcome the opportunity.

The anxiously awaited filming took place on a blustery day in early spring. Their complexions, Mrs. Tang explained to the woman in charge of makeup, ranged from raisins to months-old apples, so she might just as well save her powder and rouge for women with better reasons for looking desirable. Such self-mockery amused the TV crew. Even more surprising, the six women acted relaxed and natural in front of the cameras, but when complimented, they looked confused. She had no idea what the director was talking about, said Mrs. Cheng, the oldest and the loudest. If they were expected to be themselves, why the comment on their acting?

The documentary aired on a Saturday night and the six women became instant celebrities to their neighbors, relatives, and acquaintances. Soon it became a routine for the six friends to watch a tape of the program in Mrs. Mo's flat, which also served as the headquarters of their sleuthing business. Mrs. Mo had been widowed for twenty years, having lost her husband in a traffic accident, and at sixty-five she played tennis, belonged to a ballroom dancing club, and had a full collection of Agatha Christie novels on her shelf. With the looks of a Hong Kong film star from the forties, Mrs. Mo seemed not to belong to the group, yet it was she who had first organized the friends, inviting the other women to her flat whenever she had a day off from tennis and dancing, and later offering her home phone number as the contact for their business.

Sherlock Holmes was more to her husband's taste, commented Mrs. Tang, who was married to a retired army officer, whenever she saw the hostess's Agatha Christie collection. Mrs. Mo smiled tolerantly. She was aware that some of her friends envied her freedom. Now and then Mrs. Cheng and Mrs. Lu discussed Mrs. Mo's long-widowed situation with her, asking why she had not thought of remarrying and expressing admiration at her bringing up a daughter all by herself. Mrs. Tang, the least tactful of the six women, never missed the opportunity in these conversations to mention her own healthy and well-pensioned husband. Such petty competition, which also occurred when the women brought up their children's incomes, usually amounted to nothing more than harmless bantering. They were not about to give up the friendship that had made them famous late in their lives.

After the program was broadcast, however, their business slowed down. Perhaps prospective clients feared that the women's covers had been blown and it was unwise to hire them now, Mrs. Guan wondered aloud; or else they thought they could not afford the celebrity price, Mrs. Lu added. There was no real pressure for them to make money, in any case, said Mrs. Tang, and Mrs. Fan agreed, adding that their main goal was to raise the awareness of out-of-wedlock immorality, and that their TV documentary had made their stand known to more people than their fieldwork ever could. Such rounds of talk to ease any worry or doubt were repeated every day, though none of the six friends would admit that she was upset or disappointed by the fact that they were not sought out as they had been. While the talk went on, Mrs. Mo would brew tea and come round with a plate of nuts: green tea and pistachios on some days, red tea and cashews on others, since the tastes of the group were divided on many small things. The nuts were ground and taken in small spoonfuls, as several of the members had dentures, and when all was settled, Mrs. Mo would put the tape into the VCR player and turn on the TV.

After days and now weeks of watching, rewinding, and watching again, Mrs. Guan still felt a thrill the moment the blue screen flickered and the theme music started. Such a joy was shared by all six friends, and every viewing was accompanied by new comments and laughter. Familiar by now with every shot, they watched the program more for random glimpses of themselves. See Mrs. Cheng chat up two guards at an upscale flat complex, her cheerful nosiness not eliciting any suspicion on the young men's part. See Mrs. Lu hover patiently over a pot of watered-down tea on a bench outside a Starbucks where the cheating husband is holding an intimate conversation with a chic young woman. Thirty years of guarding the girls' dorm had taught Mrs. Lu a few things about shameless females, and every time she saw the young actress's hand covered by the middle-aged actor's hand, Mrs. Lu would relate yet another story about one of the girls from the past who had come back to the dorm after lights-out, lips too wet and cheeks flushed unnaturally. The girls would knock on Mrs. Lu's window and beg her to let them in, and often she yelled at them and said any day now she would report them to the university and they had better be prepared to move into the street with the rest of the whores. They had never taken such a threat seriously, as all of Mrs. Lu's yelling was of little use unless she could catch a pair of naked bodies in bed. Did you ever? Mrs. Fan asked one day, with obvious interest, and Mrs. Lu answered ambiguously that she might have successfully expelled a girl or two, but such decisions by the higher-ups were kept from little people like her. The discussion of the degenerating morals of the younger generation was then replaced by laughter over Mrs. Fan's secretive phone call to a wife about the cheating husband's whereabouts. Their little hen had some visitor in her nest, Mrs. Fan said over her cellphone, a cheap, bulky model that few people used anymore, her coat flapping in the wind, while in the background could be seen a blurred image of a man entering his mistress's building. Where on earth had the TV people got that hen line from, the friends laughed, as they had never used such codes in their work. Amid the laughter, Mrs. Fan sighed. No wonder her ex-husband wanted a younger woman, she said, pointing at the fine lines in her face magnified by the close-up shot, which she had paused for the friends to see. The other women stopped laughing, and Mrs. Mo, the one who dealt with any uneasiness with a perfect gesture, broke the silence and said that, husband or not, it was more important to have a fun life of one's own than to serve a king at home. Mrs. Fan nodded, and then reported that she had heard from her children that their father had just lost his new wife to a younger man and they wondered if she would be willing to go back to him for everybody's sake. But why would she want to have anything to do with that man twice divorced by now, Mrs. Fan said. It was not totally untrue, though her children's suggestion of a reunion had been rejected not by Mrs. Fan but by her ex-husband.

The five women studied Mrs. Fan, who smiled back and reassured them that she had long since passed the heartbroken stage; she might have to go out and find a younger man so that her husband would stop daydreaming about a reunion. The joke was hesitantly received and then Mrs. Mo hit the play button, and more of their glorious moments lulled them back into happy oblivion.

THE SIX WOMEN hadn't had any cases for a while when they got a phone call from a man who called himself "Dao." Not that they minded the chance to relax, the friends had been reminding one another, though after the phone call even Mrs. Mo, the calmest of the six, showed unusual animation. They had never accepted a case from a man before, but in his initial call he mentioned their TV documentary, and that alone was enough for them to make an exception.

The women invited Dao to the tea shop where they met all their clients, in a room separated from the main hall by a bamboo curtain. By now the young girls who served their tea regarded the women with awe and studied the newcomer across the big table with open curiosity. For a long time Dao seemed preoccupied, placing his teacup on the green checked tablecloth, then moving it a few squares down as if trying to position a chess piece, never looking up at the six women. Mrs. Cheng and Mrs. Tang shifted in their chairs and Mrs. Lu exchanged a look with Mrs. Guan. Many of their female clients had sounded hesitant when they first called, but once they had made up their minds to come to see the women, their stories gushed out before an invitation had even been issued.

"If you feel it easier to answer questions than just talk, we will certainly help," Mrs. Mo offered, her voice gentle and soothing. There was a girlish excitement in Mrs. Mo that Mrs. Tang was sure only she had detected. She thought of reporting this to her husband, as had been her habit for the past forty years, but more and more now the old soldier immersed himself in conversations with Sherlock Holmes, as if senility had turned him into a close friend of the famous detective. Her husband's obsession had been a major motive for Mrs. Tang to become a detective herself. She hoped for more attention and respect, but the doctors warned her that her husband's condition would only worsen, that memory loss and personality change were to be expected. She might as well enjoy her days with her friends instead of diligently gathering topics to discuss later with a husband who had always been too stingy to participate in conversations and who had, by now, stopped listening.

Dao looked up at Mrs. Mo and then at Mrs. Fan, who as always began to talk about a painful experience of her own with an encouraging smile. It was natural to be angry with the cheating spouse as well as with the perpetrator, Mrs. Fan said, using the words of the marriage expert her children had paid for her to visit—something she would never have admitted to her friends, as they congratulated themselves as the sole agents of her recovery. Natural, too, to be confused and ashamed, Mrs. Fan continued, yet he should know that such emotions were unhealthy in the long run.

"Thanks, aunties," Dao finally said, and Mrs. Mo thought that despite his vagueness, he respected their ages and addressed them properly; such old-fashioned manners were less common in his generation. "My problem is, I don't know where to start."

"Start with your wife," Mrs. Lu said. "Does she still live with you or has she left for someone else?" The man thought about the question for an excruciatingly long time. Mrs. Tang, already losing patience, picked peanuts from the plate and lined them up in front of her in formations.

"There must have been something in your mind that we could do for you when you called us," Mrs. Mo ventured.

"We specialize in marriage crises, as you may or may not know," Mrs. Cheng said. "And trust me, we've seen all sorts of marriage problems in our business."

"And we keep secrets well," Mrs. Guan added, and sent away the girls from the shop who had come in with newly boiled water. "There are things we can do better than younger people. You've seen the documentary. We're successful for good reasons."

"Look at it this way, young man," Mrs. Cheng said with a grin. "How old are you?"

"Thirty-four."

"In the old days I would be your grandmother's age," Mrs. Cheng said. It had been a lifelong regret of hers that she had married late—she had been dazzled by all the possibilities and had forgotten that time acted against a woman. At seventy-two, all she wanted was to see a grandchild, though neither of her two sons was in a hurry to marry and produce a baby for her to dote on; in the old days women her age would be holding a great-grandchild by now. "Look at it this way. You can tell us your problem as you would tell your grandmother. We've seen so much that nothing surprises us."

Dao nodded in gratitude. He opened his mouth but a deep sigh came before the words. "My wife, she still lives in our house," he said.

"A positive sign, no? Do you have children? Still share a bed?" Mrs. Cheng said. "Well, don't let me interrupt you. Go on, go on."

Mrs. Lu and Mrs. Guan exchanged a smile, but they did not stop Mrs. Cheng. The same words would have come out wrong from a different mouth, yet Mrs. Cheng, the most harmlessly nosy person one could meet in life, seemed to have a talent for turning even the most offensive question into an invitation.

"We have a son," the man said. "He just turned one."

"How is the *bedroom business* with your wife since your son's birth?" Mrs. Cheng said.

"Sometimes she says she is tired when I ask, but once in a while it is good."

Men were creatures ignorant of women's pains, Mrs. Fan thought. In her mind she was ready to dismiss the case as an inconsiderate husband unable to share a new mother's burden and casting unfounded blame on her. Mrs. Fan's husband had complained about her lack of enthusiasm in *bedroom business* after the births of both children, and she wondered why she had never seen through his coldhearted selfishness back then.

"Sometimes it takes a while for the new mother to return to her old self," Mrs. Mo said.

"But isn't a year too long?" Mrs. Tang asked. "Young women these days are pampered and way too delicate, if you ask my opinion. I don't know about you, but I served as a good wife once my baby was a month old."

"Let's not distract our guest here with an irrelevant discussion," Mrs. Guan said. "Please forgive us, young man. You must have heard that three women are enough to make a theater troupe, and among us we have two troupes. But don't let us distract you."

Dao looked from one woman to the other and returned to his study of the tablecloth. He seemed unable to grasp what had been said to him, and the thought occurred simultaneously to several of the six women that perhaps he had a problem with his brain, but before anyone said a word, he looked up again, this time with a tear-streaked face. He did not mean to be rude or waste their precious time, he said, but his problem was more than unsuccessful bedroom business between husband and wife—there was another man between him and his wife, and he did not know what to do about the situation.

"So you know the man?" Mrs. Cheng asked. It came as a pang of disappointment that there might not be any puzzle for her to solve.

"My father," Dao said. "He's lived with us for two years now."

"Your father?" the women exclaimed at the same time, all sitting up and leaning forward.

"You mean, your father and your wife?" Mrs. Tang said. "If your claim is baseless I'm ready to spank you."

"Let him finish," Mrs. Guan said.

Dao looked down at his hands folded on the tablecloth and said it was only a feeling. The reason that he had come to them, he said, was to ask the women's help to determine if his wife and his father had in fact maintained an improper relationship. "Your father, how old is he?" Mrs. Tang said.

"And why do you suspect him and your wife of having an improper relationship?" Mrs. Cheng said.

"Do you have siblings?" Mrs. Lu said. "Where's your mother?"

Dao winced at each question. Mrs. Mo sighed and with a gesture she begged her friends to keep quiet, even though her own hands shook from excitement as she poured a new cup of tea for Dao and told him to take his time.

The story came out haltingly: The man had been born the youngest of five siblings, the only boy of the family. His parents had been the traditional husband and wife of the older generation, he the king of the household, governing his wife and children with unquestionable authority, she serving him wholeheartedly. The four older sisters were married off when they reached marriageable ages, three to men picked out by the father, but the youngest sister, a few years older than the little brother, chose her own husband against the father's will. She became an outcast in all family affairs, a punishment from their father and a precaution from the rest of the family, as they would not risk the father's anger to remain in touch with the estranged sister. A few years ago, the mother was diagnosed with liver cancer. By then Dao was over thirty, and shy as he was, he had not had a date. The mother, in her sickbed, begged the father to help their son secure a bride so that she could take a look at her future daughter-in-law before she exited the world. An arrangement was made and Dao was introduced to his wife, a pretty woman, though not a virgin, as she had been widowed once, leaving her only son for her in-laws to raise.

"Did your father know your wife before you met her?" Mrs. Cheng said, thinking fast and sensing shadiness in the arrangements. What kind of father would foist a secondhand woman on his own son as a wife?

Dao said that he did not know. He had been nervous when he was introduced to his wife, and in any case, he had not thought to question the woman and his father back then.

"Did you love her when you married her?" Mrs. Cheng said.

Dao said that he supposed he loved her, or else he would not have agreed to marry her. Mrs. Tang thought he sounded uncertain. What a despicable thing for a man to be so passive.

Dao continued, calmer now, as if he had got over the initial shock of hearing his own voice. The six friends listened, all bursting with questions they tried hard to hold back so the easily intimidated man would not drown in their curiosity. Life after the wedding had been quiet and eventless, he continued, until six months later his mother had passed away, and as was common practice, Dao and his wife, the newlyweds, invited his father to come and live with them; Dao was the only son and it was a son's duty to support his father, even though at sixty his father was still strong and healthy as a bull. For more than a year now Dao had been plagued by the fear that his father had cuckolded him. Such a thought he could not share with his sisters, and the birth of the baby, a boy who looked just as Dao had looked as a bald baby, did not release him from the grip of suspicion.

"You mean the baby could be your half brother?" Mrs. Lu said.

Had he known the answer, Dao replied, he would not have approached the six friends. There was little evidence, but his wife worked odd shifts as a nurse, and there were always stretches of time when she and his father were at home together without him.

"But that doesn't mean they would cuckold you," Mrs. Cheng said.

It was a nagging fear, Dao said apologetically, and hung his head low.

"How does she treat you?" Mrs. Fan asked.

His wife treated him like a good wife should, Dao said. She cooked good meals, cleaned the house, and did not ask for expensive clothes. She put her earnings into their joint account and let him control the finances of the household. What else could a man expect from a wife? Dao asked unconvincingly.

Mrs. Cheng cleared her throat. "Back to my original question," she said, deciding by now that Dao must have some hidden illness he was too ashamed to share. "How is your bedroom business? Do you satisfy each other?"

Dao blushed and mumbled a yes. Mrs. Mo looked at him with sympathy and poured fresh tea to distract him from his embarrassment. The world was intolerant of men with sensitive hearts, but how many people would bother to look deeper into their souls, lonely for unspeakable reasons? Her own husband, dead for twenty years now, had been nicknamed "Soft Yam" by his colleagues; he was the first to be bullied and ridiculed, and had been taken advantage of in promotions. When she married him, her family and friends thought her crazy; she was an attractive girl, with better options than the man she chose for herself. He was a kind man, was the reason she had given, but it was his sadness that moved her. She had made herself an ally to his parents when she courted him, and had thought herself capable of liberating him from the sadness she could not understand. Such an innocent criminal she had made herself into, she thought, when she discovered his love affair of two decades with another man. She had always assumed that the traffic accident at the railroad crossing was a cover for a long-planned suicide, but their only daughter, then eight, adored her father, and Mrs. Mo had taken it upon herself to uphold the image of the idol in her daughter's heart and to reject all offers for another marriage. People admired her virtue and loyalty, but people were easily deceived by all kinds of facades.

"I don't understand," Mrs. Tang said. "You do all right in bed and she treats you well. Then why do you suspect her of anything? If I were you, I would be celebrating my good fortune to have found such a wife."

"And why on earth your father?" Mrs. Cheng added. "Just because the baby looks like your father's grandson?"

"Let's not interfere with our own opinions," Mrs. Guan said, trying to save Dao from further embarrassment. Mrs. Guan was finding some of her companions annoying today, their attitude unbusinesslike, but on second thought, these women had always been like this and she had enjoyed them well enough. Perhaps she was the one running out of patience. Mr. and Mrs. Guan were well maintained by their pensions from their civil servants' jobs and an annual remittance from their son in America. Still, they were witnessing a historic economic boom in the country, and it hurt Mrs. Guan not to be part of it. She had previously sold cosmetics and tonics to neighbors and friends, and perhaps it was time to invent another business now.

"But we need to understand his situation," Mrs. Cheng said. "I, for one, don't see a problem unless the young man here is hiding something from us."

It was how his father had changed, Dao said. A tyrant all his life, the older man had handed over his rule to his daughter-in-law ever since he had moved in with them. And how happy she was, Dao added. There was little reason for her, a widow who had given up her son to be remarried to a shy and quiet man, to be contented. They never behaved improperly in front of him, but he felt there was a secret from which he was excluded. "Like they built a house within my house, and they live in it," Dao said, shamelessly weeping now. What sadness, Mrs. Mo thought, and wondered if Dao would ever be able to reclaim his life. It had taken her years, but it might be different for him. Men were less resilient than women, and in any case, some sons never escaped their fathers' shadows.

"Aunties, I saw your program. You're all experienced with men and women. Could you go meet them and find out for me?"

"But how?" Mrs. Cheng said. "It's different from locating a mistress. Shall we move into your house and make a nest for ourselves underneath your father's bed? Would you divorce your wife? Would you give up the baby to your father? Tell me, young man, what would you do if everything is true as you imagine?"

As if Dao had never thought about that possibility, he looked down at his hands in agony and did not reply.

"You want us to find out for you that they're innocent so you can live in peace, no?" Mrs. Lu said. "Let me tell you, *If you suspect a ghost is sitting next to your pillow, the ghost will always be there; if you imagine a god, a god will look after you from above.*"

The vehemence of Mrs. Lu's words shocked not only Dao but also the five women. Mrs. Lu bit the inside of her cheek and told herself to shut up. Peace came from within, she often said to herself, and she had taken up the detective work with her friends in the hope that by saving other people's marriages she would finally dispel the phantom of a long-dead girl, but such hope had turned out to be in vain. She had done nothing wrong in reporting the girl, Mrs. Lu repeatedly reminded herself over the years—she had found the girl naked in bed with a male classmate and both had been expelled from the university by the end of the week. The girl sneaked into the dorm building a month later, when Mrs. Lu was busy with the mail, and jumped from the top floor. The thud, ten years later, still made Mrs. Lu shiver at night.

"Mrs. Lu here has a point," Mrs. Fan said. "We could work

for you but you have to make up your mind first. What we find out could make you more miserable than you are now, you see?"

Dao looked down at his hands, folding and unfolding them on the table. "I wouldn't do anything," he said finally. "There's nothing for me to do. After all, he's my father. All I want to know is if they've cheated on me."

Such a spineless man, Mrs. Tang thought. Her husband would have picked up an ax and demanded the truth from the wife and the father instead of crying to some strangers. Her husband had always been the quickest to react, and how unfair that he, the most virile among his friends, was the first to be defeated by age.

The only truth for Dao to know, Mrs. Fan thought, was that he would be locked in his unhappiness forever, as she herself would be. It did not matter anymore if he was cuckolded, as it did not matter to her that her husband had been deserted by his second wife. For some people punishment came as a consequence of their mistakes; for others, punishment came before anything wrong had been done. Welcome to the land of the unfortunate and the deserted, Mrs. Fan thought, almost relishing the unfairness of her fate, and Dao's.

Mrs. Guan looked at her friends. Already she could tell that they would not be able to take the case as a group, as they showed little of the sympathy toward Dao that they had shown to the wronged women. She would find an excuse to speak to him after this meeting, she decided, about the possibility of working on the case by herself. A similar plan took shape in Mrs. Cheng's mind, too, though it was not money she was after but the satisfaction of her own curiosity—Dao's description of his wife and father intrigued Mrs. Cheng: What kind of love had they fallen into that caused the father to scheme against his own son, and the wife to entertain her lover's son out of necessity? Even at her age,

Mrs. Cheng still worried that she would miss something interesting before she left this world.

Mrs. Mo observed her companions. She knew that it was her responsibility now to reject Dao gently, and despite her curiosity, she would not let his case break the friendship she had created for the lonely days she would otherwise have to pass by herself. Even as she was thinking up excuses to dismiss him, her mind wandered to the biweekly session of the dancing club that afternoon. She had discovered dancing late in her life, and had been addicted to it ever since, whirling in her partner's arm, their bodies touching each other in the most innocently erotic way. It was not a simple task to maintain intimacy with another human being by the mere touch of bodies, and to accomplish it she needed total concentration to keep her soul beyond the reach of the large and small flames of all the passions in this treacherous world.

Number Three, Garden Road

THEY HAD MOVED into number three, Garden Road forty-five years earlier, he with his new wife, she with her parents and three younger siblings. Garden Road had been a narrow dirt lane then, a patch of radish field on one side, wheat on the other. Number three, a four-storied, redbrick building, was the first to be built along Garden Road. The first to be numbered also, though no reason was ever given about not starting from the very beginning. To this day Garden Road, a four-lane thoroughfare with many shops and buildings on both sides, was missing the first two numbers, a fact known to few people, and number three, its red facade darkened by dust and soot and cracked by a major earthquake twenty years ago, stood irrelevantly between two high-rise buildings with consecutive numbers, an old relative that no one could identify in a family picture.

Of all the residents in the building, Mr. Chang and Meilan were the only ones remembering the hot July day forty-five years earlier, when government-issue furniture—tables, chairs, desks, and beds, painted brownish yellow with numbers written underneath in red—had been unloaded from flatbeds and assigned to the new tenants. Mr. Chang was in his mid-twenties then, a young recruit for the newly established research institute to build the first missile for the country. As he was waiting for his share of furniture, a toddler from a neighbor's family wobbled over and placed a sticky palm on his knee. Uncle Fatty, she called him, looking up with a smile innocent and mysterious at once. He was a stout young man but far from being fat; still, when the crowd laughed, out of their approval for the child's wit, he knew that the nickname would stay.

Apart from Mr. Chang's new wife, Meilan was perhaps the only other one who had noticed his embarrassment. Meilan was ten then, and it was the first time she had seen a man blushing. It was her youngest sister who had given Mr. Chang the nickname, so there was no other choice for Meilan but to use the name, too. Calling someone "Uncle" who was not much older than her was enough of a torture; the name itself, Uncle Fatty, troubled her long after it had stopped bothering him.

Uncle Fatty and his wife lived in a unit directly above Meilan's family. A natural musician, he played different string instruments: violin, erhu, pipa, and an exotic one Meilan had never seen. Music from that instrument, unlike the graceful serenades from the violin or the weeping folk songs from the erhu and the pipa, was loud with happy beats, but it was those songs that broke Meilan's heart to pieces before she knew it.

FORTY-FIVE YEARS was a long time, enough to broaden the muddy, nameless creek next to Garden Road into a man-made river, named Moon River after an American love song and adding value to the already rocket-high price of properties on Garden Road. "Ten thousand yuan per square meter now. Last year it was only eight thousand," Meilan said whenever there was a newcomer to the dancing party at the riverside park. Units at number three had been up for sale twelve years ago when private-owned housing had been made legal. Meilan's parents had asked their children for help so that they would not lose their home, and Meilan was the only one to withdraw all her savings to assist in the purchase. Naturally her siblings thought it her duty then, as she had just moved back in with her parents after her second divorce. It turned out to be a wise investment, and for that her siblings wrote her off as an opportunist.

"Thirty thousand yuan in '95. With that amount of money I could buy half a bathroom in this neighborhood nowadays," Meilan said often, shaking her head in happy disbelief. Like many of the street-dancing parties in Beijing, the gathering by Moon River—the Twilight Club, it was called—was attended mostly by old people, and repetitions were tolerated as they would not be elsewhere with children and grandchildren. A lucky bird she was, one of those men who liked to nod at everything Meilan said in approval would compliment her every time she mentioned her real estate success. Lucky she was, she would reply, with no children to break her back, no husband to break her heart.

Meilan was the youngest and slimmest woman at the Twilight Club, indulged by men ten or twenty years her senior. "Little Goldfish," they called her, even though she was past the age for such a girlish nickname. Indeed when she plunged into the music she felt like a playful fish, one of her regular partners holding her tight while his wife, no longer able to match his energy and enthusiasm, looked on among a group of women her age, not without alarm. Once in a while a wife would comment that Meilan did not belong at the Twilight Club. "Go to a nightclub, or a karaoke bar," the wife would urge. "Show the young people what is called aging gracefully."

Meilan smiled good-naturedly, but the next time she danced with a man whose wife had tried to offend her, she embraced him tightly and whispered so that he had to put his ear, already hard of hearing, close to her lips.

The only man Meilan had not danced with at the Twilight Club was Mr. Chang, though between the two of them they had missed no more than a handful of parties in the past twelve years. In fact, it was Mr. Chang who had introduced Meilan to the Twilight Club. She had recently returned to live with her parents then, middle-aged and twice divorced, without a child from either husband to soften people's criticism. To kill the time after work and to escape her parents' nagging, Meilan took to strolling along Moon River, and on one of those first evenings since her return, she discovered Mr. Chang, sitting on a bench with a woman. He did not recognize Meilan when her gaze caught his eyes, and the woman, in her red blouse and golden skirt, was not the beautiful wife who had, many years ago, made Meilan conscious of her own, less attractive features.

Uncle Fatty, Meilan's parents reported when she queried about him, had stayed in number three. His wife had been ill with some sort of cancer for the last year or so. Is she still alive? Meilan asked with great interest, and her parents, shocked by her inappropriate curiosity, replied that they were too old to discuss other people's health problems with the unfeeling young generation.

Now that she knew he had a wife somewhere—dying in a hospital, or at the mercy of a brusque caretaker in their unit—Meilan started to follow Mr. Chang in the evenings. He left home at half past six and went to the nearest bus stop to meet his lady friend. They strolled along Moon River, now and then resting on an available bench and talking in low voices. Twice a week they went to the Twilight Club and danced all night till the last song, "Long Live Friendship," with archaic Chinese lyrics set to the tune of "Auld Lang Syne." The first time Meilan watched a hundred old people slow-dance to the song, she was overwhelmed by a bleakness that she had never known existed. In her adulthood Meilan was considered by many as a woman without much depth; "brainless," she had been called behind her back by her siblings, the kind of wife made for a cheating husband.

Meilan was caught off guard by her tears, and she had to hide behind a bush when the partygoers bid farewell to one another. Later, when she followed Mr. Chang and his lady friend to the bus stop, Meilan was pleased that "Auld Lang Syne" had not moved him to hail a cab for the woman he was perhaps thinking of replacing his wife with.

The woman soon was replaced by a younger, prettier-looking woman, who did not last long. A couple of women later, his wife died, but the news was a few weeks old when it reached Meilan. She did not remember having detected any sadness in Mr. Chang; at least there had not been any change in his evening routine. By then she had created a few opportunities to encounter him in the building, but he only nodded at her in the same unrecognizing manner as if she were one of those less fortunate who had to rent in number three. She studied herself in the mirror. Even if his deteriorated eyesight and memory prevented him from recognizing her from her girlhood, she did not see why she could not compete with the women he was dancing with twice a week. Perhaps she needed a different setting to meet him instead of their dusty, stale-smelling hallway. Meilan spent half a month's pay to take a dancing class, and after that she showed up at the Twilight Club like a princess. The hem of her long skirt brushed the sandaled feet of her partners in the summer, and in winter the men competed to hold her hands nestled in a pair of white suede gloves. Little Goldfish, soon the men renamed her; there was no excuse for Mr. Chang not to see her and perhaps desire her in ways she did not care to imagine.

The Twilight Club had become a center of Meilan's life since she was forced into early retirement at the age of fifty. She accepted small harmless presents and dinner invitations from men with wives, but once a widower made a move to differentiate himself from her other admirers, she discouraged him with subtle yet resolute gestures. In time, death came for some of the old men, but one had only to avert her eyes to forget such inconvenient disruptions. With a flat, a small pension, and many admirers, Meilan had little more to ask from life. If there was one imperfection, it would be Mr. Chang—what right did he have to ignore her for twelve years, all while he was busy dancing with those not-so-young women who had to take buses to the Twilight Club?

MR. CHANG CIRCLED the flat: the kitchen, the living room, the bedroom their twin boys used to share. He slept in one of the single beds now. The other bedroom, where he had spent the thirty-three years of his married life with his wife, was entered every spring and autumn when he brought her clothes to the balcony for airing. Once upon a time the lingering scent of sunshine on the clothes, mixed with that of camphor, had filled the flat with the peculiar presence of another warm body and left Mr. Chang drowsy for days afterward; now that number three was dwarfed on both sides by high-rises and Garden Road was often congested with long queues of honking cars, the clothes came home with a cold strangeness to the touch. The liveliness that took longer to leave the clothes than for a body to be cremated, a slower death for which Mr. Chang had not been prepared, made him wonder how much he had not known about the life that he had once thought of coming to completion at the deathbed of his wife.

Mr. Chang poured tea for himself. Each time he finished a round in the flat he swallowed another pill with half a cup of tea. At least an hour of his morning would be covered by the handful of pills. Another two hours by the three morning newspapers he subscribed to. Cooking, an hour, and eating, with the new, ill-fitted denture, another half hour. The afternoons were less intimidating, for he allowed himself to nap as long as he could. The evening papers arrived before four o'clock, and by half past six, with some leftovers from lunch in his stomach and clean clothes on, he was ready to meet his friend at the bus stop.

They were always his friends—not girlfriends, as many of them might have mistakenly thought—coming into his life and then leaving, one at a time. Some of them were easier to break up with than others; one of them, about five years ago, had gone to the extreme of threatening to kill herself for him, but he had known, as she had too, the flimsiness of the threat. Passion of that sort could be taken seriously only when one was in his twenties, a novice of love and of life in general. And not to his surprise, even the most persistent of the women eventually left him alone. After all, there had been no intimate touches to be accounted for; he had only strolled along Moon River and danced at the Twilight Club with them. It was they who had nurtured their own hope, even if they could blame him for misleading them in the first place.

When an old friendship came to an end, a new one began without a problem. For the records Mr. Chang kept at a dozen matchmaking agencies, the few key details he provided—a retired scientist with a sizable pension and a flat on Garden Road—were enough to attract certain women in their midlife dilemmas. He did not go through the big binders to choose someone but let his name remain to be chosen by desperate women, for whom he had not many specific requirements except for two rules: He was not to go out with a mother—a child could become a complication in time, and by all means he had brought up two sons of his own and had no intention to help raise another child, grandchildren included; and he was not to befriend a woman who had never married. Divorced women in middle age, with no housing of their own nor a great job for long-term stability—enough of them were plagued by their futures in this city and there was no reason to put his peace at stake by wading into the more treacherous water.

Mr. Chang had never thought of remarrying, though for a while his fellow dancers at the Twilight Club thought one or another of his friends would become his new wife. They complimented him on his ability to attract women fifteen or twenty years younger than he was, and perhaps secretly they also envied him for the many opportunities they themselves did not have. In time some of them joined him in his widowhood, and a few of them remarried, joking with him of their taking the lead now. Mr. Chang smiled and promised to hasten, but eventually, as he had expected, people started to treat him more as a joke. An old donkey who loved to chew on the fresh grass, they must have been saying behind his back. He'd better watch out for his stomach, some of them would perhaps say, but they forgot it was the heart that would kill a man; a man never died from indigestion.

IN LATE APRIL the regulars at the Twilight Club decided to change the party schedule and meet four times a week instead of two. Spring in Beijing was as brief as a young girl's grief over a bad haircut and they might as well not waste the good days before the sauna weather set in, though no doubt by then they would have more reasons to keep the schedule despite the heat. Amid the excitement, the absence of Mr. Chang went unnoticed except by Meilan, and when he didn't show up for the next two parties, she decided that it was her responsibility as a neighbor to check on him.

A little before five she knocked on his door. It was a decent time for a single woman to drop in at a widower's, with dinner as an available excuse if the meeting was unpleasant. She had put on her favorite silk blouse of sapphire blue and a matching skirt, secretly hoping that, if she were not to find Mr. Chang with a grave illness, they would perhaps show up at the Twilight Club together that night.

Mr. Chang looked alarmed when he opened the door, his round-necked undershirt and threadbare pants reminding her of her own father in his old age. "Little Goldfish?" he said. Though the question was inappropriate for a greeting she was glad that he recognized her. She told him her name, and he showed little recollection. "I'm the first daughter of the Lus, downstairs," Meilan said. "Remember, Uncle Fatty? My little sister gave you the name."

He had to excuse himself to change into more formal clothes so that he could calm himself. His wife had always called him by that name; "Aunt Fatty," he would reply, with forced cheerfulness till the very end of her life, when her body was wasted by the cancer. One would hope for certain things to be buried, but no, a woman he did not want to dance with had come and knocked on his door, claiming her partial ownership of a name she had no right to use. Mr. Chang's hands shook as he buttoned his shirt. If he lay down on the single bed, would the woman take the cue from the closed bedroom door and leave him alone? But she would knock and break into the bedroom, she would call an ambulance if he insisted on ignoring her questions, and no doubt she would, later at the Twilight Club, brag about how she had saved his life by being a considerate neighbor.

Windows in his unit opened to the same view as hers did, and Meilan was surprised that she had overlooked this fact despite the time she had spent imagining his life. The last time she had visited the unit she had been twelve, and in the living room there had been a few articles of furniture identical to theirs. She wondered now if he had sold the ugly-colored furniture with red painted numbers underneath. Her own parents had saved every piece, but after their deaths she had hired two laborers to dispose of the furniture as they wished. She regretted now that she hadn't saved a few pieces; had there ever been an opportunity for him to pay her back a visit, the furniture might provide a topic of shared memories.

Mr. Chang entered the living room, and Meilan did not turn from where she stood in front of the window. "Remember the pigpens?" she said, lifting her chin at a man washing his brand-new Lexus in the narrow lane between number three and the next building. The pigpens had been there in 1977 when she had come home to her parents with the news of her first divorce. The man at his Lexus worked on diligently, unaware that he was being watched just as full pens of pigs had once been watched from the windows of number three.

Mr. Chang sat down on the couch before the guest did. An ill-mannered host, she must be thinking of him, but he had not invited her, and he would let her draw any conclusion she wanted to. Of the women at the Twilight Club he had avoided her more than others. A rabbit should not be chewing on the grass around his nest, Mr. Chang had told a few old men when they had hinted that, as neighbors, he and Little Goldfish could develop some convenient romance. They laughed at his cunning reply, but they, unwise old souls who could be deceived by a flirtatious gesture from a no longer young woman, could not see that certain women, Little Goldfish being one of them, were to be shunned for their shrewdness.

"We used to name the pigs after people in number three," Meilan said, and turned around with a smile. "Of course you were one of the grown-ups then, so you wouldn't know our tricks."

"I didn't know you moved back," Mr. Chang said.

"I bought the unit downstairs for my parents," she said. "They didn't want to live elsewhere."

The same with his wife and him, Mr. Chang replied, though it was only half the truth. They had helped both sons with their purchases of bigger, more modern flats so they could marry their dream lovers, and in the end, number three, with its rumbling pipes and cracking walls and the garbage chute that still attracted flies years after it had been sealed, was what Mr. Chang and his wife could afford.

Meilan nodded and sauntered to the couch. He stood up quickly and watched her take a seat close to where he had been sitting. Tea? he asked, and when she said yes, he was both horrified at her insistence on extending the visit and relieved that he had an excuse to leave the room. When he returned from the kitchen he sat down in an armchair across the room.

He had his shirt on now, buttoned to the top, and Meilan had to restrain herself from telling him that his shirttail was escaping from under his belt. The glass top of the coffee table had tea stains; a bowl of leftover noodle soup was sitting on a pile of newspaper. The flat was not one where a man could entertain a lady friend; she felt an urge to absolve him of all the women he had danced with.

"I heard about your wife's passing," Meilan said, eyeing the framed pictures of his wife on the wall, mostly enlarged black-and-white snapshots taken, judging from the clothes and the young look of the wife, before anyone in number three had been able to afford color film. It was strange to study his wife through an older woman's eyes; years ago her beauty had been stifling to Meilan, but now she detected melancholy in the young face. Such a woman would let herself be defeated by an illness. "A good wife you had," Meilan said. "I'm sorry about your loss."

It had been eleven years, but the way she said it made the pain fresh again. He said that he had been sad to hear about her parents' passing, too, as if by reminding her of her own loss he would be spared. It was different with one's parents, she argued, and he had little to defend himself. The teakettle whistled, a prompt excuse for him to withdraw from her gaze.

"Have you thought of remarrying?" Meilan asked when he returned with the tea.

She must have seen his friends at the Twilight Club, so it was natural for her to regard him as an old donkey fond of fresh grass. It was better that she, or anyone else in the world, think that way. He shook his head without giving more explanation. Instead, he asked her about her marriage and her children, as if it were a game of Ping-Pong that one had to win with a tactful performance.

"No husband, no child."

"You own a flat on Garden Road," he said. There was little else to compliment in her situation.

"Funny thing is, we moved here when I was ten," Meilan said, "so there must have been another home before this, but I have little recollection. Am I not a lucky one to die in the only home I've known?" It was meant to be a joke, but she was surprised to see that he looked pale and shaken. She had always liked to talk about her own death as if it was an event to look forward to, her secret superstition being that death, like a man, would make itself conveniently unavailable once it knew it was desired.

The only home for him, too, he thought. His sons had tried to persuade him to sell the unit in number three after his wife's death and he had refused. It was not his responsibility to make them understand him; time would come and teach them about love, which they thought they knew about already.

Meilan studied the old man shrinking into the depth of the armchair, his eyes looking past her and dwelling on some distant past she had no place in. How many times in his life had he let himself truly see her? She remembered years ago—when gas pipes had not been installed in number three and when propane tanks had been rationed—she had often hidden behind a pile of coal bricks on the third floor landing and waited for Uncle Fatty to come back from work. How old was she then? Twelve, or perhaps thirteen, too old to pretend to be playing in the sooty hallway, but she persisted. Once, a rat came out from nowhere and jumped onto the coal, not more than five feet from where she squatted. Neither the rat nor Meilan moved for a long moment, until Uncle Fatty and his wife walked upstairs. The rat scurried away, frightening his wife with its swift movement, and Meilan remembered him looking past her to search for the offender. She had been born ten years too late to bear any meaning for him, she remembered weeping to her journal.

"I've always thought that one of your lady friends would be good enough to marry into number three," Meilan said, laughing lightly. "Have you realized you're the only one to bring your own partner to the Twilight Club?"

He would no longer, but such information he did not have to share with a stranger. After the relapse of her cancer his wife had told him to start searching for a replacement; she said she would like to see him taken care of so she could leave in peace. He obliged her as one would oblige any fantasy of a dying loved one, but he could not stop himself from strolling and dancing with strangers after her death. He would do anything to keep her alive from day to day, even if it meant being called an old donkey and using other women's hope as an anesthesia. A week ago, when he had had to break up with his latest friend and call the matchmaking agencies, none of them had provided any new names who had shown interest in his file. A clerk at one of the agencies had even suggested that he no longer pay the fee to keep his file active; her words were subtle but there was no way to make the message less humiliating.

"Of course everything gets harder at our age," Meilan said. Ten years could be an abyss when one was twelve, and what a relief one did not have to stay twelve all her life. She adjusted her necklace of cultured pearls and sipped the tea. "So if you ask me, I'd say you're the smartest. It's better just to have a few dances together. Beyond that things get complicated."

"So you've always been single?" Mr. Chang asked with some curiosity. The woman, uninvited and at ease in his home, was different from his friends. Was it because she owned the patch of roof above her?

"Married twice, lost twice to mistresses," she said. "No, you don't have to feel sorry for me. The way I look at it—a bad marriage is like a bad tooth and it's better to remove it than to suffer from it."

Mr. Chang leaned forward. He had some vague recollection of her from years ago, but hard as he tried, he could not connect the woman to the young girl, whom his wife had once commented on as being intense and sad for her age. He had never doubted his wife, for whom the world seemed to be more transparent, many of its secrets laid out for her to see, but could she have made a mistake about the girl, or had time alone been able to transform a sad and serious girl into a loud and graceless woman?

"Come to think about it, at least I don't have to grieve over the death of a spouse," Meilan said. She was insensitive, she knew, but why should she pretend to be someone other than herself, even for him?

"That's to be congratulated," he said with sincerity, but perhaps she took it as a sarcastic comment, as she shrugged without replying.

The light dimmed in the flat. Evenings in Mr. Chang's unit, as they were in Meilan's, came earlier in all seasons, their windows shadowed by the high-rise next door. In the soft light Meilan fixed her eyes on his face, unscrupulously. "What would your wife have said about your lady friends?"

She had told him that he needed another woman in his life so she could rest in peace; would she have less peace had she known that not one but many had been in his life, coming and going? Mr. Chang shook his head. "*The dead is gone, the live lives on,*" he said. The same saying must have been quoted by all the widows and the widowers in this city when they accepted a substitution.

"The live lives on only to ignore a longtime neighbor," Meilan said. She wondered if she sounded like a hurt woman. What she meant, she explained, was that they were both good dancers, and wasn't it a surprise that they had never danced? Unless it was more than a dancing partner he had been searching for, she added with laughter; she herself had no interest in anything other than dancing, she said, dancing being all that mattered to her.

The woman, with her cunning smile as if she had seen through him, looked familiar. Mr. Chang felt a moment of disgust mixed with fascination. Then it came to him, not the woman in front of him but another one, with her hand between his legs, not moving it much but nevertheless applying pressure from each of her fingers. He had been thirteen then, taking a train ride for the first time in his life, to the provincial capital for middle school; the other passengers, his uncle included, had been dozing off in the dimming light of the northern plain. He could have gripped the fleshy wrist and removed the hand from his lap, he could have yelled for her to stop, or at least stood up and moved to another seat, but in the end, he had done nothing, because when he looked up she was smiling at him, her teasing eyes saying that she knew all about his secret, and that he was as sinful in this little game of theirs as she was.

Mr. Chang shifted in the chair. The phantom limb of a youthful swelling from half a century ago and the wetness afterward made him unable to breathe in the twilight. He had never told his wife about the incident; she had not been the kind of woman who would make a man relive a humiliating memory like that.

She did not mean to embarrass him in any way, Meilan said; only she was curious why he had not thought of dancing with her. Mr. Chang shook his head. Some people were destined to be friends, he said, and others strangers.

A man could break a woman's heart with that reply, and Meilan had to tell herself she was lucky that she had not had a heart for all of her adult life.

Neither spoke for a moment, and when Mr. Chang asked if Meilan needed another cup of tea, she knew that her time was running out. "Do you still play music?" she asked, eagerly grabbing the first topic that occurred to her.

"*The one who understands the music has ridden the wings of the crane to heaven,*" he said.

She thought of telling him how she had listened to the music coming from his unit years ago, through open windows in the summer evenings, behind piled coal outside his unit on winter nights. But a love story told forty years too late could only be a joke. Instead, she asked him about the strange instrument she had never seen. She might as well solve one mystery if this turned out to be her only chance to talk with him.

He looked at her as if surprised by her memory, and without a word withdrew from the living room. A moment later, he came back with a round-bellied instrument. He plucked the strings and shook his head at its off-key tuning. "My father-in-law brought it from America but neither he nor my wife knew how to play it," he said. "It's a banjo."

"Where did you learn to play it, then?"

"I figured it out myself. It was not that hard. My wife used to boast to her friends that I was the only banjo player in Beijing."

"Was that true?" Meilan asked, watching him smile dreamily, remembering an old joke, perhaps, between husband and wife.

"I've not met another one in my life."

"Am I not a lucky one to meet the only banjo player in this city, Uncle Fatty?"

Mr. Chang nodded, trying to recover some old tunes. Meilan stood up and swung slowly to the music. In the soft twilight her face looked beautiful in a strange way that reminded him of his wife, but the woman, with her blind cheerfulness and loud voice, would not feel in his music what his wife had once felt. Perhaps this was what his wife had wanted for him, a woman who understood little, an antidote to death and loneliness.

"I have a great idea," Meilan said when the music stopped. It had taken forty years for him to play the banjo for her once, and neither of them had forty more years to waste. "We should move into one unit and sell the other."

Why? he asked, aware that he had not appeared as shocked or offended as he should have. If he told the story of the train ride to the woman in front of him, would she laugh at him? Or perhaps she would tell an equally unseemly story, a joke that would crack them up like a pair of shameless oldsters at the Twilight Club.

"Garden Road is hot now, and we'll make good money."

"What should we say we are if the police come to check our household register cards?"

"Neighbors, roommates, coinhabitants," Meilan said. "How much space does one need at our age?"

Indeed, he thought. In the semidarkness he plucked the strings again. Sooner or later one of them would have to stand up and turn on the lamp, but for now he would like to think of himself as happily occupied, playing an old song on an older banjo.

Sweeping Past

THEY HAD BECOME sworn sisters in Ailin's backyard fifty years earlier, Ailin being the oldest of the three and the one to come up with the idea. They were twelve going on thirteen, their bodies just beginning to fill the gray Mao jackets handed down from their mothers. By then sworn sisterhood, like many other traditions, had been labeled as a noxious feudal legacy, and they had to bribe a neighbor's daughter to take Ailin's younger siblings to the marketplace for sugar canes so that the three girls could be free of prying eyes—it would take the little ones a sweet long time to chew from one end of the sugar canes to the other. Mei had stolen some yam liquor from her father's cabinet, and they each took a sip of the strong liquid before pouring it on the ground. "*Let the heaven and the earth be the witnesses of the beginning of the rest of our lives,*" Ailin read a pledge she had adapted from old novels in which men and women chose their sworn brotherhood and sisterhood beyond the bond of blood, and Mei and Lan repeated after her that they, sworn sisters from now on, would stick through thick and thin till the day they were to leave the earthly world together.

Later they went to the only photographer in town to have a picture taken. They were in their best outfits: moon white blouses with bows of the same color tied on the ends of their braids, pants with soft-colored floral prints. The photographer, a bachelor in his late thirties, watched the three girls giggle with excitement as he adjusted the lamps, and was moved by something in the girls' faces that was beyond their understanding. In the final prints, he wrote, with a fine-brush pen, a line from an ancient poem: *As innocent as new blossoms, unaware of the time sweeping past like a river.* Embarrassed yet unable to bring themselves to confront the photographer, the girls pretended that they did not notice the annotation to their sworn sisterhood.

Nine years later, the photographer, with his German-made cameras as evidence for his being a capitalist spy, was the first one in town to be beaten to death by the young Red Guards. By then Mei and Lan were both expecting their first babies, and Ailin, pressured by the other two's achievements, rushed into marriage with a man whom she had barely known and would take years to fall in love with. He was not the first man the matchmaker had introduced to her, nor was his family the one best able to afford good betrothal gifts, but it was like the old saying: *The one to show up at the right time beats the earlier risers.*

On the morning of the wedding, while her two sworn sisters helped Ailin make up her face, she remembered, to her surprise, where the long and gentle fingers of the photographer had touched her chin when he had adjusted the angle of her face years ago. If she closed her eyes she could almost feel the momentary coolness when she was shielded from the bright light of the lamps, big and small, by his raised arms. Remember what the photographer wrote on our picture, Ailin asked, and then said how true it was that time swept past when they were the least prepared. Mei and Lan, both glowing in their new motherhood, laughed at Ailin for being a sentimentalist. Wait until this very night to discover what you haven't known about life, said Mei, always the most outspoken one, without lowering her voice; Lan blushed but then agreed with a coy smile, and for a moment Ailin was intimidated by a looming void of which her two sworn sisters seemed unaware.

THE PICTURE WAS buried with a few pieces of her maiden clothes in a trunk that had been rarely opened in her married life, and when it was uncovered again, it was not by Ailin but by Ying, Ailin's fourteen-year-old granddaughter on her summer holiday from Lisbon. Who were these girls? Ying asked her grandmother as she put aside the picture and tried on a blouse from the trunk. The moon white silk fabric had taken on a dull yellow hue, just like the faded picture from fifty years ago, but she seemed to be impressed by herself in the old-fashioned blouse. She parted her hair, dyed reddish yellow, in the middle and braided it, but the hair was unruly from her perm, and after a few trials she let go and focused on a tortoiseshell comb missing a few teeth.

They had been best friends, she and the other two girls, Ailin said, but did not explain the ritual of sworn sisterhood for fear of being laughed at, which happened sometimes when she talked about the past with her granddaughter. Ying picked up the picture again and studied it. Sweet, she said, as one would speak of a puppy.

If her granddaughter was home for stories Ailin would tell her stories, but she knew that even though the girl acted nonchalant when her childhood friends admired the pictures she brought home, in which she posed in an exotic city with stately buildings, grand statues, and blue harbors with white boats, Ying already had too many stories of her own to shoulder. Five years earlier, after the death of Ailin's husband, her only son had decided to emigrate to Portugal, and Ailin, knowing that her opinion was the last thing sought from her, had given him the money he had requested without voicing any doubt. Ailin had thought of suggesting that they could leave their only daughter for her to raise, but Ying had been the one most eager to leave for a foreign life.

She was a good helper in the restaurant, Ailin's son soon called to report, and became even more useful when she picked up Portuguese and learned to deal with the paperwork and officials for her parents. Every summer she came back to Ailin's home for two weeks of vacation, an award for her contribution to the prospering restaurant, but apart from quietly showing off her new life to friends and neighbors, Ying was also in charge of purchasing handmade tablecloths and napkins, decorated with the embroidery the province had been known for in the past thousand years and still cheap if one knew which village to go to.

Life was good, and the business had never been better, Ying reported every summer, with fewer details each year, and Ailin learned not to ask for more than what was provided. If the girl wanted to tell stories, Ailin was all ears, but Ying was at an age where the line between the real and the imagined was blurred, and the tales she thought impressive invariably bored Ailin, though she was careful not to show it.

TOWARD THE END of Ying's stay the girl brought home a poster-sized print of Ailin's picture with her sworn sisters. The store had Photoshopped it for better effect, Ying explained. The three girls in the sepia-toned print smiled dreamily, as if a shared mystery had cast a mist that separated them from the rest of the world. What was this for? Ailin asked, and the girl replied that the picture was to be part of the new decorations for a section of the restaurant divided from the main floor. There were other pictures she had gathered, too, Ying said, old photos she had sought from her friends' parents, and the store would have them ready in a day or two.

Ailin looked at the picture. She was sitting on a stone bench, her knees drawn to her body and clasped in both hands, as directed by the photographer. Look slightly upward as if being summoned, he had told her, though by whom he had not said. Mei and Lan stood behind her, each placing a hand on her shoulders and pointing the other hand to where all three were expected to look. All of it had been staged, and the painting of bamboo trees and waterfall on the background curtain, already faded fifty years ago, was recognizable perhaps only to Ailin's eyes now. Still, the long-forgotten details came back with the enlarged images: The coiled ends of her braids, slightly burned even though it was hard to see in the picture, were the result of impatient curling with a pair of hot tongs; the jasmine blossoms in their top button holes were from Mei's neighbor, a boy their age with a shy smile who liked to offer Mei the blooming flowers from his mother's garden, but before any fruitful connection could be made from all the fragrant presents, the boy had to move away when his widowed mother remarried into another province; Lan, the prettiest of the three, had to be begged once and again by the photographer not to turn her face away, though if looking closely, one could detect the shying away of her face from the lens, and the photographer had skillfully caught her eyes just before she had averted them.

"How much does it cost to make this?" Ailin asked as she fingered the fabric of the print.

Ying gave Ailin a number that took her aback, and Ailin commented that despite the amount of money spent, the picture looked even older than it was.

"That's the effect I need."

"Did you talk to your parents before making this?"

"Why should I?" Ying said. "They'll love it if I tell them that this is what the guests have been asking for. Besides, they say the restaurant will be mine someday, so why can't I make the decision now?"

Ailin thought about lecturing her granddaughter on filial respect, but Ying would only roll her eyes and laugh at her outdated and useless wisdom. "I don't see why anyone wants to look at some girls from ages ago while eating at your restaurant."

"All three of you look very young and innocent. Very Chinese."

"We certainly didn't take the picture to entertain some foreign devils," Ailin said dolefully.

"But you don't mind, do you?" Ying said. "And your friends—will you not tell them about this? I don't want them to come to me and ask to be paid."

The girl was too young to worry about such things, Ailin thought, saddened by the fact that her granddaughter had less space and time to dream than Ailin herself had once had at this age. She would not let the secret out to her friends, Ailin replied, but Ying looked doubtful.

"But you may forget," she said. "I know what it's like with old people. You make a promise one day and the next day the promise means nothing because you have all this time on your hands and you need to tell them every bit of news."

"I'll never see them again."

"Are they dead?"

They did not live in town, though neither had moved very far away. The distances could be covered easily by a two-hour bus ride, but Ailin had not sent word to Mei and Lan about her husband's funeral. It had occurred to Ailin before that similar losses might have been kept from her as well, though she had always believed that in the case of a death among the three, the news would find its way to the other two. On what ground to be so blindly confident? she pondered now, and Ying, studying Ailin with a detached sympathy, asked again if her friends had died on her. They were probably still in good health, Ailin replied; only they no longer talked. But why? Ying pressed. Circumstances, Ailin said, and added that fifty years was a long time to keep up.

Ying seemed dissatisfied with the answer. "You don't stop being a friend because of circumstances," she said. She herself stayed close to a couple of friends through Internet phone calls, birthday cards, and days spent together on her holidays. Every summer she gave the friends presents she bought with money she earned, clothes and shoes said to be in fashion in Europe.

Life was crowded with many small worries that could replace a friendship with indifference—meals to be prepared, diapers to be changed and washed, critical in-laws and bosses to appease, illness and exhaustion to recover from—and beyond that there was what the photographer had called the sweeping past of time, but Ying was right that one did not discard the sworn sisterhood due to some minor changes in circumstances. "Something happened to us a while ago," Ailin said finally. "I told a very bad joke, and neither of them wanted to be my friend anymore."

"A triangle can be unforgiving and unstable for friendship," Ying said. "What kind of joke was it?"

"They both had their first babies before I had your father—a boy and a girl, so I suggested that they arrange a marriage between the kids," Ailin said. "It was meant to be a joke."

"And of course one of the families took it more seriously than the other. It was a silly joke, if you ask me, but it was sillier to stop being friends because of the joke. So don't blame yourself, Nana," Ying said. Ailin had never seen her granddaughter act brusquely protective, but perhaps it was what was required of her when she had to speak for herself as well as for her parents. "*There would've been no trouble in the world if not for the stupid people who make stupid mistakes,*" Ying added.

Only it had not been proposed as a joke, nor had it been received as one. The two babies were born a day apart, both as beautiful as their mothers. There would be more children coming to the three families, but the first two were special. Their mothers were sworn sisters, and what could be a better destination than a marriage, so that the two children would continue loving each other beyond playmates, beyond brother and sister? It made sense when a marriage was semiofficially arranged for the two babies; it made Mei and Lan happier that Ailin had been the one to propose it—they worried about her feeling left out, she could see, and with more enthusiasm than either mother she prepared a lavish meal for the small ceremony. None of the three husbands attended the ceremony, treating it with dismissive amusement, as a harmless feminine fantasy. The three men got along all right, but they would not have chosen to be friends if not for their wives; none of them had been told about the sworn sisterhood.

"What happened?" Ying asked. "Did one of the families change their mind?"

"Something horrible happened," Ailin said. "The boy killed the girl by accident."

Ying gave a low cry but the shock was at once replaced by fascination. "When did that happen? Why did he do that? How old were they?"

"Not much older than you," Ailin said, and right away regretted making the connection. "They were sixteen. They went out for a field trip all by themselves and he strangled her by accident."

Ying made some exclamation in a foreign tongue. "That could not be an accident. He could've pushed her into a river by accident, but strangling? How could that happen by accident?"

Ailin shook her head. There had not been much to ask from the boy. The fact that he had ripped her blouse had been enough. The two children had known all their lives about the existence of a marriage arrangement; naturally the boy had expectations, but the girl fought and scratched his face and arms, perhaps out of fear of the urgent rudeness that had turned the boy into an unrecognizable creature.

"Did he rape her?"

The girl's ease with voicing the word unsettled Ailin. At fourteen, she and her sworn sisters had not known much of the cruelty life had in store. "He didn't mean to harm her," Ailin said in his defense. She had always loved the boy, a most generous big brother for her own son, six years younger; she had been selfishly relieved that he was not old enough to understand the situation when the scandalous murder filled the local newspapers.

"But he killed her. I bet this was how it happened. He wanted to have sex, and she didn't want to. He got out of control," Ying said. "Did he get a death sentence?"

Ailin nodded.

"He made a stupid mistake but perhaps not enough for a death sentence," Ying said. "But of course this is China—a life for a life."

It was the same thing Lan had said when Ailin had begged her to show some leniency toward Mei's son. A life for a life, Lan said, not meeting Ailin's eyes; why should she think of giving the boy a future when her daughter had no future left? Unable to reply, Ailin lit some incense in front of the girl's black-framed picture and prayed to her for a change of heart on her parents' side; in the picture the girl had Lan's beautiful features and bashful smile, and Ailin wondered if there had been another boy whom all three of them had not been aware of to account for the girl's vehement resistance.

Look what you've got us all into, Mei yelled to Ailin outside the courthouse after the sentence had been read. As Mei was screaming in Ailin's face, Lan, winning yet having nothing to share with her sworn sisters anymore, hastened past them with averted eyes. It was the last time Ailin had seen either of her sworn sisters. The news of both families moving away was reported to her by her husband long after they had left; he had clumsily frolicked with their son in the backyard afterward so that she could remain undisturbed in her mourning.

Ying studied the girls in the picture again and asked Ailin to point out the one with the murdered daughter and the one with the murderer son. "I wonder which one of your friends hates the other more," she said.

"They don't hate each other as much as you imagine," Ailin said. She had owed Mei a son and herself a daughter—Lan had written back ten years later when Ailin had sent her a letter, hoping to renew their connection—and no matter what excuse Ailin would find for herself, she was the only one of the three to be indebted. "They both blamed me," Ailin finished.

Ying replied that it was ridiculous for Ailin's friends to think so, and that Ailin herself must be crazy to take on responsibilities that she had no business claiming. Ailin shook her head and did not argue with the girl, who, despite having accumulated wisdom beyond her age, was too young to understand that hatred, as much as love, did not come out of reason but out of a mindless nudge of a force beyond one's awareness. That Mei and Lan had lost their children would not be enough for them to keep their hatred alive. It had been Ailin's idea to arrange the marriage; it had been her idea to become sworn sisters in the first place.

Ying seemed eager to continue the argument with Ailin, yet Ailin was not in the mood anymore to offer the girl a chance to dispute what she did not understand. Had Ailin not been stubborn in holding on to her girlhood so that no man could replace her sworn sisters, she might well have got married and had a baby at the same time as Mei and Lan; it could have been Ailin's son who was arranged to marry Lan's daughter, and he might or might not have got the three families into the tragedy even if the girl decided not to honor the arrangement. Ying might have not been born but there might've been another girl in her place, with her name, who would perhaps be content in living her life out in the provincial town, but how could Ailin make the girl understand that all the existences surrounding her, solid and reasonable though they seemed to be, could be changed if the fantasy of a lifelong sisterhood had not occurred to Ailin on that spring afternoon fifty years ago?

After waiting in vain for a long moment, Ying looked defeated. "Well, if they hate you as much as you say, the more reason there is to put up the picture so they will be looked at in my restaurant while they don't know it," she said.

And they could smile on the wall into the indifferent eyes of foreign strangers, as if time had stopped at the photographer's cramped studio fifty years ago, Ailin thought, and turned away from the poster before her sworn sisters caught a glimpse of her moist eyes.

Souvenir

THE MAN NOTICED the girl first, moving cautiously from one storefront to the next, not glancing even once at the shop windows. She wore a white dress, more like a smock, with a pink and purple floral print, and her bare arms and ankles were innocent as a small girl's, bony and smooth. The man watched her walk past him on the roadside bench and stood up. You remind me of my wife when she was your age, he practiced in his mind. His cane bumped into the backpacks on the ground, which belonged to the two college students sitting next to him on the bench, and they looked at him with disapproval before resuming their intimate conversation, the boy's lips touching the girl's earlobe. They had hinted, when he had first taken the seat next to them on the bench, at their unhappiness at his intrusion, but he had refused to leave, having every right to the bench as much as the young couple did.

You remind me of my wife when she was your age, he said now to the girl. It was not the first time he had started a conversation with a young woman with the line, but he meant it more than any time before. The way she maneuvered through the late-afternoon street—vigilant, as if she was aware that anyone, anything, could run her over without the slightest idea of her existence—was how he remembered his wife—not only as a young woman when they had first met but also as an older woman in the next forty years of their marriage. She had been taken advantage of by many unfriendly strangers cutting into the lines in front of her, colleagues getting promotions that belonged to her, three miscarriages, and a tumor in her liver.

She passed away six months ago, the man added now. We don't have children.

The girl looked at the old man, unconvinced by his widower's sorrow. This was not the first time she had been approached this way, older men claiming that she reminded them of their dead wives and first loves. She was never harsh with them. Even with her physics professor, who took every opportunity to touch the arms and backs of his female students, she did not flinch as the other girls did; the graze of his hands was no more harmful than another man's recognition of his own dead wife in her. They were in as much pain as she was, and they did not add to her suffering.

Have you tried the chrysanthemum tea? the man said, pointing to the window display of the pharmacy where the girl had stopped. My wife used to say it helped to get any poison out of someone's system.

The girl sighed noticeably. She would learn every bit of information about his wife if she did not stop him; not that she minded being told about and compared to a dead woman, but she had her own love to take care of on this evening. She nodded to the man and went for the door of the pharmacy, wishing that he would take his leave and find another girl in the street.

The man followed her into the store. Fluorescent lamps lit the place from the ceiling and from underneath the glass counters. Two middle-aged women, one sitting behind the cash register and one behind the counter at the opposite side of the store, exchanged information about their husbands' annoying habits, agreeing and encouraging each other as if they were deeply engaged in a verbal Ping-Pong game. Another customer listened while studying pairs of reading glasses but then left without buying. It was one of those long evenings, the man thought.

The girl walked from counter to counter and feigned interest in various products. She did not know how to stop the man from following her, since he had every right to be standing in the same store that she was, but soon it would be nightfall and the women would close the shop without asking her what she needed. The girl looked at the clock on the wall and panicked. It was all as she had planned it, that the pharmacy would be free of prying eyes in the last ten minutes before closing and she would be spared embarrassment; she did not foresee the tenacity of a lonely man.

There's a good wonton stand across the street and I'll buy you a bowl of wonton soup, the man said to the girl.

His wife must have liked wonton soup, or else she must have cooked good wonton soup for him. The girl thought about being old and having few comforts to hold on to. She was twenty-two and found it hard to be comforted by the little things in life. For the past two years she had seen bigger events than she had been prepared for, protests that led to bloodshed that led to arrests and interrogations; the tragedies would not be personal if not for her having fallen for a boy hero—she had not been the only one to admire his flamboyant gestures in front of Western reporters' cameras, but two years later, she was the only one to go to his parents' flat and sit with him every night. Don't keep your hope high, his mother had warned the girl earlier on, but she had not believed that the spirit he had shown in the square would be so easily crushed by the interrogations. She had gone to his parents and begged to see him until they had to accept her presence; still, they told her that the boy, officially a madman now, would not pass the test for a permit to get married.

Marriage is for those who still believe in the mundane, she replied and later told her parents so. She went to sit with the boy and listen to his long monologues on history and philosophy and the fatality of humankind; she noticed repetitions but did not point them out to him, nor did she ask what he thought of her presence in his bedroom. Perhaps she blended in with the furniture well, but even a piece of good furniture might save someone's life by miracle. He touched her face and arms sometimes, absentmindedly, as someone deep in thought would stroke a cat. The tenderness of his hands kept her hopeful of his recovery; after all, he had not been handled with any consideration in the two-month detention.

It's just a bowl of wonton soup, the old man said, more vehemently than he had intended. The girl's quiet rejection shamed him; his wife would have smiled and thanked him because she knew the invitation bore no ill intention. Even if she were indeed unable to join him, she would have given him a good excuse instead of letting him stand in the middle of the shop like an idiot. The world is not as bad as you think it is, he said to the girl. Enough young women these days were treating him as if he were as old and non-feeling as a half-dead tree, but he could not stand that she, who reminded him of his wife in another life, was being one of them.

The girl looked at the man. His sudden rudeness was a relief. She did not have to be responsible for his feelings, after all, even if he had not lied about his wife. The girl moved closer to the cash register, where in a locked glass case packs of condoms were on display. The girl glanced at the half-naked men and women, all foreign with blond hair, printed on the packages. A pack of those, comrade, she said, and wished that only she herself noticed the trembling in her voice.

What are those? We don't sell "those" here, the woman behind the cash register said.

The condoms, the girl said.

Which one?

That pink pack.

What size? They come in three different sizes, the woman said, and the other woman laughed audibly across the store.

The medium size, the girl said.

Are you sure?

The man watched the girl's face and neck burn with shame. Such a young woman, he thought, not experienced enough to know that all married people with respectable jobs had condoms distributed monthly to them by the birth control officers in their working units. He wished the women would be adamant in not selling the condoms to the girl; he wanted to suggest they require her marriage certificate, but before he opened his mouth, the woman asked for the marked price and then threw the pack to the girl. It slid on the glass counter and then fell onto the floor.

Young girl, the man said. Do you know what you're doing?

The girl watched the man step on the naked couple with one foot. Please, sir, I paid for them, she said. They belong to me.

She's not like my wife, the man thought. He remembered one time running out of the monthly ration of condoms from his work; he had begged his wife to ask the birth control officer in her working unit, but she had cried and said she would rather die instead of going to ask a man for them. He would rather die now, the man thought, to make her alive again, but what was the point of wishing for that? It was a better arrangement that he was left behind; without him she would be bullied every day by people like those women behind the counters.

Please, it's getting late, the girl said. Had she been a different person she would have found a sharp voice and ordered the man to return to her what by law belonged to her; she would have turned to the two women, who were enjoying the scene for their end-of-the-day shift, and told them that they had better stop feeling good about themselves, because after all, they were old and loose and not as desirable as she was. The women would curse her as if she were a madwoman, and they would try to get rid of her and pretend that they were not stung by her words, but for the rest of the evening they would stay furious and their meals would remain undigested, a big lump of stone in their stomachs where her poisonous words sat, and she would walk away with a triumphant pleasure, but the truth was, she was not that person. She was the girl who went to buy condoms and planned to give herself to the boy she loved; the boy had been beaten so badly that he would never become a husband, his parents had told her, but she was the kind of girl who did not believe their words. She believed that her love would save and change him.

The old man moved away his foot. He could go on chiding the girl but he was tired. Perhaps it was good that they had not had children; his wife would be heartbroken if their daughter had turned out to be like the girl in front of him.

The girl bent down to pick up the condoms and clutched the pack in her fist. Someday, when she became an old woman, she would show the pink pack to her children, a souvenir of her hopeful youth. She was aware of the old man's shaking hands, just an arm's length away from her, and she was aware of the two women watching with ridicule, behind the counters. She wondered how much they understood love, and love despite the fatality of humankind.

Gold Boy, Emerald Girl

HE WAS RAISED by his mother alone, as she was by her father. She wondered if his mother, who had set up their date, had told him about that.

Siyu was thirty-eight, and the man, Hanfeng, was forty-four. Siyu's father, after supporting her through college, had remarried, choosing a woman thirty years his junior. The woman had a young son from her previous marriage, whom Siyu's father had taken on as his responsibility. The boy was now in his last year of high school, and Siyu, having told her father many times that he deserved peace and simplicity, maintained a respectful distance from his new family. Each year she spent New Year's Eve, and sometimes other holidays, with Hanfeng's mother, who had been her zoology professor in college. There was no way to predict when the older woman would be in the mood to invite Siyu, so she tried to keep herself uncommitted, which meant that most of the holidays she spent alone.

"Professor Dai must miss her students these days," Siyu said after she and Hanfeng had exchanged greetings, although she knew it was not the students that his mother missed but the white skulls of mammals and birds on her office shelves, the drawers filled with scalpels and clamps and tweezers that she had cleaned and maintained with care, and the fact that she could mask her indifference to the human species with her devotion to animals. The first time Siyu had seen Professor Dai, on a campus tour during the opening week of college, the older woman had been following a strutting owl down a dimly lit hallway; she paid little attention to the group of new students, and stooped slightly the whole time, as if she were the mother of a toddler and had to watch out for minor accidents. When a boy stepped over to take a closer look at the owl, she scooped up the bird and glared at him before striding away.

"Retirement is a strange thing for her," Hanfeng said. His mother had always despised women who grabbed every opportunity to matchmake, but within days of his return to China she had mentioned a former student she thought he should meet. His mother did not say much else, but he could sense that it was marriage she was thinking about. Twenty years of living away from her had not changed that in him: He always knew what was on her mind before she said it, and he wondered if she was ever aware of that.

The teahouse where Hanfeng and Siyu were meeting, at a hillside pavilion in the Summer Palace, had been chosen by his mother, and she had suggested that they also take a long stroll along the lakefront. It was early March. The day turned out overcast and windy, and secretly Hanfeng hoped that the wind would not die down, so they could forgo the romantic walk. He wondered if Siyu was wishing for a different scenario. He could not yet read much from her face. She smiled courteously as she gave him a few facts about White Peony, the tea she had ordered for them both, but the smile and the words seemed to come with effort, as if her interest in interacting with him could easily fade. Her body was slender, and her hair, black with noticeable strands of gray, was kept straight and at shoulder length. He wondered why the woman, who was beautiful in an unassuming way, had never married.

"Do you find Beijing a different city now?" Siyu said. It must be a question that he was asked all the time, but it would not do anyone any harm, she thought. It was not the first time that Siyu had been set up with a stranger—since she had turned twenty, neighbors and acquaintances, pitying her for not having a mother to fuss over her future, had taken it as their responsibility to find a husband for her—but with those men she had known from the beginning that she would not bother trying to impress them. Over the years, she had developed a reputation as unmatchable, and nowadays only the most persistent of the matchmakers would mention a widower or a divorcé, in his fifties or sometimes sixties, as a possible solution. The first time such a prospect was presented in an enthusiastic speech, Siyu had the odd feeling that she was now expected to marry her father; only later did she realize that she was no longer a young woman.

Siyu worked as a librarian in a zoology institute, and her life had not changed much from that of a college student. In her mind, she might still be the eighteen-year-old who had set her alarm clock early so that by six o'clock she would be sitting on the bench under an ancient ginkgo tree in front of the biology building. At half past six, Professor Dai would arrive on her bicycle—a tall, rusty, heavy-built one that would have better suited a peasant or a street peddler—and she would nod at Siyu almost imperceptibly as she locked it up. It had taken two years for Professor Dai to cross the courtyard and ask Siyu about the thick volume she had been reading every day. Charles Dickens, Siyu replied, and then added that she was trying to memorize *Great Expectations*. Professor Dai nodded, expressing neither surprise nor curiosity at the task that had already made Siyu an eccentric in the eyes of her classmates. Siyu did not explain to them that her grandfather—her mother's father, whom she had never met—had once memorized volumes of Dickens on the small balcony of a Shanghai flat, a feat that had eventually led him, before the liberation, to a high position in a bank run by Englishmen. It was Dickens who had in the end killed Siyu's mother: As a daughter of the British capitalists' loyal lapdog, she had hanged herself when her own daughter was four months of age, barely old enough to be weaned.

Hanfeng looked at Siyu's face, detecting a familiar absentmindedness. His mother, too, asked him questions to which she seemed scarcely interested in knowing the answers. He wondered if this happened to women who lived by themselves. "Too many cars," he replied, nonetheless—the standard response he gave when asked about his impression of Beijing these days. "I miss the bicycles."

Hanfeng had returned from the States a month earlier. He had told his former colleagues in San Francisco about his intention to settle down in China, and they had joked about moving with him and becoming the forty-niners of the new gold rush. He went along with the joke, making up ambitious business plans that he knew he would not carry out. His mother was getting old, he explained to his friends; the thought that he, too, was no longer a young man in need of adventures he kept to himself. Semiretired was how he liked to think of his situation, but within days of returning to Beijing he realized that what he had made in the States at the tail end of the dot-com bubble would not be sufficient to support a life of idleness, as he had hoped. Still, he was not eager to go out and seek employment. He deposited half his money into his mother's account and told her that he would take a break; she did not ask about his plans, in the same way that she had not questioned his decision to leave or to come home.

At seventy-one, his mother was as independent as ever, and she loathed most activities that a woman her age enjoyed: taking morning walks with a companion, gossiping and bargaining at the marketplace, watching soap operas in the afternoon. Hanfeng had never wondered how his mother spent her days in retirement until his return, when, all of a sudden, the three-bedroom flat that must have seemed empty to her became crowded. He had been the one to cook for the two of them when he was a boy, dividing the meals in half and eating his portion alone; his mother, her preoccupation with her research a ready excuse, had eaten at odd hours then. Since his return, he had taken over the cooking again, and now that neither of them was eager to go out into the world to fulfill any duty, they ate together.

The idea of renting a flat had occurred to Hanfeng, but as soon as the thought formed he dismissed it as a waste: He had left for America right after college, a move intended to claim a place for himself—a whole continent, in the end, as in twenty years he had drifted from New York to Montreal, then Vancouver, and later San Francisco—and a life that had to be lived away from a mother, but with the return to China he no longer felt the urgency to have his own place. Freedom is like restaurant food, he once told an old friend in the States, and one can lose one's appetite for even the best restaurants. Pure nonsense, replied his friend, who, unlike Hanfeng, had long ago settled down with a partner, a house, and two dogs, and talked of adopting a baby. Take a break, he said, urging Hanfeng to return to California after he refreshed himself with his homemade dumplings and noodles. Hanfeng, however, could envision himself living a bachelor's life in his mother's flat, reading the same newspapers and comparing notes on the stories that interested them both, wandering freely through the flat when she went out for her piano lessons twice a week.

The piano was the only thing that kept his mother actively engaged with the world. Soon after Hanfeng's return, she had asked him to go to a recital she was playing in, at a local music school. It was attended by men and women Hanfeng's age, who seemed nervous when their well-trained and nicely dressed children took the stage. His mother was the only one who went up without a puppetlike show. She gazed at the sheets of music for a long moment, then started to pound on the keys with a seriousness that took Hanfeng by surprise. He had thought the piano was merely a retirement pastime for his mother, and had protested mildly when she mentioned that her goal was to be good enough one day to play four-hand with him. Hanfeng had not told her that he was no longer playing, even though a rented piano had always been the first piece of furniture to fill an empty flat in each city he moved to. Small children giggled in the audience, and a few older ones smirked, pitying the old woman for her stiff arthritic fingers, which would never again be as good and agile as theirs. Some parents shook their heads at their children disapprovingly, and it occurred to Hanfeng that he was becoming a parent for his mother, that he would be the one to protect her from the hostility of the world.

The thought baffled him. His mother had always been a headstrong woman, and with her grayish-white mane and unsmiling face, she appeared as regal and intimidating as she had ever been. Still, seeing her through other people's eyes, Hanfeng realized that all that made her who she was—the decades of solitude in her widowhood, her coldness to the prying eyes of people who tried to mask their nosiness with friendliness, and her faith in the notion of living one's own life without having to go out of one's way for other people—could be deemed pointless and laughable. Perhaps the same could be said of any living creature: a caterpillar chewing on a leaf, unaware of the beak of an approaching bird; an egret mesmerized by its reflection in a pond, as if it were the master of the universe; or Hanfeng's own folly of repeating the same pattern of hope and heartbreak, hoping despite heartbreak.

Siyu asked a few more questions, and Hanfeng replied. When there was nothing much left to say, he curled his fingers around the teacup and studied its shape, and Siyu pictured him as a young boy, spreading his slender fingers on the cold keys of a piano. His mother must have told him, when he complained about the open windows in the winter, that playing would keep the blood circulating in his hands. Siyu did not know why she imagined that; it was as unfounded as all the other things she had made up about him. In Professor Dai's flat, there were framed snapshots of Hanfeng playing in piano contests at five, eight, ten, fifteen. There were snapshots of him when he had first arrived in America, with his bright-colored T-shirt, long and flying hair, and broad smile, as picturesque and unreal as the Statue of Liberty in the background.

Siyu had been eighteen when she first saw those photographs, when she was sent as a representative from her class to deliver a New Year's present to Professor Dai. No one had wanted that job; Professor Dai's coldness was known to be hurtful, and it made sense that Siyu, with her mild eccentricity, would be the one chosen. But that day, to Siyu's surprise, Professor Dai did not simply dismiss her from the doorway, even though she immediately placed the present, a framed painting of a golden carp, next to the wastebasket. Instead, Professor Dai invited Siyu into the flat, moved the papers that covered the dining table onto the piano bench, and let Siyu sit while she went to the kitchen to make tea. Her son was the one who played the piano, Professor Dai answered when Siyu asked, and pointed out the pictures of Hanfeng. Very vaguely, Siyu had thought that he was the kind of boy she would like to have as a boyfriend, a prize badge that she could wear to make other girls jealous. Years later, she knew it was not the thought of the boy that had made her wait on the bench outside the biology building in the mornings during college; nor was he the reason she continued to befriend Professor Dai in a manner allowed by the older woman. Occasionally, Siyu would carefully study the pictures of Hanfeng in Professor Dai's flat, and when they ran out of things to say about animals she would ask about his life in America. When Professor Dai called and asked her to meet Hanfeng, Siyu wondered if the matchmaking had come as a result of a beguiling impression she had left of her interest in a good-looking bachelor.

The waitress came to offer a fresh pot of tea. Hanfeng turned to Siyu and asked her if she was ready to leave. They had spent almost an hour talking, and he had fulfilled his mother's wish without humiliating the woman with his lack of interest. Siyu looked out the window at the willow trees, their branches waving like unruly hair in the wind. Not a great day for a walk, Hanfeng said. Siyu agreed, then asked him if he needed a ride.

"I'll take a cab home," he said.

"I'm driving past your mother's place, in any case," Siyu said. Her own flat, a small studio that she rented from a retired couple, was only minutes from Professor Dai's flat, but Siyu thought she would appear too eager if she mentioned that.

Hanfeng wished that he had made up an excuse—a lunch with a friend in another district; an exhibition or a film to see—but it was too late to correct himself now.

A WEEK LATER, Hanfeng's mother asked him if he planned to see Siyu again. They had finished their breakfast and were reading that morning's newspapers, plates and bowls scattered on the table between them. Hanfeng's mother did not raise her eyes from the page as she asked, but he knew the question was not as haphazard as it seemed. Should he? he replied.

"Do you dislike her?"

It took more than an hour over tea for him to say that he disliked a woman, Hanfeng thought, but he just shook his head slightly. He was not surprised by his mother's question. *Do you dislike piano?* she had asked, when he wanted to give up the instrument at twelve for games that he could play with boys his age; *Do you dislike engineering?*, when he thought of pursuing a literature degree in college rather than the one she had chosen for him. Before he left China, she told him that she might not have been a good mother in the worldly sense, but she considered herself successful in having given him two things: practical skills with which to earn a living, and music as the only trustworthy companion and consolation for his soul. Twenty-three, and in love with a childhood friend who was dating a chirpy girl, Hanfeng did not believe that either of his mother's gifts would in any way contribute to his happiness. America, at first glance, seemed a happy enough place, and when his friend called with the news of his engagement, Hanfeng sought out companions. All he wanted was to have some fun, he replied when more was asked of him; "have fun"—wasn't that the phrase that replaced words of farewell in many Americans' lexicon? But eventually the reply came back to taunt him: I thought we would have some fun and that's all, his last lover had said, a Chinese boy, a new immigrant, as Hanfeng himself had once been, whom Hanfeng had helped support through college.

He should ask Siyu out to a movie, his mother suggested, or a concert. When he showed a lukewarm reaction, she said, "Or ask her to have dinner with us here."

"Wouldn't that be too quick?" Hanfeng said. Even though Siyu had been introduced to him by his mother, a dinner invitation, after meeting only once, seemed to imply an approval of sorts from both him and his mother.

"She is not a stranger," his mother replied, and proceeded to check the calendar on the kitchen wall. Saturday was a good day, she said, and when Hanfeng questioned Siyu's availability at such short notice, his concerns were dismissed. "She'll rearrange her schedule if she has to," his mother said, and wrote down the date and Siyu's number on a piece of scrap paper.

Hanfeng wondered if Siyu had felt similar pressure from his mother. What would she have said to Siyu—*I would like you to date my son*? Knowing his mother, he wondered if she had simply mentioned that her son needed a wife and that she thought Siyu would be the right person for the role. "Why has she never married?" he asked.

"I imagine for the obvious reason of not having felt the need to get married."

"Does she want to get married now?" Hanfeng said. He had expected his mother to reply that Siyu had not met the right person—and then he could have questioned why his mother thought him a good choice for her.

"She didn't say no to the date last time, no?"

When Hanfeng called Siyu to invite her to dinner, the line was quiet for a moment. He waited for her to find an excuse to turn down the invitation, or, better still, to tell him that she had obliged his mother with their last meeting and the sensible thing to do now was to make their mutual disinterest known to his mother. Instead, Siyu asked him if they could possibly meet once more before the dinner. Anytime after she got off from work would do, she said. He wondered why she needed to see him when all could be settled on the phone, but he agreed to a late-afternoon meeting that day.

There was a power outage at the coffee shop where Siyu had suggested they meet. Apart from the light of a few candles on the counter, the inside of the shop, a long, narrow rectangle, was almost pitch-black. Siyu, who had arrived a few minutes earlier and taken a seat by the only window, explained to Hanfeng that the place was always quiet, and more so today, as the coffeemakers were not hissing. A sulky young girl placed a pot of tea and two cups heavily on the table. Siyu apologized for the shop's unfriendliness after the girl returned to the counter. "I'm about their only regular customer, but for three years no one has acknowledged me," she said.

"Why do you still come here?"

"It's quiet. I can assure you it's not easy to find a quiet place like this in Beijing," Siyu said. "My theory is that the proprietress is a rich man's mistress. She does not want the shop to make money for him, and he cannot close it, because it was his present to her."

Hanfeng looked around, but no one was there besides the girl at the counter. "They seem to hire unhappy people," he said.

"The proprietress is a beautiful woman," Siyu said. Hanfeng nodded. He had no further questions, and she could see that he was one of those people who would not return to the place. She wished she could tell him that, apart from the beauty of the woman who once in a while showed up at the coffee shop with an air of authority, there was little evidence to support her guess. Yet there had to be an explanation for the sad, lifeless appearance of the shop. She thought of telling him this, but he was part of the world that did not seek her explanations. The world had made up its mind about her oddity in her spinsterhood.

They sat in silence for a moment. In another place, a more romantic setting, lovers' murmurs would have been well masked by soft jazz coming from hidden speakers, their faces illuminated by candlelight, but here there was no music and the candles were lit out of necessity. The idea of getting to know Hanfeng better before having dinner with him and his mother seemed, like all the other ideas that had occurred to Siyu, a regrettable mistake. When he did not help find a harmless topic of discussion, she asked him if he was aware of his mother's wish to see him get married.

"I suppose all mothers worry about their children's marriage status," Hanfeng said vaguely. He had thought that his mother had long ago accepted who he was; when he had visited in the past, she had never pressed for any details of his American life, sparing him the pain of explaining himself. "Doesn't your mother?"

She had no right to feel let down, Siyu thought. Nevertheless, it disappointed her that Professor Dai had not told him much about her. That she had been raised by her father was, from a young age, the first thing people said of her. "I never met my mother," she said. "My father brought me up by himself."

Hanfeng looked up at her. Before he could form an apology, she said there was no need for one. She had grown up not knowing her loss, so there had not been any real loss. She wondered if that was how Hanfeng thought of his father. Professor Dai had never mentioned her late husband, but Siyu had once had a summer job in the department office, and had heard other professors and the secretaries talk about how he had died in a snowstorm when his bicycle skidded in front of a bus. An accident that no one could be blamed for, but Siyu had sensed the others' disapproval of Professor Dai, as if she were partially responsible for the unfair fate that befell the man; the dead husband, by contrast, was always praised as the gentlest person.

"What was it like to grow up with only a father?" Hanfeng asked. He had little recollection of his father, but there were photographs, taken when Hanfeng had turned a hundred days, six months, one year, and then two years old. In all four pictures, he was flanked by his parents, who looked serious and attentive. They would have been called "gold boy" and "emerald girl" at their wedding, enviable for their matching good looks. It must have been his father's idea to have a family picture taken at every milestone of his life, since after his father's death Hanfeng had never been in the same photograph as his mother.

Siyu replied that she imagined it was not very different from growing up with only a mother. There was no other parent to whom they could compare the one they had, and love did not have to be balanced and divided between two people; the claiming of loyalty was unnecessary. Siyu did not say these things, but there was a gentleness in Hanfeng's eyes where before there had been only aloofness, and she knew that he understood.

Hanfeng turned away from Siyu's gaze and looked out the window. A woman in a heavy mud-colored coat was riding a bicycle and threading through the long line of cars in the street. A young child, bundled up in a gray shawl, so that its gender could not be determined, sat on a bamboo chair affixed to the back rack of the bicycle, as unfazed as the mother was by the impatient honking of drivers around them. Hanfeng pointed out the child to Siyu, knowing that both of them had traveled the streets of Beijing in that way, he behind his mother, she her father.

After the woman and her child had disappeared from sight, Siyu said that when she started to ride her bicycle to school at twelve, her father would get up every morning and run after her until she reached the school gate. She used to be ashamed of being the only one escorted to school by a running father, but she could never say no to him.

"He must be the most loving father in the world," Hanfeng said.

Siyu nodded. A door behind the counter opened and then closed, and for a moment it seemed that the flickering candles would be extinguished. She had had to squeeze the hand brake often on the downhill ride to the school so that her father's panting would not be so loud that other people took notice, and only when she was much older did she realize that her father had insisted on running beside her so that she would not become one of the wild youngsters who sped and broke an arm or a skull in an accident. She had always been aware of his love for her and for her mother, even though he had not said much, but in the end she had been the one to make up grand excuses for her absence. You're still my only daughter, he said to her when she decided not to attend his wedding; you're part of the family, he said when she told him that she would not be coming home for the Lunar New Year. He did not need her to complicate his life, she replied, knowing that he would stoically accept her proposal of a monthly lunch as their only way of remaining father and daughter.

Ungrateful and coldhearted she must seem in the eyes of old neighbors and family friends, but how could she stay in his sight when she was going through her life with a reckless speed known only to herself, all because of a love she could not explain and did not have the right to claim in the first place? I wonder if I made a mistake by bringing you up alone, her father had said to her at their most recent lunch, taking it as his failure that she had not found a husband. I was afraid of what a stepmother would do to a girl, but perhaps a woman would have made a difference, he said, less guarded and more talkative now in his old age. Siyu shook her head and denied that he had anything to regret. That she had grown up without a mother could be a ready explanation for anything—her oddness in her teenage years, her choice of an unremarkable job despite her excellence in schoolwork, her singleness. Were people to know her secret, they might easily conclude that she had spent her life looking for a mother in her love of an older woman, but Siyu did not believe that things would have turned out any differently had she had a mother.

A beautiful and sad woman, Hanfeng thought as he looked at Siyu's face. As beautiful and sad a woman, perhaps, as his mother had once been. Could this account for his mother's wish for a marriage between Siyu and him? Hanfeng had been surprised, at first, that a former student would remain close to his mother. She had not been the kind to pick favorites among her students; nor had she ever encouraged any personal interaction with them, as far as he knew, though he could see why Siyu, motherless and with a gentle and loving father, might seek out a professor despite, or perhaps because of, her sternness. But Siyu seemed to know his mother only in a peripheral way, as a pupil, and Hanfeng wondered if this was why his mother had allowed the younger woman to remain a friend. When Hanfeng was ten, a woman had come from a southern province to see his mother. An unannounced visit, he could tell, when his mother had returned home in the evening and found him shelling peas alongside the guest, their knees almost touching, on two low stools. The woman, who had told Hanfeng that she was a very old friend of his mother's and was planning to stay with them for a week, left the next morning before he awoke. He was puzzled but intuitively knew not to ask his mother about it. Still, the image of the woman's face, pale at the sight of his mother, and her hands, which let the peas fall into the pile of shells, stayed with Hanfeng. He could not pinpoint when he understood that there had been betrayals between the two friends, but by the time he left home for college he knew that he would never learn the true story, his mother having long ago decided to live alone with the secret until her death.

AT THE DINNER, both Siyu and Hanfeng felt a shyness around each other, but Professor Dai did not let the awkwardness deter her. "When you are young, you marry for passion," she said, looking first at her son and then at her future daughter-in-law. "When you're older, you marry for companionship."

Hanfeng glanced down at his plate. One day she would die, his mother had said to him the night before, after he had listened to her stumble through a Chopin piece on the piano. There was nothing to grieve about in her death, but she would like to see that he did not repeat her fate. Repeat? Hanfeng asked, pretending that he did not understand and knowing that she could see through him. She would like him to marry Siyu, his mother had said. There were many ways to maintain a marriage, and she expected theirs to be far from the worst.

The same message had been conveyed to Siyu, when Hanfeng was sent to buy a bottle of wine for dinner. She was helping Professor Dai lay the table, and when she looked over, the older woman paired the chopsticks without meeting her eyes. Siyu had never mentioned the strangers she had been matched up with over the years, but one New Year's Eve, Professor Dai had told Siyu that she shouldn't get married if it was not what she wanted. They had just finished dinner, and sitting across the table from Professor Dai, Siyu could see the prints of bamboo leaves on the curtain lit up by the fireworks outside. Professor Dai had opened a bottle of wine that year, an unusual addition to the holiday meal, as neither of them was the type to celebrate. You could feel trapped by the wrong man, Professor Dai said. Her voice, softened by the wine, was less steely and almost inaudible beneath the booming of the fireworks. You would have to wish for his death every day of your marriage, she said, but once the wish was granted by a miracle, you would never be free of your own cruelty. Siyu listened, knowing that the older woman was talking about herself, knowing also that both of them would pretend to have forgotten the conversation after that night. Other conversations, on other New Year's Eves, were never mentioned again. One year, Siyu told Professor Dai about her mother's suicide; another year, Professor Dai mentioned that her son had no interest in marriage. Professor Dai's acknowledgment of Siyu's decision to purchase a secondhand car so that the older woman could avoid taking a crowded bus or enduring a chatty cabdriver was hinted at but not directly stated, and so was her gratitude for Siyu's alertness, when she failed to answer Siyu's weekly phone call and Siyu discovered the older woman on the floor by the piano, having suffered a stroke.

She had remained unmarried for Professor Dai, Siyu thought now, and she would, with her blessing, become a married woman. She would not wish for her husband's death, as his mother had, because the marriage, arranged as it was, would still be a love marriage. Siyu had wished to be a companion for Professor Dai in her old age, and her wish would now be granted, an unexpected gift from a stingy life.

"So this is an engagement dinner, then?" Hanfeng said, feeling that it was his duty to say something to avoid silence among the three of them. He doubted that he would feel any deficiency in his life without a wife, he had said the night before, and his mother had replied that Siyu was not the kind of woman who would take much away from him.

"We don't need any formality among us," Professor Dai said now, and told Siyu that she should move in at her earliest convenience instead of wasting money on rent. Siyu looked down the hallway, knowing that the room which served as a piano studio for Professor Dai would be converted into the third bedroom, the piano relocated to the living room. She could see herself standing by the window and listening to Hanfeng and Professor Dai play four-hand, and she could see the day when she would replace Professor Dai on the piano bench, her husband patient with her inexperienced fingers. They were half orphans, and beyond that there was the love for his mother that they could share with no one else, he as a son who had once left but had now returned, she who had not left and would never leave. They were lonely and sad people, all three of them, and they would not make one another less sad, but they could, with great care, make a world that would accommodate their loneliness.

Acknowledgments

As always, I am deeply grateful to:

Sarah Chalfant and Jin Auh, for taking extraordinary care of my work; Kate Medina and Nicholas Pearson, for their continuing support; Cressida Leyshon, for the many great discussions about stories.

Amy Leach and Aviya Kushner, for being indefatigable friends.

Dapeng, Vincent, and James, for their love.

Mr. William Trevor, for his generosity and kindness.

Gold Boy, Emerald Girl

Yiyun Li

A Reader's Guide

A Conversation Between Brigid Hughes and Yiyun Li

Brigid Hughes is the founding editor of A Public Space, *a Brooklyn-based independent magazine of literature and culture that debuted in 2006. Previously she worked at* The Paris Review, *where she succeeded George Plimpton as editor upon his death in 2003.*

Brigid Hughes: To get things started, can I ask you about influences? You mention William Trevor in your acknowledgments, and you published an essay in *Tin House* about his influence on your work. What authors or books have mattered to you?

Yiyun Li: I like to think that one writes stories so they could go out and talk to other stories. William Trevor's stories have made space for my stories to venture out to the world, to be on their own, so my stories talk to Trevor's stories constantly. For instance, the title story, "Gold Boy, Emerald Girl," was written especially to talk to a Trevor story, "Three People."

Of course stories, like people, can't just stay sheltered by those to whom they feel close kinship. Stories also like to have discussions and sometimes arguments with other stories. A few writers who have been constantly on my mind when I write: Elizabeth Bowen, Graham Greene, John McGahern, J. M. Coetzee. So they have been influencing me too in each of their own ways.

BH: Can I ask what specifically "Gold Boy, Emerald Girl" and "Three People" were talking about with each other?

YL: "Three People" [from Trevor's collection *The Hill Bachelors*] is, as the title suggests, a story about three people: an aging father; his unmarried, middle-aged daughter; and a man close to the family who the father hopes will propose to the daughter so she will not end up in solitude after her father's death. Unknown to the father—I don't want to give too much away of the story—the daughter and the man shared some dark secret between them. The final passage of the story goes like this: "The darkness of their secrets lit, the love that came for both of them through their pitying of each other: all that might fill the empty upstairs room, and every corner of the house. But Vera knows that, without her father, they would frighten one another."

When I started to work on "Gold Boy, Emerald Girl," I imagined writing a story about three people too—an aging mother, a grown-up son, and a woman—and the mismatch between the latter two would not be any better than between the couple in "Three People." The story is set to a tone similar to that of "Three People," though I do remember writing toward the end and feeling overwhelmed by the bleakness and fatalism of "Three People," working on the final line of my story to catch the same music but with some gentleness: "They were lonely and sad people, all three of them, and they would not make one another less sad, but they could, with great care, make a world that would accommodate their loneliness."

BH: Do you think your characters in the new stories are lonelier, or rather more isolated, than in *A Thousand Years of Good Prayers,* the first collection? I'm thinking of that opening line from "Immortality"—"His story, as the story of every one of us, started long before we were born"—and that sense of being part of something bigger than oneself, history, or community, which seems much less the case with the new stories. Do you notice differences between the two collections?

YL: I would like to think that the stories in *Gold Boy, Emerald Girl* were more mature than the stories in *A Thousand Years of Good Prayers*!

But I know exactly what you are asking about. "Immortality" was the first full-length story I wrote, about nine years ago, and I was very aware at the time of how China and its past (and present) cast a long shadow over at least two or three generations of characters. Many of the stories in the first collection were written out of meditations on the inescapable fate of many of the characters being trapped by political and ideological turmoil in the past century.

Are my characters lonelier or more isolated now? In a way, yes. In choosing solitude, my characters are also trying to regain some of the control of their own fates—rather than being members of a chorus, they allow themselves to become outcasts, sometimes illogically, sometimes stubbornly. But I don't think they are passive characters. I like to imagine that some of the characters in the first collection (in "Persimmons," for instance, or "Immortality," or "A Thousand Years of Good Prayers") allowed themselves to be carried away by history and politics as long as they did not drown—and one tended not to drown if one did not fight against that torrent. Many of the characters in *Gold Boy, Emerald Girl* made the decision of not letting themselves be swept away. They held on to anything—loneliness, isolation, and even death—to be themselves.

BH: Is that also what Professor Shan is saying when she tells Moyan, in "Kindness," "The moment you admit someone into your heart you make yourself a fool. When you desire nothing, nothing will defeat you"?

YL: By forbidding Moyan to fall in love with anyone, in a way Professor Shan is acting as cruelly and inhumanely as the unfair and harsh world from which she is trying to shelter the girl, though the latter, in following the advice of the older woman, also defies her in her own way. Twice in the story—at the beginning and at the end—Moyan says, "I have never forgotten any person who has come into my life." And indeed she is able to remain true both to her words and to her promise to Professor Shan: She is able to love without making herself a fool.

BH: When you emigrated from China, *The Letters of Shen Congwen* was one of the few books you brought with you to the United States. He wrote about, and was criticized for, his disinterest in politics and lack of commitment to the class struggles of his time. You recently translated some of those letters, and in an introduction wrote that "relevance is always a useful tool for lesser minds to attack true artists." What is the connection between the politics of the present day and fiction—does one inform the other in any way? What does it mean to be a political writer?

YL: I have always resisted being called a political writer. Take Shen Congwen as an example—his commitment to his arts was not influenced by the ideology of his time, which, in one sense, made him apolitical, but in another sense his resistance was also highly political. Once I was asked by an editor to write something relevant to our time—in his letter he framed relevance with examples of a Mumbai slum, or a Chinese sweatshop, or a war-torn zone in Africa. Certainly we need stories from these countries, these places, but his letter reminded me of the criticisms Shen Congwen received in his time.

BH: How would you like your books to influence the reader?

YL: If books are like people, mine are not the prettiest ones, or the loudest ones, or the quirkiest ones one meets at a party, nor are they, I hope, too frivolous or too scared of truths to matter to the readers. I would like to imagine that the readers can have a conversation with my books—they can agree or disagree with the characters fairly and honestly.

Questions and Topics for Discussion

1. It seems that none of the stories from the collection can straightforwardly be called a happy story, yet happiness is never far from the characters' minds. For instance, in "Kindness," Moyan describes her happiness looking at trees, saying, "I loved trees more than I loved people; I still do." In "Souvenir," the unnamed young woman believes that she was happiest when she sat with a young man who had gone crazy from torture, because she could be like a piece of harmless furniture to him. What are other instances of happiness for the characters in this collection? What have the characters given up to achieve their happiness, and what do these compromises reveal about the characters and the time they live in?

2. Every one of the stories in the collection includes a love story, or several love stories. What are the moments in these stories when love transcends the bleakness and "fatality of humankind," as the young woman in "Souvenir" calls it at the end of the story?

3. Many of the stories are set in China at a time when the modern world clashes with traditions, creating situations that baffle the characters and change their lives in one way or another. For

instance, in "The Proprietress," a young woman finds herself the object of a great deal of media attention when she petitions to have a baby with her husband, who is on death row. What are some other situations that you find especially fascinating or perplexing in these stories? Do you think these situations are particular to life in China, or are they more universal?

4. The beauty of human memory is that, at any given moment, each of us is living multiple lives, anchored in different time periods—our decisions and perceptions about our lives reflect not only the present moment but also what has been carried on in our memories. History, especially Chinese history in the past fifty years, has given Li's characters richly layered memories. Which of their memories moved you most, and why?

5. Many of the stories feature older characters—an old woman unwilling to give her son and daughter-in-law control of her life in "The Proprietress"; Teacher Fei, the retired art teacher, and his mother in "A Man Like Him"; the six friends who establish a business to fight against extramarital affairs in "House Fire." What do you think Li, a writer in her thirties, has done to make these characters believable? What makes their stories important and compelling?

6. Many of the stories are set in China, which, in the past thirty years, has transformed itself with dazzling speed. Yet in any society, during any given period, human nature evolves at a much slower pace. What beauties and follies of human nature have you have seen in the characters that seem to have remained unchanged, despite the surface excitement of a new country and a new millennium?

7. The centerpiece of the collection is the novella "Kindness." What sorts of kindness and unkindness are present in the novella? And in the other stories? How do the characters in these stories come to terms with the kindness and unkindness of their fates?

8. Despite the major and minor tragedies many of these characters have to live with, there are moments in each story when a character allows him- or herself to envision a future that is at least a little better than the past, or the present. In "Number Three, Garden Road," the two neighbors allow themselves to be "happily occupied" in the falling dusk with the music of an old banjo; the title story, "Gold Boy, Emerald Girl," ends with Siyu's thought that "they were lonely and sad people, all three of them, and they would not make one another less sad, but they could, with great care, make a world that would accommodate their loneliness." What are other instances when the characters, despite the harshness or bleakness of their lives, do not lose their ability to imagine a better future?

9. Li grew up in China, and English is not her first language. Is there anything about her writing that would indicate this to you, if you didn't know already? What do you think makes her writing stand out, as a writer in a second language?

PHOTO: © YE RIN MOK

YIYUN LI is the author of *A Thousand Years of Good Prayers* and *The Vagrants*. A native of Beijing and a graduate of the Iowa Writers' Workshop, she is the recipient of a MacArthur Foundation fellowship, the Frank O'Connor International Short Story Award, the Hemingway Foundation/PEN Award, the Whiting Writers' Award, and the *Guardian* First Book Award. *Granta* named her one of the best American novelists under thirty-five, and *The New Yorker* named her one of twenty U.S. writers under forty to watch. Her work has appeared in *The New Yorker, A Public Space, The Best American Short Stories, The O. Henry Prize Stories,* and elsewhere. She teaches writing at the University of California, Davis, and lives in Oakland, California, with her husband and their two sons.

ABOUT THE TYPE

This book was set in Sabon, a typeface designed by the well-known German typographer Jan Tschichold (1902–74). Sabon's design is based upon the original letter forms of Claude Garamond and was created specifically to be used for three sources: foundry type for hand composition, Linotype, and Monotype. Tschichold named his typeface for the famous Frankfurt typefounder Jacques Sabon, who died in 1580.